"Hey, Fran?"

She lifted her head. "Yeah?"

A caring look crossed his face, tinged with something she'd call apprehension if it wasn't Archer, ever calm and in control. "I've been checking my watch, and are you sure—"

The lights went out.

A void enveloped them. She couldn't see six inches in front of her, let alone Archer in his chair.

The dog startled, shifting under Franci's forward bridge.

Franci sat back on her heels.

Bands tightened from her back to her belly. And in the pitch dark, she couldn't focus on anything but the ramping intensity.

No. Not tonight. She moaned, spreading her knees wider and pressing her face into the comforting floof in front of her.

"Yeah, I thought so," Archer said quietly.

A clunk of wood sounded—him putting the guitar back on its stand.

"Going to be tough to make dinner with no power," she said.

And even harder to deliver a baby.

Dear Reader,

Welcome back to Oyster Island! It's all decked out and gorgeous for *A Hideaway Wharf Holiday*, including a Santa dressed in scuba gear at Otter Marine Tours, which is fully booked with divers looking to enjoy the outstanding visibility of the winter water. Of course, Franci Walker hasn't been able to dive in eight months, and she's more than ready to welcome her baby into the world. She knows motherhood will be unpredictable, but a rather stormy delivery serves up more holiday surprises than she'd anticipated— including some unexpectedly close quarters with her protective, serious and way-too-attractive coworker, Archer Frost.

Falling for Archer comes with barriers that even Franci's best efforts might not overcome. After a devastating accident led to the death of his best friend and to his divorce, the former coast guard rescue swimmer doesn't believe love has a place in his life anymore. But babies come with new possibilities and so much love, and Franci's precious arrival is no different. I'll let you in on a secret: I wasn't originally planning to set this story during the holiday season. Much like Franci's pregnancy, it's a happy accident that Franci and Archer's romance happens when all the love and hope of the winter holidays can bring healing to even the most wounded hearts.

Keep up-to-date on Love at Hideaway Wharf and exclusive extras by visiting my website, www.laurelgreer.com, where you'll find the latest news and a link to sign up for my newsletter. Come let me know your thoughts on *A Hideaway Wharf Holiday* on Facebook or Instagram. I'm @laurelgreerauthor on both.

Happy reading!

Laurel

A Hideaway Wharf Holiday

LAUREL GREER

———

HARLEQUIN
SPECIAL
EDITION

HARLEQUIN®
SPECIAL EDITION™

Recycling programs for this product may not exist in your area.

ISBN-13: 978-1-335-59430-3

A Hideaway Wharf Holiday

Copyright © 2023 by Lindsay Macgowan

For questions and comments about the quality of this book, please contact us at CustomerService@Harlequin.com.

Harlequin Enterprises ULC
22 Adelaide St. West, 41st Floor
Toronto, Ontario M5H 4E3, Canada
www.Harlequin.com

Printed in U.S.A.

USA TODAY bestselling author **Laurel Greer** loves writing about all the ways love can change people for the better, especially when messy families and charming small towns are involved. She lives outside Vancouver, BC, with her law-talking husband and two daughters, and is never far from a cup of tea, a good book or the ocean—preferably all three. Find her at www.laurelgreer.com.

Books by Laurel Greer

Harlequin Special Edition

Love at Hideaway Wharf

Diving into Forever

Sutter Creek, Montana

From Exes to Expecting
A Father for Her Child
Holiday by Candlelight
Their Nine-Month Surprise
In Service of Love
Snowbound with the Sheriff
Twelve Dates of Christmas
Lights, Camera...Wedding?
What to Expect When She's Expecting

Visit the Author Profile page
at Harlequin.com for more titles.

For my writer friends. I would have stopped writing long ago were it not for your daily support, humor and inspiration. Thank you.

Chapter One

A shadowy form lurked around Otter Marine Tours'
two-tiered front counter, covertly examining the point-
of-sale system.

"Hey! What are you doing here?" Franci Walker
called out from the doorway to the staff change area,
having just taken her hundred-and-second bathroom
trip of her shift. "The front door was locked!"

Except this intruder owned the place, so he had a key.

Still, he was supposed to be packing for a trip around
the UK, not interfering with Franci's temporary management role.

Her brother turned, expression sheepish as he quickly
exited the shop's scheduling program. Half brother,
technically, though they rarely made the distinction.
She was closer to Sam than she was to anyone else in
the world. And with a fresh haircut and beard trim, he
was as spruced up as he ever got.

"You look more spit polished than Archer's boots were on Veterans Day," she teased. The island residents had held their annual ceremony for the holiday a few days ago, so the mental picture of her coworker, Archer Frost, in his dress uniform was fresh in her mind.

The recency was obviously the *only* reason she'd be thinking about Archer.

Nerves shadowed Sam's green eyes. "Why'd you have to bring up clothes? Nothing I own is classy enough to wear to the restaurant party."

Sam's fiancé, a chef, was funding his friend's high-end bistro in London, so Kellan and Sam were both invited to the grand opening. And with flying that far, they planned to visit Scotland and Kellan's birthplace in Ireland, too.

"Go shopping on Oxford Street," she said gently. She was ready to pry him away from the business with a shoehorn. She couldn't wait to have two weeks in charge, to prove him correct in asking her to cover for him while he was away. She'd been building to it, having taken on more and more of the office-management tasks the further along she'd gotten in her pregnancy. It was time to show him everything she'd learned.

It was also time to ease his worries. "Kellan's people will all like you, Sam."

"As if they don't resent me for stealing him from them."

She shook her head. Her soon-to-be brother-in-law had come to Oyster Island on a mission to complete his late sister's outdoor-adventure bucket list. He'd fallen in love with both Sam and the small community, enough to add a foraging-and-cooking business onto Otter Marine Tours. After relocating to Washington State in the spring, he was nothing but ecstatic about his new life. How could any of his London friends resent Sam for contributing to Kellan's happiness?

"'Stealing' isn't the right word," she insisted. "Kellan chose to stay on Oyster Island. And you two are perfect for each other."

"I know." Hissing out a long stream of air, he raked a hand through his auburn-tinged brown hair. The lights over the counter glinted off his silver engagement ring. "You're sure you're up for being in charge? No one would blame you if you wanted to rest while you can."

She rolled her eyes. Sam and Kellan being out of town would be a vacation for her, too. Then again, Sam's worrying was only the tip of the iceberg. Everyone had an opinion about her becoming a single mom.

"It's just pregnancy," she said. "It's a good thing."

Getting to bring smiles to her family members' faces would be the best. Ever since the car accident she and her dad had been in two years ago, there had been too much frowning. Her family too often treated her like she was going to fall apart because she'd been behind the wheel.

She thought they'd been on an upswing. Her dad's physical therapy was helping him have more pain-free days than before. Between that progress and Sam falling in love with Kellan, her older brother was no longer Captain Worrypants—or at least he was chill on days he *wasn't* leaving the island for a two-week trip to his fiancé's past life. But the closer Franci got to her delivery date, the more her family hovered.

The next biggest worrier was Franci's best friend, Violet, though she got a pass because she was also Franci's midwife. Everyone else needed to cool their jets.

"But your due date," Sam said, tapping a rapid beat on the counter with a pen. "And missing Thanksgiving…"

"All things we talked over. It will be fine."

"Ask for help if you need it," he said. "Archer will be able to—"

"I don't need an assistant, Sam." Nor did her brother's lead divemaster give off "assistant" vibes—he'd served in the Coast Guard, first as a rescue swimmer and then as a diver. He was all leading, all the time.

The fact Sam had chosen her to take over for him instead of Archer filled her with pride.

Jitters, too.

Fine, panic.

After taking a deep breath, she said, "Sam, I've got this. Please, go. If you miss your ferry and your red-eye, Kellan's business partner *definitely* won't like you."

Sam blanched.

"I'm *kidding*. Oh, man, you are in a bad way, aren't you?" She wrapped her arms around him as best she could given her belly. A couple more days, and she'd be at thirty-seven weeks.

He squeezed her gently. His deep exhalation ruffled the hair that had long escaped her messy bun. "I'm just nervous."

"I told you—Kellan's London crew will like you."

"It's not only Kell's friends. It's deserting you when you're this pregnant, and leaving the business during storm season." His words were strangled. "I'm so sorry this is when Rory scheduled the restaurant launch."

"Babies are always late in our family. I'll still be ridiculously pregnant when you get home. And I know the storm-season protocols. I'll even get the holiday decorations up, so you don't need to do it when you get back."

One more thing to add to her list. Where had she put the damn thing, again?

"And what if Kellan and I get there and he wants to stay…?"

"Not happening. Kellan Murphy is head over heels in love with you." She cupped her brother's bearded cheeks. "He'll probably be more eager to get back to Oyster Island than you will be. Forest + Brine is fully booked for winter. As if he'll want to miss cooking for all those eager stomachs." She hugged him, then went behind him and pushed him toward the rear door. "Now get…out…of…here. Don't forget, I want a stuffed corgi and a bag of real Scotch mints. The kind with packed powder inside, like we used to get from the Vancouver ferry when we were kids. Not the chewy stick-to-your-teeth ones."

Sam was thirty-eight to her own twenty-five, but he'd lived on Oyster Island almost his whole life, so he'd often traveled with her and their dad and their youngest sister, Charlotte, even into adulthood.

He took a deep breath, gave her another half squeeze and palmed her bump for a second. "Go easy on your mom, okay, kid?"

A sharp elbow bounced under Sam's hand.

Franci smiled. She didn't have a partner to share the journey, so her family had belly-touching privileges. "The baby's saying goodbye."

He shook his head in amazement. "I'm going to miss that while I'm gone."

"It'll still be here when you get home." She kissed his cheek. "Travel safe."

"I'll talk to Archer, make sure he's good with you leaning on him if you need to."

Franci's face heated. "Leave it, Sam."

Putting *need* and *Archer* in the same thought was dangerous business.

Lean, too. Archer Frost had a big, brawny body made to be used as a support beam. And ever since Franci's pregnancy hormones hit, she'd been losing her ability to ignore her coworker's fine attributes.

Exactly why she *wouldn't* be leaning on Archer in Sam's absence.

"I know what to do if I need help. Trust me." She made a shooing motion with her hand.

Sam sucked in what appeared to be the deepest breath ever taken by a human. The tension melted from his face, and his smile turned genuine. "You're right. You do." His smile widened farther. "And I get to go eat some excellent food in London before playing planes, trains and automobiles through Scotland and Ireland."

"It'll be a whirlwind, but you'll love every second of it. It's only logical to make a holiday of it after the grand opening." Sam adored traveling—he'd even flown to Australia to declare his love for Kellan back in March. The sweet gesture still got talked about over coffee at Hideaway Bakery.

And in Franci's loneliest moments, she let her heart ache over never having found that same life-changing love with anyone.

Romantic love, of course. Maternal love? That was already overflowing, and she was still at least three weeks from meeting her baby, likely more. Rubbing her stomach with one hand, she gave her brother one last wave.

The door finally shut behind him. The shop never felt empty—scuba and stand-up paddle equipment and racks of outdoor clothing crowded the space—but she lived for the few times a day when there were no other people around and she could enjoy the calm. A moment to take some grounding breaths and reassure herself she wasn't being overconfident in believing she had the shop—and life—well in hand.

She made her way through the store, tidying the stacks of equipment and clothes customers had mussed up over the course of the day. The ventilation system hummed overhead, the only sound. The old swimming pool clock on the wall reminded her that in ten minutes, the afternoon scuba tour would dock. Soon after, her favorite divemaster would stroll in and her ability to think would flood out the open door to the boardwalk, leaving behind a mental vacuum instead of management brilliance.

She was already at a deficit with pregnancy brain.

Thankfully, no one else knew about her little hormone-induced situation of not being able to keep her eyes off Archer Frost.

Stop it. There is no situation.

She had way too much to organize between now and her due date to add a head-turning scuba diver to the list.

Painting and nesting and work—oh, my.

The stack of paint chips she'd snagged at the local hardware store sat next to her water bottle on the front counter, waiting for her to choose the perfect color once her shift was over. How was she supposed to decide, though? They were all beautiful.

So she'd put it off a little longer. She for sure had time. Her mom had gone far overdue with all of her pregnancies, and Franci expected her own would be the same. She wasn't worried, and the people who loved her shouldn't be, either.

She had things under control. A successful full-time job, albeit a little altered from usual since she couldn't lead dive tours at the moment. A new cozy rental out on a gorgeous piece of farm property on the other side of Oyster Island. A flourishing pregnancy.

She was going to be a mother.

She was healthy.

And she could handle the flipping dive schedule and sales terminal while her brother went to the UK to support his man.

Without "leaning on Archer."

If she tried that, even once, she'd never want to stop.

Archer Frost guided Otter Marine's motorized wagon over the lip at the top of the boat ramp, wanting to finish cleanup before the sun set and he lost light. Then again, if he dragged the task out, he could delay replying to the series of texts he'd received while out on the water.

His godson, Daniel, was brimming with excitement over registering for his scuba certification course.

Got any advice, Arch?

Yeah, plenty.

Most of it having nothing to do with diving.

The wheels of the cart thumped over the wooden tread of the harbor boardwalk, echoed by Archer's uneven steps. Too uneven. He'd rushed while getting out of the boat, rotating his prosthetic knee to climb over the gunwale instead of opening and lowering the accessible gate. He hadn't been precise enough to get his foot facing forward again in the rush of eight divers offloading their tanks and gathering their gear. Hopefully he could fix it with a bit of fiddling. If he'd broken his dive leg and hadn't noticed, it would be a monumental pain in the ass. He'd just been to see his prosthetist on the mainland to tweak his everyday leg, the computerized model he used when he wasn't diving or running. He didn't want to have to make another ferry trip, especially not with Sam flying off today. Archer would loathe leaving Franci short-staffed. She had enough on her plate.

His phone buzzed in the pocket of his shorts. Likely Daniel with another diving question.

He'd answer them tonight, when he could get his fingers to complete a full sentence without his eyes going blurry. But the thought of his godson going underwater…

Archer should not be the one doling out advice.

Daniel's dad should be around to do that.

And because of Archer, he wasn't.

His chest tightened. Gritting his teeth, he steered the cart toward the tank cage. The metal structure bookended one side of the row of converted houses centering Oyster Island's front promenade. The pastel exteriors were a bright splash of color anchoring the wild beauty of the cove. Archer had lived on Coast Guard bases from the Arctic to Hawaii to the Gulf Coast, and nothing felt like home as much as this charming little collection of businesses and people, tucked safely away from the elements. Getting to show guests and tourists all the wonders Oyster Island had to offer, on the surface and underwater, was a privilege he didn't take lightly.

He'd sent today's lucky clients ahead with Nic, Otter's young part-timer, to organize and return any rented equipment. No doubt they were all inside, being directed to drop their fins and buoyancy compensators in the correct bins. Franci would be there, coaxing out stories of the day's adventures with her sunny smile, and lamenting not getting to join in on the undersea exploration.

He missed being in the water with her, too. His best friend's younger sister was a blast to have on tours, always the positive energy, always enchanted by the small things.

His Veterans Affairs counselor would probably tell him he needed more of that energy in his life.

Archer disagreed. He'd made his peace with a whole lot of garbage in order to make the physical progress necessary to do the job he loved, but being Suzy Sunshine wasn't ever going to be his vibe.

Didn't mean he couldn't secretly enjoy Franci's particular brand of joy, though. On the periphery of his life, at least.

His cell vibrated again. *Damn it.*

He yanked it out, making the case creak in his grip. If Daniel was this excited, Archer couldn't ignore—

The notification was from Sam.

Relief washed through him as he tapped on the text thread.

Sam: We're off—do me a favor

Archer: Depends on the favor

Sam: Keep an eye on Fran for me

Sam: Without her noticing I asked

Archer suppressed a snort. The closer Francine got to her due date, the more Sam's watchdog habits were kicking back in. Hopefully the vacation would calm him the hell down. And besides, Archer didn't need to watch out for Franci on Sam's behalf. He already did it for his own sake. But secrecy was key there.

Archer: As if she'd notice something unless I wanted her to

"A" school, where he'd done his aviation survival technician training, had been a long time ago. Even so, a guy didn't forget how to hide his discomfort while enduring some of the toughest physical tests possible.

Came in handy when said guy couldn't stop thinking about his best friend's much-younger sister.

Groaning at his foolishness, he sat on one of the boardwalk benches and took a minute to get the alignment right on his prosthesis. Then he attacked the empty steel tanks like they were a gnarly underwater hazard to be cleared and finished the job faster than usual. Franci aside, he had one thing to do while Sam was away: make sure all the diving tasks were taken care of with no fuss.

With the canisters inspected, filled and stored, he locked the cage behind him and headed for the ramp at the back entrance of the store. He checked his dive watch. Close to five. Franci would have locked up and headed home by now. He hadn't gotten to say goodbye.

Damn. Maybe he wasn't as good at this covert-checking thing as he'd thought.

He reached for his keys, but the door was unlocked. Wait, she was still here? A protective streak ran up his back. With all the guests gone, she should have thrown the dead bolt on the back entrance. He entered the rear storeroom.

"Franci?"

"Hey, Hawkeye." The lilting voice came from somewhere on the shop floor. A silly nickname. He swore she kept a mental list of famous archers from books and movies. Waiting to see which one she'd pull out next was entertaining as hell.

He stalked into the space, then nearly tripped over thin air. He had to swallow to keep from croaking. "Yoga hour, I take it?"

She was using one of the inflatable SUP boards in place of a mat, minus the detachable fin. Her downward dog was a thing of beauty.

She made *everything* she did beautiful. Her red curls were piled on top of her head, and she wore bright pink leggings and a loose T-shirt. She'd always been curvy, with a figure he'd only ever thought of as lush, but pregnancy enhanced all that. Her feet were bare, her toenails a vibrant indigo.

A million fascinating details.

He wanted to know them all.

They aren't for me to learn.

Some days, being thirty-seven felt like he had a lifetime ahead of him, and others he felt as old as the rotting pilings from the original ferry dock he could see from his place on the north side of the island.

She shifted into a lunge and pointed a flat hand in his direction, a fierce gestating warrior. "Want to join me? Once the last client left, I couldn't resist loosening up."

"Bridge too far for me this evening." He forced himself to admit the truth. His back ached and his hip pinched. Time to get home, switch to his chair and take a long soak in his bathtub.

"Cool cool." Curiosity danced in her gaze, those wide eyes flecked with more shades of brown than he knew the names for. "And here I was going to ask you to come help me paint."

He straightened. "The hardware store carries the pregnancy-safe kind?"

"Yeah, but I haven't narrowed down a color yet."

He chuckled. Of course she hadn't.

"I was kidding about asking you to help," she said, then nibbled her lip, making the small, curved scar at the corner of her mouth stand out. "Even if I had the paint, I wouldn't subject an innocent victim to the chore."

"I can make time for it," he said. Having a project would be better than thinking about Daniel's dive training. It also fit under the umbrella of him keeping an eye on Franci for Sam's sake. "Not tonight, but soon. Tuesday? I don't have anything planned for my day off."

The shop was closed once a week, so she wouldn't be working, either.

Her cheeks went bright red. "I wasn't serious."

"I am. Think about it," he said.

Making a noncommittal noise, she shifted into warrior pose with her other leg and arm forward.

Goddamn. Her rock-solid balance, round hips, strong thighs… A man could explore those curves for days and barely scratch the surface.

He swung his gaze from her. "I'm going to rinse off the salt before I head home."

"Be quick—I think Nic used most of the hot water."

Swearing, he went into the staff change area and shut the door with too much force. The shower turned icy halfway through but didn't do anything to cool him off.

He toweled off, put on his walking leg and got into his after-work sweats and hoodie. He slung his duffel bag with his other prosthesis and his ocean-damp clothes over his shoulder. With any luck, Franci would have headed home. He'd have to text her, insist on coming over on Tuesday to pitch in with her painting.

First, I need to text Danny.

He pulled out his cell to finally reply to his godson's messages. A simple "That's exciting, kid" would be fine.

But when he put his thumbs to the screen, he couldn't make them move. Frowning at the device, he left the staff room.

"What's wrong?"

He jumped, dropping his phone.

"Shoot, sorry." Franci winced from her seat at the lower tier of the counter. She'd started using an exercise-ball chair a few months back. She bounced in place, holding a stack of paint chips like a rainbow fan. "My fault. I'd offer to pick it up for you, but I think I'd get stuck."

"I've got it," he murmured, grabbing the corner of the desk for balance and swiping the device off the floor.

"Everything okay?" she asked.

Finally managing a Wow, awesome to Daniel, he pressed Send and pinched the bridge of his nose. "That should be *my* question for *you*."

"Why?"

He motioned to her ever-rounding stomach.

"Nah. Same old, same old in the baby-growing department. And I'm not the one scowling at my phone like I got summoned for jury duty."

"I'm not scowling," he grumbled.

"Lies, Legolas."

Shaking his head—she hadn't pulled out that particular "archer" name in a while—he motioned to Franci's collection of paint chips. "What are your favorites?"

Her cheeks reddened. "All of them."

"Pick one," he said. "I'll grab you the cans you need and bring them to work tomorrow morning."

"Why?"

"To give you a break," he said, trying to keep his tone neutral.

"I can lift paint cans. They're not too heavy. And before you ask, I have a painting mask to wear with the right filter."

"I wasn't going to ask." Though he had wondered about that while he was in the shower. He rubbed the back of his neck. "I need to go to the hardware store anyway. I need to, uh, replace the seal around my kitchen sink."

"I appreciate the offer, but I've got this."

"I didn't say otherwise."

"It's always implied, Archer."

"Maybe with other people. Not me," he said. "I know you're capable—"

"Thank you."

He lifted an eyebrow. "Interrupting me when I'm about to give you a compliment?"

"When it's likely accompanied by a *but*? Yes."

"Again, not from me. You're capable. And you're close to your due date, and going it alone—"

"Aha!" She threw up her hands. "That 'and' was totally a 'but.'"

"No, it's stating truths. You are very pregnant *and* you are going it alone *and* you can do things by yourself, but sometimes, a coworker offers to run an errand for you and slap some paint on a wall, and it's not a damn crime."

She blinked. "'Coworker,' huh?"

The quiet disappointment killed him.

"Uh…"

"I know. You're Sam's friend first," she said, sighing. "And you probably still see me in pigtails. But I thought we'd started to progress to friends, separate from my brother."

Christ. He did *not* see her in pigtails. He *should*, given he'd noticed a few gray hairs setting up shop over his temples while she'd be hitting the clubs if she didn't live on a remote island hours away from Seattle.

But he didn't.

Or at least, his instincts didn't want to.

He refused to entertain them.

"Coworkers *and* friends," he said gruffly.

She grinned. "Good. And as your friend, I'd feel even worse asking for your help. You've already adjusted your schedule so much for me."

"And? Your point?" As soon as she'd found out she was pregnant, she'd had to stop diving and had switched to Zodiac, kayak and SUP tours, leaving Archer with more diving assignments. Life was more comfortable underwater than above, so he didn't mind.

"I feel like an inconvenience," she grumbled.

"Never. I'd be happy to help, Franci." *Watch over her* without *her noticing*. "But I won't force the issue."

"Hmm." She rubbed her belly near her ribs.

He shot her a look of concern.

She waved it off. "Dang baby elbow. It's pointy. So, you're going to the hardware store anyway?"

"Yes," he said, lying through his teeth.

She plucked two of the color cards from the stack and laid the bright aqua next to the pale yellow. "What do you think—Sea Glass Blue or Lemon Sherbet?"

He studied the selections, then pointed at the paler color.

"The other is too bright?" she asked.

"No, the yellow is like early-morning sunshine. It suits you."

"Suits a baby's room, you mean."

The blood drained from his face. He had no business commenting on what suited her or not. No right to connect her bright smile to a freaking paint chip. "Yeah. That."

"Okay. Lemon Sherbet it is."

He jerked a nod.

She handed him the rectangular card. "This brand, the zero-VOC type. I'll need two gallons."

"Hardware store opens at ten. I'll bring it with me for my shift." He let out a relieved breath. "Honestly, it's nice to have an easy problem to solve."

Her smile fell and his world went a little darker. "You think I'm a problem to solve?"

"No. *No*," he said. "I'm just... My godson is... Never mind." He hitched his duffel higher on his shoulder. "I'll see you in the morning."

He couldn't be honest with her. Franci Walker *was* a problem.

Just not for the reason she suspected.

Chapter Two

"No squishing my niblet!"

Lifting an eyebrow at her protesting best friend, Franci paused her struggle to get the zipper on her makeshift maternity dry suit fastened over her baby bump. She and Sam had jury-rigged a Frankensuit out of a few used models of different sizes. Fitting into it was getting to be a laborious task the closer she got to her due date. But the alternative—staying off the water—wasn't happening.

"I'm not squishing anything except my pride," Franci insisted.

Violet Frost slurped the dregs of her bright orange breakfast smoothie with a silicone straw. Her dry suit, lightweight for kayaking during the winter, fit like a glove, of course. Violet was a good five inches taller than Franci, strong and vital like her older brother. She had the same deep blue eyes as Archer, too, and that beautiful dark hair with a tendency to curl when wet. Ready for a morning paddle, Violet wore a slouchy turquoise knit cap over her two long braids.

"Pregnancy's the most beautiful thing in the world," Violet said. "It's also a hell of a kick to the ego."

Franci laughed. Violet would know. Not from personal experience—she hadn't been pregnant—but she'd been Oyster Island's nurse-midwife for three years and had seen it all by this point.

A beam of sunlight shone across Violet's shoulders. Her friend sprawled in Sam's office chair, enjoying an early breakfast from the Hideaway Bakery. She had arrived, drinks and pastries in hand, a few minutes after Franci. They were going to steal a half-hour paddle before Franci had to dive—figuratively—into her Sunday of running the shop.

Franci usually abhorred getting up early for work and had to admit she was often late, but she'd needed to be more than on time this morning. Somehow, she'd prove to everyone around her, and to herself, that when the demands of single motherhood swamped her, she'd be able to float above the current.

The glass in the window of the back office glowed as the morning sun rose over the small peninsula protecting Hideaway Wharf from the elements. A perfect morning for an early kayak—sunshine, calm waters.

"So much for storm season." After tilting the blinds to direct the sun away from her eyes, Franci got back to her task, yanking on the zipper. It was supposed to fasten diagonally across her swollen abdomen, but it gaped like the mouth of a Halloween mask. "Damn it.

I've grown out of this, and there's no way to alter it further without wrecking the seals."

"Sorry, hon. I'll be able to deliver your baby like the best of them, but I'm not crafty like you."

Ugh, what was she going to do to stay dry? "Maybe if I wear an extra insulating layer, I could find some Gore-Tex pants and a waterproof jacket of Sam's."

Expression dubious, Violet nibbled on her blueberry muffin.

"If I ever have another baby, I'm going to make sure to plan the due date better." *Or plan the pregnancy in the first place.* "Summer deliveries only. No fussing with dry suits and cold-weather gear."

Violet coughed. "Babies don't like to follow schedules."

"Yeah, kinda clued into that back when I peed on a stick and saw a plus sign." Her precious nugget was the product of a week-long fling with a tourist, a guy visiting from Idaho. He was going to help her out with child support but didn't want to be involved in parenting. Some difficult conversations awaited her in the future, when she'd have to explain Brad's decision to her child. She'd have to be enough for two parents.

She could do it, though. Her child wasn't going to grow up wondering if her mom loved her.

Violet had been supportive from the minute she found out, at least. Sam, too, and his mom and her wife. Rachel and Winnie were Franci's landlords. Her little bungalow was located on the edge of their hobby farm. And her dad had come around, after some initial surprise. Rachel had helped there. She still managed to be friends with Franci's dad, despite their divorce.

Franci's mom? Not so much. Alina struggled to acknowledge Franci and Charlotte, let alone her ex. It was like her mom had expected them to take sides after the divorce, and had been pissed off that her daughters still loved their dad. Alina chose to focus on Franci's stepdad and younger half brothers.

Maybe she'd find room to love a grandchild, though.

Hopping a bit, Franci tugged at the zipper but got nowhere. She hung her head. "I give up."

"Want me to try?" Violet offered.

"No." She sat on the edge of the desk and held out her hand. "Muffin, please. I need to eat my feelings."

"Do you want midwife Vi, or best friend Vi?"

"Best friend. You know that with my family history of late deliveries, I'm going to pop this one out at forty-two weeks on the nose. I honestly appreciate the encouragement to cut out added sugar for the sake of trying not to have a massive baby. But we have a deal." Inside the Bloom Midwifery office on the other end of Wharf Street, Violet had free rein to remind Franci about all the healthiest pregnancy habits. Outside the office, the nagging was a no go.

Violet handed over the pastry.

Franci took two gorgeous bites of sweet pillowy cake and then handed it back. "Okay. Feelings sated. Time to figure out what I'm going to wear."

Her friend yawned. "We could postpone."

"On a miraculously clear day in November? No way."

They went to the staff change room. Franci spun the dial to open Sam's locker.

She groaned. "It's empty. He must have taken his stuff home to wash before his holiday."

Curse her brother and his incessant forward planning.

Violet plucked a set of waterproof overalls and a rain slicker off an overflowing hook on the wall. "These would fit."

"Those are Archer's."

"And?"

"I'm not sure he'd be good with me using them."

"I'm good with it for him." Violet's younger-sister vibe was as strong as Franci's, though there were only five years between Vi and Archer, a way smaller gap than the one between Franci and her own brother.

"Seriously, we don't have the kind of relationship where I have free rein to borrow his raincoat."

Violet rolled her eyes. "He's all bark and no bite, hon."

"He doesn't bark at me. He just considers me a colleague." Yesterday, she'd had to drag his admission of friendship out of him like he was a boat anchor stuck in a tidal flat.

"You're overthinking this," her friend said. "And we're running out of morning."

"Fine." Franci clutched the waterproof material, picturing being surrounded by Archer himself instead of his rain slicker. *Oh, no no no.* She needed to get outside and clear her head.

She pulled on the too-long pants and tightened the toggles around her ankles to keep the hems from dragging. The jacket smelled like whatever spicy soap he used, mixed with salt air and a bit of boat gas. She zipped it up, barely getting the thick fabric over her belly. The getup wasn't going to breathe well, but she'd at least stay dry. So long as they got back to the dock in time for her to return the outerwear before he noticed she'd borrowed it, she'd be fine.

Ten minutes later, they were climbing into their kayaks. Her boat wobbled as she sat.

"Whoa!" she said, catching the edge of the dock for balance. She did not need to end up in the drink in this makeshift getup.

Violet yelped, face pale above her short red life vest. "Easy, now. No swimming in November."

"Yeah, yeah."

They made it into the next bay to the west and back without getting drenched. Franci felt twenty pounds lighter. With every dip of her paddle into the lapping waves, she deposited a bit of tension. There was nothing like the view of the shore from the sea. Craggy trees, bold splashes of evergreen against steely gray cliffs and the winter-pale sky—she could breathe out here.

Violet helped, too, chatting about her overdue client on Orcas Island, agreeing with the choice of yellow for the baby's room and asking about how many times Sam had called since he landed in London.

"Only twice," Franci said, shaking her head at her overprotective brother. Being with Kellan had softened him some, but he'd always be a sheepdog.

They approached the pilings bracketing the entrance to the harbor.

The wind blew gently. She sucked in the fresh air. "I'm thinking the forecast is wrong. If there's an atmospheric river on its way, it's being mighty sneaky."

"Maybe it'll miss us," Violet said.

A phone shrilled.

Franci straightened. "Is that your emergency number?"

Violet fumbled in the waterproof compartment of her kayak. "Crap, yes." She answered with a hello, followed quickly by "uh-huh," "you're doing great," and "I'll be on the next ferry."

Franci smiled when Violet hung up. "'Overdue' is soon becoming a delivery?"

"Seems so." Violet winced. "I gotta speed if I'm going to catch the ten-thirty boat."

"You go on ahead."

"I don't want to leave you."

"This is my job, Vi," she said gently. "I'll be fine. Leave your kayak on the dock—I'll put it away."

"Use the accessible docking thing, okay?"

"Mmm-hmm." They had a contraption where people with mobility needs could secure their kayaks and safely step out without being at risk of pitching into the water. Franci hadn't needed it so far, though. Daily yoga did wonders for her balance. "Go deliver a baby. Practice for this one." She patted her bump.

"Right." Violet dug her paddle into the water in smooth strokes, quickly disappearing around the rocky breakwater that protected the hodgepodge of boats in the harbor from the worst of the winter waves.

Franci took her time. She did need to get back to the shop before Archer arrived for his eleven-o'clock tour, but she had a few minutes yet.

The ferry was pulling into the dock adjacent to the harbor.

Wait. It was already ten after ten? *Damn it.* She stepped on the gas, paddling hard herself. Once she'd skimmed up to the dock, she grabbed on to the wooden lip, tossed her paddle up, yanked her spray skirt free and pulled herself upward.

And went nowhere.

What the hell?

She hoisted herself again. *Nothing.* Had her belly seriously grown that much in a week? It couldn't have. Was the extra fabric from the bulky jacket to blame? She groaned, gave one last hoist and made it partway on her side.

Her boat slipped away from the dock.

"Oh, shit!"

Hanging on to the edge, thighs still stuck in the cockpit, she hung, torso close to brushing the water. She scanned the web of docks for the nearest person. Of course it was empty.

She clutched tighter, biceps and triceps screaming. Squinting at the ramp, she caught movement. "Hello?"

A familiar figure appeared, backlit by the sun, along the path from the parking lot toward the shop. Didn't react to her shout, though.

Come on, Archer. Hear me.

Thirty more seconds, and she'd be swimming. She took as deep a breath as she could, her diaphragm compressed by baby, and let loose with a bellow. *"Help!"*

Archer dropped the paint canisters on the sidewalk and ran toward Franci's ringing plea. He couldn't see her, but he knew what her howl meant—move faster than he ever had. Sprinting in his walking leg could leave him hobbling tomorrow, but his gut told him to push.

The metal ramp shrieked in time with another *"Help!"* as he bolted down the angled surface, desperately scanning around sailboat hulls and fishing boats to see where she was.

"Franci?" he bellowed.

"By the *Queen*!" she called back, voice weakening.

His lungs heaved, and as he rounded one of the local trawlers, he finally spotted her, clinging to the end of the branch where they stored the kayaks in a specially built cage. Face white as a sheet between her rainbow beanie and olive green slicker, clutching the edge of the dock like she was a sea star.

"Jesus, Francine. Hang on."

She whimpered.

He made it to the end of the dock and knelt carefully. Wrapping his arms under hers and around her back, he finally exhaled.

"Don't let go," she squeaked.

"Never." He rose taller on his knees, dragging her legs and the boat closer to the dock. "Put your arms around my neck."

"I'm too heavy. I'm going to pull us both in."

"If I can rescue people off a sinking boat while dangling from a rope in a hurricane, I can lift you out of a kayak, Francine."

"Okay."

She was kind not to point out he hadn't rescued anyone since having to be rescued himself.

Since requiring a rescue so time consuming that

his teammate—his best friend—had ended up with the bends.

Since that nitrogen sickness had led to Eduardo's fatal heart attack.

Goddamn it, he couldn't let that distract him right now.

"I'm going to stand slowly. Let the kayak go. I'll fish it out once you're up."

He flattened his right foot and rose, managing to lift them both enough to get his prosthetic leg under him, too. Thank God he deadlifted in the gym on a regular basis. By the time he had her secure, she was on her toes, shaking, her arms banded around his neck.

"You're good," he said. "You can let go."

"N-no."

"Okay, then." He shouldn't like being the person she clung to, but he couldn't bury the feelings of relief. *Not just relief. Comfort. Mine as much as hers.* "Breathe."

She let out a squeak.

"Yeah, I hear that. Breathe *with* me, then, okay?"

He set an easy rhythm, and was happy when the rise and fall of her chest slowed to match his. His own peace was a facade, though. He could control his inhalations and exhalations all he wanted, but his heart rate refused to calm.

"Close call." He shifted her arms lower, wrapping them around his waist so she could relax off her tiptoes.

"I know how to s-swim."

"Doesn't help much when the water's forty-eight degrees and you're not properly dressed for it." He didn't put much stock in prayers, but he was willing to get back on his knees and say his thanks for having shown up early after hitting the hardware store this morning.

"Y-you spent half your l-life in frigid ocean t-temperatures. I w-would have been f-fine."

"I wore a buoyant survival suit," he said. "And haven't in a lot of years." Most of his friends had been in disbelief when he'd moved from being an aviation survival technician to a diver. Coast Guard diving was difficult and well respected, but the prestige of being an AST made it one of the most competitive jobs in the armed forces. Coasties waited years for the chance to rappel from a hovering helicopter to save boaters in peril. But he loved being under the water.

He should have listened to everyone. Would've kept saving lives on the surface instead of losing one of the ones he'd held most dear.

His ex-wife had told him as much.

Thankfully, today had a better outcome.

He narrowed his eyes at Franci's baggy outfit. "Is that my jacket?"

"Uh, yeah... Glitch with my dry suit. Violet figured it was fine to borrow this even though I told her you wouldn't like it but she insisted and I was itchy to get out on the water, but then I got stuck in the flipping boat because of the extra fabric and I don't think I'll ever *not* feel embarrassed—"

She stepped away, blowing a breath through pursed lips, hands resting on the top of her stomach. Her face was too pale, her lips white around the edges, and damn it, he wasn't ready to let go of her yet. At least she'd gotten her breath back enough to spout one of her classic run-on sentences. He'd never been so happy to be the recipient of so many syllables.

"What does my sister have to do with anything?" he asked.

"She was with me, until she had to race off to catch the ferry." She narrowed her eyes. "You thought I'd gone out on the water alone?"

He jammed a hand in his hair. "Wasn't sure what to think."

"Jeez, Robin Hood, have a little faith in my judgment." Frowning, she eased into a squat, then knelt and reached for the kayak.

"I can do that."

"You've been on your knees enough. The shell's light."

"I don't want you doing a header into the water if you're still shaky."

She lifted the craft from the water with the ease of a person who'd done it a thousand times before.

Sam's request was turning him into an overprotective bear.

"Consider the squats as me practicing for labor," she said lightly, standing awkwardly before lifting the kayak to the struts inside the cage.

"As long as it's only practice," he grumbled. "You've hit your drama quota for the day."

Her stricken look was like a speargun to the chest.

"I'm kidding," he said, rushing to get out the assurance. Anything to wipe the hurt from her eyes.

"Obviously," she returned just as quickly.

Ha, right. As if anything was obvious when it came to Franci Walker.

Chapter Three

It took until the afternoon for Franci to wind down from the shock of her eventful exit from the kayak. She rubbed her bump for the umpteenth time.

Sorry, peanut. Overestimated myself.

Or underestimated the size of her stomach while wearing Archer's jacket, to be more specific. She'd thought the worst-case scenario would be him being grumpy about her borrowing it, not a near miss on a November ocean plunge.

Had Archer not been there, it would have been a frigid morning, or worse. Being left with bruised pride and sore triceps and shoulders was a small price to pay.

Her body was telling her to rest, and she wasn't going to ignore it. So long as the storm in the forecast didn't cancel the kayak tour scheduled for two days from now, it would be her last one. She'd make sure to use the accessible dock for getting out of the boat, and would ensure Kim, the other Otter Marine tour guide scheduled on the trip, was close by.

With that decided, she couldn't focus enough to check on the supply orders Sam had left her to complete. Knowing she was going to be useless with anything clerical, she headed for the small storeroom and took out the boxes of holiday decorations. All the businesses on Wharf Street hired the same artist to paint winter scenes in their windows, but she always made sure to add extra touches around Thanksgiving. This year, it seemed smart to do it even earlier. She didn't want to count on being in the mood to decorate a few days before her due date.

Deciding on decor for the baby's room seemed impossible, but she could handle the shop. She started with light strings tacked around the edge of the front windows. Halfway through, she realized she needed the step stool. She stared at the three-stair rise. Would using it be smart? After the morning's adventure, she wasn't so sure. If Archer came in from his dive tour and saw her off the ground, even with the support rail, he'd probably frown for the rest of the week.

The bell jingled, letting her off the hook from making the decision. She let the half-hung string dangle and peered around a rack of wet suits. "Hi, there—oh! Dad!"

"There's my fancy Franci." He was wiping his feet on the mat and leaning on his cane. He had a bulging cloth shopping bag in his other hand.

She stopped short—he wasn't smiling like usual. "Is something wrong?" she asked.

"Popped into the bakery for a coffee just now and heard a hell of a story from Rachel."

She winced, glad she didn't have to give details. Where would she even start? The weirdest parts stood out.

The jade green of the water.

A streak of black and gray clothing as Archer sprinted toward her.

And other sensations, too, impressed in her mind, hard to shake. Mainly, how being able to bury her face against his broad chest, of being supported—no, *cradled*—had been necessary in that moment. And without it, she might have fallen apart.

"Made the wrong call," she mumbled. "Glad I didn't get hurt."

Or worse, the baby.

He nodded slowly. "I know you want to be everywhere and do everything, but maybe for the next few weeks, you might consider slowing down?"

Her cheeks heated. "Already ahead of you. I spent the morning begging Nic to start his full-time tour guide hours a couple weeks early so I can stick to cashier detail."

He nodded in satisfaction. Rolling his shoulder and stretching his neck, he said, "Let me get the high ones for you."

She suppressed the urge to ask him if his shoulder was feeling okay enough to reach above his head. If she wanted him to back off about his concern over her pregnancy, she needed to extend the same to him when it came to his recovery.

She'd walked away from being T-boned at the intersection in front of the elementary school with a scar on her face, a broken arm and a dislocated shoulder. Painful, but temporary. Greg, on the other hand, had borne the brunt of the impact in the passenger seat, and sustained all sorts of pelvic and back injuries. His chronic pain broke Franci's heart. It had been an accident, and someone else's fault, but it had taken her a long while to get to the place where she didn't feel guilty for having been behind the wheel.

She handed him the string. He easily reached the cup hooks they kept screwed into the upper window frame.

Man, she missed being able to do everything she liked to do.

It's temporary. Five and a bit more weeks at most.

And between Sam being gone until the end of the month, and all the myriad festivities in the lead-up to all the December holidays, it would have been a busy period of time even if she *wasn't* expecting her baby to arrive sometime after Thanksgiving.

She glanced at the bag her dad had put on the floor. "Early Christmas shopping?"

"No such thing as too early."

Maybe not, though Franci usually left her shopping for December 23. "Who's it for? Charlotte?"

Charlotte had graduated high school in June and still lived with Greg.

"Your sister wants gift cards. This is for Ali," he said, cheeks going ruddy.

Franci chuckled. She still found it a little odd how Alice Wong had gone from the neighbor who made the best chocolate chip cookies to the person Franci occasionally caught kissing Greg in the kitchen, but she was happy to roll with it if it kept said father smiling. He hadn't smiled enough in the past two years. And with not having much of a relationship with her step-dad, Franci was enjoying at least one of her parents partnering up with someone who showed interest in her and Charlotte.

Maybe when the baby arrived, her mom and step-dad would carve out more family time. She didn't want to hope, but she couldn't help it. The baby was already not going to have a father. How would Franci explain an absent grandma, too?

She sighed, forcing a smile for her dad. "What did you get Ali?"

"A new herb dryer."

Franci's jaw dropped. "*Dad.* An *appliance*?"

He laughed. "And these."

Producing a small hinged wooden box from his pocket, he flipped open the lid. A pair of dangling aquamarine earrings nestled on a layer of navy velvet.

"That's more like it," Franci said primly.

He winked. "I'm not screwing this one up, Francine. Third time's the charm."

She truly wanted him to find that happiness.

She also wanted something similar for herself.

One step at a time.

First, she had to figure out motherhood.

A gust of wind whipped against the back windows of the cottage so hard, Franci jumped. A thump followed. Had she not known better, she would have thought a branch hit the roof. But she'd seen storms like this be-fore. Despite her doubts yesterday with the weather

being beautiful, the forecast was following through on
its promise for a Monday howler. Nothing she couldn't
manage. She had hot water in her kettle, a good book
to read and a backup generator if the power went out.

She'd also been able to head home early after sending emails to all the clients who would get rescheduled
or refunded. A wind this strong meant a small-craft
warning, so no tours of any kind would be running for
a few days.

She'd even started prepping the baby's room, thanks
to Archer collecting her paint yesterday. He was planning to come help her tomorrow, but she'd left the task
long enough and wanted to at least get a bit done before he pitched in.

Once the walls had the first coat on them, she could
take on the crib. Maybe. She wasn't sure how much
more painting she had in her today—her back was sore
after the dock incident yesterday.

She stared at the patchy first layer of paint on the
wall.

Well, first she'd finish the baby's room. *Then* she'd
rest.

Another blast of wind rattled the windows. She swallowed her irrational bolt of nerves and lifted the roller.

She rolled a pretty yellow coat over half a wall before
taking a break to stand back and knead her lower back
muscles. Damn, they'd fused into some knot. She took a
deep breath, muffled by the mask she wore for painting.

*Breathe in, create space. Breathe out, release the
tension.*

Create space. Ha. Her little one wasn't leaving room
for anything today. Holding her left hand to her spine,

she reached with the roller to swipe another swath of pale summery light on the wall.

Bang bang bang. Bang.

Shrieking, she dropped the roller. "Oh, damn it!"

She had a drop cloth protecting the floor, but still, the shutters rapping the siding shouldn't startle her that badly.

Ding-dong.

The doorbell. Not the wind.

She groaned, rescuing her roller. Once she had the paint-slicked tool back in the tray, she took off her mask and made her way to the front door. Who would have come all the way from the wharf in this storm? She wouldn't want her dad to be out—with his mobility issues, the last thing he needed was to slip on the slick ground because he'd come to check on her. Charlotte was no doubt busy with her boyfriend or her online college courses. Maybe Rachel or Winnie, her landlords, had braved the sideways rain and wandered down the driveway from their larger, gingerbread-esque house? Though the bakery wouldn't close with the wind, so they were unlikely to be home yet.

Fear jolted through her veins.

Silly, getting scared. There was no one on Oyster Island out to hurt her. She peeked through the peephole in her front door.

A familiar olive green slicker filled the fish-eye viewer.

Her heart leaped.

Oh, good grief.

She yanked open the door and backed up, waving a drenched Archer into the house. Honu, his black Labrador, bolted past them both, immediately heading for the kitchen. "Come in! God. You're going to short out your knee it's raining so hard."

Exasperation shadowed his blue eyes to navy. "This model is nearly waterproof." He shut the door and shook himself out on her doormat. "Goddamn, it's a typhoon out there."

"A bomb cyclone, I heard," she said. "Why are you out in it?"

"Making sure you're okay." He hung his jacket on the coat tree. He only had a thin T-shirt underneath. *Oh my.* The cotton blend had a worse crush on Archer's shoulders than Franci did. The material clung to the angles and hard lines.

"Staying awhile?" she croaked.

"Not in the mood for company?"

For yours, these days? Always.

"You could have just called," she pointed out. Her spine stiffened in irritation, and the added muscle tension jabbed at her hips. "It's not like I asked you to check on me."

"No, *you* didn't," he said under his breath.

"What does that mean?"

His cheeks reddened. "Nothing. And I *did* call you. Three times. And some texts. You weren't answering."

She put her hands on her hips. "Persistent much, Hawkeye?"

He crossed his arms over his broad chest.

Her mouth went dry.

Most days, he was Archer Frost, dive instructor.

The level of sternness currently turning his face to concrete was 100 percent Petty Officer Archer Frost, diver first class, with a chest full of medals and an impeccable service record until the one day everything had gone wrong.

He let out a gust of irritation that was likely felt by the wind sensor at the top of Teapot Hill. "Forgive me for panicking when my friend's eight-plus-months-pregnant sister doesn't answer her phone, Franci."

He pulled his cell out of his pocket and tapped the screen.

God, why was it so hard for him to call her *his* friend? Her ribs tightened and she rubbed the little knob of baby foot by her navel.

"I'm clearly fine." She only managed a half hearted protest. He wasn't entirely wrong. If Violet were pregnant, Franci would be checking on her three times a day.

A buzz sounded from the coffee table in the living room.

"So it *is* working. You were ignoring me?" He looked a little hurt.

"I was in the baby's room. Painting." The knot in her back twinged again and she dug a thumb into it. "Might get enough done today to free you from helping tomorrow."

His expression softened. "Let me give you a hand now. Please."

Ugh, when he said *please*...

Gruff Archer was easy to deny. Annoyed Archer, too.

But how was a woman supposed to say no to manners and alarmingly tender blue eyes?

"Fine. There's not much left to do, anyway."

Only the entire part near the ceiling. NBD.

"Got a towel so I can dry off my shoes?" he asked. "I forgot a spare pair."

She'd learned enough about his prosthesis to know it wasn't adjusted for him to walk around barefoot for long lengths of time. She went to her laundry room to grab an older dish towel and brought it back to him. While she waited for him to dry off his sneakers, she eased onto the floor and into butterfly pose to work out the kinks in her back and hips.

"Stiff?" he asked.

"Mmm." He didn't need to know kayaking was the culprit.

"How about you do whatever stretching you need to do to loosen up while I finish your painting?"

She made a face. "The only thing that's going to fully loosen me up is delivering this baby."

Archer glanced out the window and blew out a breath. "Let's avoid that, yeah?"

"Obviously." She got on her knees and palmed the wall.

He made a grumbling noise.

"What?" she snapped.

Leaning over to cup her elbow, he mumbled, "Know one thing I've learned over the past four years?"

He smelled like the rain. And soap.

And kissing.

Why did Archer Frost smell like kissing? What did that even *mean*?

With a little bit of pressure from his hand and a little bit of help from the wall, she managed to stand without looking too much like a harbor seal phlumping across a dock. Her grumpy and tired-of-her-backache self wanted to snap a quick retort to his question-that-might-be-admonishment, but his tone was genuine, not know-it-all.

"What've you learned, Archer?" she asked softly.

His hand was still under her elbow, strong and steady. "Pride can make life a hell of a lot more difficult than it has to be. Or so my VA PT used to tell me."

She lifted her chin. "Didn't pride get you from lying in a hospital bed to exploring the deep blue sea again? At least in part?"

"Yeah. But so did a lot of helping hands."

Honu returned from his inspection of the kitchen and insisted on a scratch from Franci, rubbing his big head against her knees.

"Did I not drop any food for you? Are you so hard done by?" she said, obliging with some intense scritches. The dog kept her company at work some days, and she rarely turned down his need to be loved on. "You need a blankie to lie on? Honu, come."

She laid a crocheted blanket out by the living room couch. The dog sacked out and was headed toward dreamland in seconds.

"You spoil him," Archer said.

"He deserves it. He's a prince among dogs."

Wind rattled the front window. Archer looked over sharply. "Christ, I thought things were getting gusty at my place."

"Yeah, I've got the flashlights ready for later," she said. "And the battery-powered lantern Sam got me for a housewarming gift." Kellan had given her a beautiful Le Creuset Dutch oven in her favorite turquoise color, but Sam hadn't been able to resist the practical.

Then again, she couldn't be too mad about it today. The clouds were so gray and thick, it already looked like twilight and it was still hours until sunset. She let out a long breath. The weather didn't seem as fierce now that she had company.

As long as she didn't make it obvious she really, really liked having Archer around, it should be fine accepting his help.

"I haven't mustered the energy to use the stepladder to edge near the ceiling," she said. "Feel like putting your unnecessary height to use, Legolas?"

"You were going to climb a—" His jaw slammed shut, the muscles ticking. His throat worked. "Yeah, I can reach the ceiling."

"Follow me, then."

The little cottage felt thirty degrees warmer with Archer in it. The baby's small room sweltered like a damn furnace. She stripped to the thin tank she had on under her hoodie and adjusted the high waistband of her leggings.

Archer's gaze darted everywhere except on Franci. "Got an edging brush?"

She pointed to her painting tools. "I'll keep going with the rolling."

"I could finish that, too, if you want to take a break," he said, scanning the walls with a critical eye. "Not much more to do here. Color looks great."

Exactly. She had almost managed by herself.

"The rhythm of painting is helping. You know how it is with stiff muscles—better to keep moving." After putting her mask on, she retrieved the roller she'd left and set to using it with a vengeance. Anything to keep her eyes off the way the US Coast Guard logo on his shirt rippled across his pecs with each measured, skilled stroke of the brush.

They'd worked in silence enough that it wasn't usually awkward, but tonight their lack of conversation echoed like the underwater hum of a passing tanker's propellers.

He was managing to create perfect edges without painter's tape. What was he, a painting unicorn? And why was it so attractive?

Everything about him is attractive.

And he never looked at her that way. Archer Frost was all business, platonic—fraternal, even.

Was it even possible to get him to see her otherwise?

Clearly not while she was pregnant. It seemed to make his protective side kick into overdrive.

Sigh.

"You must have the steadiest hands in the world," she said.

His grip bobbled. Swearing, he wiped at a smudge on the ceiling with a rag. "Sometimes."

Sadness swamped his face for a second. He pressed his lips together, the emotion vanishing behind rigid determination.

She wanted to know what was hurting him. She'd seen that look before, and wished he felt comfortable enough to open up. But what if asking hurt him worse? Everyone on the island knew the details of his accident. If pointing out his skill with a paintbrush had somehow taken him back to that time in his life, she'd feel terrible. Or did it remind him of physical therapy or something? Or maybe his divorce? He'd had more than his fair share of difficult times in the year prior to his return to Oyster Island. There had to be a way to help him carry those burdens. Could she do that somehow?

Would he let her?

His expression certainly didn't welcome a deep dive into his past. He refocused on painting, having to move the ladder every twenty seconds because he was so damn fast.

Tidy, too. Nary a fleck of paint on his T-shirt, whereas her tank sported as many sunny yellow freckles as her face had pale brown ones.

"Are both your parents going to Hawaii with you this year, or just your dad?" she asked. The Frosts holidayed there every year in December, a tradition from back when Archer was stationed in Honolulu.

"Only Dad. With Violet not willing to take the time off, my mom decided to hold off this year."

Franci winced. The roller made a sucking sound as she slicked it in the W shape she'd learned in a YouTube video. "My pregnancy got in the way of your family's fun. I'm so sorry."

Violet refused to be anywhere but Oyster Island until Franci was past six weeks postpartum.

"Don't worry about it. Dad and I will get a ton of diving in, so that's great. Mom's going to head to Tennessee for a couple extra weeks with my sister and the kids, so she's happy. She gets to pitch in while my brother-in-law is deployed. And with you on your own, it's crucial Vi stays. Some things are more important than a beach holiday."

"Pssh. I have family to spare."

She would be on her own, though. Without a partner, she had some lonely moments ahead of her.

Dealing with Brad's decision not to be an active father was odd sometimes. He wasn't emotionally attached to the baby and was tied to his job in Idaho. She didn't resent his choice not to relocate, or his reasoning that it was easier not to build a connection across state lines. And she was thankful he was putting up zero fuss about child support. But…she wanted this baby so badly. So empathizing with him about feeling the opposite challenged her sometimes.

"You're frowning over having lots of family?" Archer asked.

"No, I fell down a bit of a rabbit hole of feelings," she said. "Hazards of pregnancy. But I don't like dwelling on Brad's choices. How was the dive tour yesterday?"

His face darkened and he lowered his edging brush. "I get there's no easy answer when it comes to being a parent, but he sure didn't make the same decision I would have."

The insistence on his face triggered every nervous-to-be-a-single-parent molecule in her body. She could *not* let herself wonder how her life would have been different if a night with Archer had led to her pregnancy.

She needed to change the subject.

"I miss diving with you."

Raising an eyebrow, he scooted the ladder to edge over the top of the door. "I get it. When you're used to being in the water every day, it's shit when you can't be."

Oof.

At least she'd known she'd get back to diving fairly

soon after delivering. He'd probably had many a sleep-less night, unsure of what his recovery would look like.

"I hope I wasn't whining." Her back tensed and she groaned, putting her roller down to dig her knuckles against her stupid lumbar vertebrae.

"I'd be whining, too, if I was pregnant."

"No, you wouldn't," she grumped. "You'd be all stoic and hard jawed, and you wouldn't have thrown your back out by nearly falling out of a kayak."

"You did what?"

Damn. "Nothing."

She stepped back to examine her work.

The ladder creaked behind her. A soft touch brushed her shoulder.

"Want me to work on it for you?" he murmured.

"Work on what?"

"Your backache. It's easier to hit the knots from my angle."

He was a few inches behind her. The heat of him ca-ressed her bare shoulders. Strong fingers, roughened calluses...

He pulled his hand away.

Why? No! She glanced over her shoulder.

Guilt etched his face. "Sorry. I crossed a line. Never mind."

"No, it's fine. Uh, have at it."

Stretching his palms across her lower back, thumbs at her spine and fingers splayed on her hips, he pressed tender circles along her unhappy muscles.

"Mmph." She couldn't help the embarrassing moan. His hands were sucking out all her good sense.

"Relax." The low timbre hummed down her spine,

the sound loosening the tautness even more than his fingertips.

Leaning back, she rested her shoulders against his hard chest. Not so much to send him off-balance, but enough to steady her jellying knees while leaving him enough room to manipulate her muscles.

"Was the paddling or getting stuck on the dock to blame?" he asked.

"Not sure." She closed her eyes. The warmth of his body and the tender ministrations were like a hazy cloud around her. She was tempted to take off her mask—this close, she bet the spice of his soap would cut through the smell of fresh paint. "Wasn't bothering me when I was out yesterday. It's been pretty steady since I left the shop this morning."

As if she'd summoned it, an aching spasm bloomed under his hands. She hissed.

He stilled. "Shoot, sorry."

"No, no, you were helping. It's just the weight of the baby."

"If you want to ice your back, I can clean up here," he offered.

Yawning and overstimulated, she didn't have the will to keep caring about finishing the walls. Rest, ice and then a heating pad. Not as good as having Archer untangle her twisting muscles, but safer. The longer he touched her, the higher the chance she'd make a face that would clue him in to just how much she was enjoying it. She didn't have a military-grade stone face like he did.

"Okay. I'll go find an ice pack, and make us a pot of tea, too." She walked to the small utility room at the back of the cottage, put her mask on her tool shelf and made her way to the kitchen, rubbing her tight belly. Yeah, she was definitely overdoing it.

She padded to the counter and turned on the kettle, then reached for the beautiful pottery teapot she'd gotten for a song at the farmers market during the summer when one of the local potters had sold off all her stock and moved away. She added a few bags of peppermint tea to the pot, grabbed an ice pack from the freezer and a dish towel from where it hung over the oven handle and made her way to the couch. Propping herself on a wedge of pillows, she set a timer on her phone and stretched out, tucking the chilly pad under her back.

Honu waddled over and rested his head next to her bump.

"Hey, fuzzball." She stroked his silky ears. Oh, yeah, this was better. The soothing rattle of the kettle, the quiet clatter of Archer cleaning up the paint and tools, the howl of the wind, the chill on her tense spine.

Until it wasn't, and another spasm made her muscles clench. Why was it coming and going?

Am I...

Could I be...

No. She was thirty-seven weeks along. It was too early. Had to be Braxton Hicks from activity. She'd rest, and then give Violet a call for reassurance. Her friend had been up all night with the delivery on Orcas Island and had only made it back to Oyster Island a few hours ago.

After a couple more minutes, her phone alarm went off, reminding her to remove the ice. She slid the pack out. Archer was in the utility room with the sink running. The kettle had clicked off, but she couldn't bring herself to get up. It was comforting to have someone in the house, taking care of a few little things. She pulled a plush blanket off the back of the couch and covered herself, soothed by the sounds of the storm, running water and heavy male footsteps.

The sounds eventually shifted to quiet guitar.

She opened her eyes.

Wait, when had she closed them?

She bolted upright, the quick movement bringing on a painful spasm.

Archer sat in the armchair by the window, fingers plucking a pretty arpeggio on the strings of the instrument she kept telling herself she'd learn how to play.

He was pretty, too. Rugged and broad, sure. Dark hair a little mussed, the first hints of gray glinting in the light of the lamp on the table next to him. Eyes shut, lost in the melody. His long lashes fanned on his cheeks. The tune sounded a bit familiar, but she couldn't place it. Not surprising—they had opposite tastes in music. Their arguments over late-nineties rock versus more recent pop hits occupied most days when they were in the shop together. He never missed a chance to remind her of their generational divide.

She hadn't heard him play in a long time. There was something precious about music when it came from his fingers.

Rain lashed the window behind him, as if a hose was spraying against the glass. It was dark out. Five thirty, according to the clock on the microwave.

"You let me sleep for so long." She put a hand to her complaining back. Frustration rose. Clearly, lying down hadn't been the solution.

He opened his eyes. "You needed the rest."

"And you waited for a couple of hours?" She stood and stretched, not sure how to feel about him sticking around. She loved it. She also suspected he was doing it out of obligation, and she hated being an obligation. And what had he been up to? No way had he been sitting there playing guitar for that long.

"I was working. After I cleared away the drop cloths, I put together the shelves for you, the ones in the box in the middle of the room. Wanted to build the crib in your utility room, too, but it'll be a two-person job."

She'd been ignoring that fact for days.

Gratitude swamped her. He didn't seem put-upon over the shelves, so she was going to take it as a kind gesture from a friend. Accepting help from Archer was easier than from her family members.

"We should get Violet over here soon," he said. "Deal with the crib."

"'We'?"

"It's a big piece of furniture. The more the merrier."

Remembering she'd left the tea bags in the pot, she made her way over to the counter. Every step jarred her pelvis, and her stomach felt heavy. Had the baby dropped while she was sleeping or something? Violet had warned her it could be imminent. But if walking was going to grind like this for the next three-plus weeks... *Yikes.*

The teapot had a cozy on it, a blue-and-white-striped one knit by Winnie. Having Sam's mom and stepmom as her landlords was a damn delight. Made up for her own mom being too busy with her second family to care much about Franci. Winnie and Rachel had Franci wrapped tightly in their loving wings, and she was ever grateful for it.

"Did you make tea?" she asked Archer, who'd switched to a livelier song, one of Pearl Jam's newer hits.

"Yeah. I saw you'd prepped it, so I poured in the water and used the knitted thing to keep it warm."

She shook her head and served herself a mug of tea, the peppermint fragrant in her nose. Something didn't make sense, all the coddling. If he'd slotted her into a friend's-pregnant-little-sister category, then why was he—

Oh, son of a *biscuit.*

"Sam," she said.

Archer performed a complicated chord progression. "What about him?"

"He's why you're here. Did he ask you to check on me because of the storm?"

His fingers stilled on the strings. "Not specifically."

The front window shook, as if it was calling him out on a lie.

He didn't look like he was being dishonest, though.

"So you're here because you want to be?"

"Wouldn't be here otherwise."

She put her hands on her hips. "Yes, you would. If you thought I was in trouble, you'd be here in a second, no matter what."

"Again, because I'd want to be." He coughed and glared at the window. "Storm's getting worse."

Honu whined, as if backing up his owner's concern. He trotted over to Franci and leaned against her leg, tipping up his face to stare at her.

Franci booped the dog's nose. The howl outside was downright eerie. She shivered, which sent a twinge from her tailbone.

More than a twinge.

She took a breath and gripped the dog's thick scruff. She needed to chill. She was just on edge from the storm and the busyness of painting.

Leaving her tea on the counter, she grabbed her yoga mat and went to stretch. "Play me something peaceful for a bit, and I'll pay you with dinner."

"Deal." He spun into a relaxed version of an Adele song, the one Franci belted out at work any time she was in the mood to annoy her brother. The notes knit into her fluttering nerves, smoothing them out. She got on the floor on her knees, spread them and shifted into child's pose.

A cold nose nuzzled her armpit, burrowing under until the entire dog was under her chest. She went with it, relaxing into his furry body. Honu let out a big breath and closed his eyes.

"Less than helpful, sweetie," she chided.

Archer full on laughed.

Wow, what a sound. So rare. She pushed up on her palms to do cat/cow with a Labrador chaser. To look at Archer's face, too, because there had to be a smile to go along with that laugh, and she'd be foolish to give up a glimpse of a full flash of white teeth and the sun crinkles at the corners of his eyes.

He loved to point out how old he was, but damn, age looked good on him.

Maybe that explained her reaction to him. Did him

being older all of a sudden look better now that she was going to be a mom?

Nah.

If her attraction stemmed solely from the twelve extra years he had on her, she'd also have a thing for Sam's other best friend, Matias, the local bartender. But nothing shimmered inside her when Matias smiled.

Looking away, she focused on her breathing and on arching her sore back. She hissed in pain.

The music stopped.

"Hey, Fran?"

She lifted her head. "Yeah?"

A caring look crossed his face, tinged with something she'd call *apprehension* if it wasn't Archer, ever calm and in control. "I've been checking my watch, and are you sure—"

The lights went out.

A void enveloped them. She couldn't see six inches in front of her, let alone Archer in the chair.

The dog startled, shifting under Franci's forward bridge.

Franci sat back on her heels. "Archer?"

"Sit tight. I've got my phone here somewhere."

Bands tightened from her back to her navel. And in the pitch-darkness, she couldn't focus on anything but the ramping intensity.

No. Not tonight. She moaned, spreading her knees wider and pressing her face into the comforting floof in front of her.

"Yeah, I thought so," Archer said quietly.

A clunk of wood sounded—him putting the guitar back on his stand.

"Going to be tough to make dinner with no power," she said.

Archer cleared his throat. "And even harder to deliver a baby."

Chapter Four

Archer didn't panic. Never.

Not when he'd walked in on his wife getting more than her spiritual needs met by her pastor. Not in nearly sightless underwater conditions when the munitions sweep he'd been charged with leading turned ugly. He'd gotten close when he woke at Walter Reed National Military Medical Center and realized Eduardo had died after the blast. His teammate, his best friend, gone because of a freak chain of events set off by a slip of Archer's hand. The first thing Archer had seen after his surgery was Clara's and Daniel's shattered faces, somehow full of worry for him even though he was the reason they only had memories instead of a living husband and father. He been wracked with heart-wrenching guilt then, not panic.

So why was a fist squeezing his throat now?

He sat in the chair in the black hole of Franci's living

room and forced himself to take stock. She let out a low noise, muffled by Honu's fur. Distress laced the sound.

He swore under his breath. He could handle his own pain. Did daily, having learned all sorts of techniques to manage the phantom sensations that came with being an amputee. But apparently all the knowledge in the world of energy therapy couldn't stop him from freaking out when Francine Walker groaned.

His heart was going to break his ribs if he didn't get his pulse under control.

First, he needed light on the situation. After pulling out his phone, he turned on the flashlight and pointed it at the coffee table.

The beam framed Franci, too, who was still on her knees on the floor clinging to his dog.

"Want to flick on your lantern? We'd better preserve our cell batteries." Not that his had a dependable signal anywhere on this side of the island. Service was notoriously bad.

"It could just be a backache," she said stubbornly, turning the dial on the lantern. The beam lit all but the corners of the living room.

He flicked his phone's flashlight off. "We can't deal in 'could' right now."

"Well, I've never been in labor, so I don't know," she snapped, shifting from kneeling to having her legs crossed. She didn't have much of a lap, but Honu insisted on filling what was left of it. The dog propped his head on top of Franci's belly.

"We should rename you Velcro." Franci's voice had lost the sharpness. She wrapped her arms around the dog.

"He's good at sensing emergencies."

"We don't know for sure what this is, so I wouldn't call it an emergency."

Felt like one to him, but his job was to keep her calm. "No, you're right. It isn't. Gotta admit it's a dilemma, though."

"A small one."

Small. Ha. No power, a storm of the decade outside and she was about to have a baby.

But they had time. No snap decisions necessary. Every day of his sixteen years with the Coast Guard, he'd woken up, made choices, solved problems.

He leaned forward, resting one elbow on his sound knee and one on his socket. "So let's make a plan."

The lantern cast shadows on her face, highlighting the strain by her temples and jaw. "You're fidgeting."

"Huh?"

"With your phone." She nodded at his hands. "You never fidget."

He forced his hands to still where, yes, he had been peeling his phone case from the corners and snapping it back on. "Are you in pain right now?"

She shook her head and used the coffee table to stand. "I should call Violet."

"Yes."

She retrieved her phone from the kitchen counter, tapped at the screen and closed her eyes. "Of course there isn't a signal."

"Yeah, mine's got zero bars, too."

"Thank you, Rachel and Winnie, for including the landline in the utilities." She pulled an old telephone out from behind her toaster and lifted the receiver, then held it by the cord and let it spin and untangle before lifting it to her ear.

Her brows knit. She pressed the hook a couple of times and put it to her ear again. "There's no dial tone." More rapid-fire attacks on the button. "We *need a dial tone*."

"Hey." He shot from his chair as fast as his mechanical knee would let him. "Let's see what's wrong."

She wasn't his to soothe, his to touch. But like earlier when she'd been digging her fists into her back, he was helpless to do anything but provide comfort.

Squeezing her shoulder with one hand, he jiggled the plastic clip in the socket with the other.

A faint droning hum sounded from the receiver.

Her shoulders dropped by an inch, and she let out a gust of relief. "I would have thought of that. I may be Gen Z, but I know how to plug in a phone."

"And my aging millennial ass is telling you it's okay to be overwhelmed."

Though I'm right behind you with the overwhelm.

He breathed as deeply as he could without tipping her off to the claws of fear digging themselves into his chest.

"Talk to Vi, and we'll go from there."

She dialed the phone but had to enter the number three times because her shaking fingers kept slipping. He almost grabbed the device from her to enter it himself, but knew she needed to complete the task herself to feel in control. Anything he could do to boost her confidence, he would. It was going to be a long night.

Her eyes shut and she set the handset back in the cradle. "No answer."

"Maybe the storm's affecting her connection, too. Try again."

She did. "Still nothing."

"Okay. We'll give it a few minutes."

Franci braced her palm on her back. "With the power out, I wonder if I should be closer to Hideaway Wharf, maybe at my dad's place or Violet's…"

"Not the medical center?" If the decision was his alone, he'd have her there in two minutes, but he knew enough from Violet's stories to know there was rarely a need to rush with first babies.

"I'm not delivering in a hospital setting. Not unless it's an actual emergency."

The ferocity in her tone went beyond a belief in home birth. He raised an eyebrow at her.

She didn't elaborate and dialed another number. "Dad?" A pause. "No, your other daughter." A strangled laugh. "The one that might be in labor."

"'Might'?" Archer murmured.

She waved a hand. "Hush." A pause. "No, Dad, not you. Archer." She sighed. "Nope, at my place. He came by to help with something." Her cheeks flushed enough for the lantern light to catch the pink hue. "Uh, *not* to help with delivering my baby, no. I'm sure he'll be on his way home soon. Honu's going to need dinner at any time."

Archer snorted. Fat chance. His dog could eat table scraps for one meal.

"Is your power out?" she continued. Her nose scrunched at what had to be an affirmative from her dad. "Oh, dear." A hum. "No, I think… Damn it. I don't know. Maybe I'll head up the driveway to see if Rachel and Winnie are home, or if they're still at the bakery. Let me talk to Archer. I'll call you back."

The receiver clunked in the cradle. A huge breath gusted from her, loud enough to compete with the storm. She gripped the counter and groaned.

"Hey." Everything inside him clamored to help, to soothe, to lift the burden. The urge muscled past his determination to keep his physical distance. He rested a palm between her shoulder blades and checked his watch.

"Twelve, by my count."

"Right. Twelve." A minute passed of her taking long breaths and clutching the granite.

"Lean on me, if you need."

"I've got it." She pursed her lips and blew like she was extinguishing a candle. "Okay. That was... Well, it was something."

"You handled it. You've got this, Francine. And I'm not leaving you until you tell me to go away. Actually, I'm not leaving you until you have someone else with you, and you *also* tell me to go away."

Her gaze sharpened. "Let's head to the wharf and find Violet."

Relief gushed through him faster than the rain from the gutter spouts. "I'll drive you."

She nodded.

"Got a hospital bag ready? You should bring it in case you end up laboring at her place."

"No."

"No?"

She made a face. "Don't look at me like that. All the women in my family deliver late. Always. Plus, I'd planned to deliver right here in my house. Figured it was too early to think of contingencies."

It was never too early to think of contingencies, but he wasn't going to argue with her. They'd have to pack a bag now.

"Let's gather what you need."

With Archer holding the lantern, they carefully made their way down the hall, Honu on their heels. Franci collected some things from her small en suite and her drawers before she paused, another whimper escaping her.

"Getting intense again?" he asked, folding the clothes she'd passed him and neatly stacking them in her duffel bag.

"I think…" A puff of breath. "I can call that a contraction."

He coughed. He'd been calling them *contractions* in his head since he'd noticed her wincing when they'd finished the painting hours ago. "Anything you need from the baby's room?"

She shook her head. "Everything's still in the basement. I'll go get—"

He grabbed her forearm to stop her. "No. You sit. Let Honu snuggle away your worries." *Given I can't.* "Tell me what I'm looking for."

Handing him a flashlight from her bedside table, she recited a list of things to retrieve. "There shouldn't be any tripping hazards, but be careful."

He always was.

And there weren't any tripping hazards. There was, however, half an inch of water on the concrete in the unfinished space.

Whistling in surprise, he scanned the room with the narrow beam of light. Where the hell was it coming from?

Nowhere obvious, nor did he have time to look into it in detail. And the last thing he was going to do was tell Franci and give her one more thing to worry about. This was a problem for her landlords. He ferried the three boxes of baby things upstairs to the living room one at a time in case she needed the rest before the water got cleaned up, then pulled up the number for Hideaway Bakery on his cell and entered it into the landline.

"Hi, this is Rachel." Sam's mom's voice was more strained than usual. "Everything okay, honey?"

"Well, that's some greeting, Rach."

"Huh?" She paused. "Who's this? Where's Franci? The call display…"

"Ah, so you do have power at the wharf," he said. "It's Archer. I'm at Francine's."

"You're at… Well, now." Curiosity entered her tone. "What's going on? I didn't know you and Franci—"

"We're not." Christ, if that got around the bakery, it would be all over Oyster Island as soon as power got restored. "She needed a hand with something."

"Oh. A *hand*."

"Rachel. I didn't call for gossip. There's water in the basement, and I don't have time to deal with it. I need to drive Franci into town."

"Water… *Oh*. And *town*." Rachel's tone reached the stratosphere.

"What am I missing, Rach?" Blood echoed in his ears, a rhythmic *whump whump whump* he'd yet to get fully reined in.

"Well, a road."

"What now?" He clenched the phone hard enough his knuckles ached.

"The road. It's blocked."

Whump. Whump.

"*Miller* Road?"

It was the only route connecting the few dozen properties on the back side of the state park to town. Including his own house.

"Yeah. Kitsch Creek overflowed, brought a bit of a mudslide and some rocks with it. Took out a few wires. No one called to tell you?"

"No cell signal out here."

Rachel swore.

"Exactly," he said, repeating the profanity. "Franci's in labor. Early. But still."

A screech on the other line.

Also appropriate.

"She's with you," Rachel said, panic rising in her tone. "She's with you. At least she's with you."

"Not sure I'm the best person."

"You were a damned medic, Archer. I'd say you're more than competent."

"Didn't deal with many maternity cases. One delivery in a hurricane—" which was way too similar to this situation for his liking "—but it's not exactly my specialty." Though he did keep his advanced first aid up-to-date. Technically, he knew what to do.

It wouldn't get that far, though. They'd find a way to get to Violet. Though a boat was out, given the small-craft warning, and they weren't going to be able to walk around a mudslide.

"If the basement's flooding, you shouldn't stay in the house," Rachel said.

"I know. I'll take her to my place. I won't have power, either, but I do have a generator."

"I'll call around, see if I can get you some help. The San Juan Fire boat might be nearby. Or the Coast—"

Her offer trailed off in a hiss.

"Coast Guard," he finished for her. "Hopefully it doesn't come to that. Let's aim for her laboring at my house for a while, the storm dying down a little, and someone bringing a boat to my dock and getting her into town."

"Like I said—I'll call around."

And I need to tell Franci we're not going anywhere fast.

He ran through a few more logistics with Rachel. With her house being just up the driveway from Franci's cottage, she and Winnie would be stuck in town for the near future. Rachel confirmed they had a key to Sam and Kellan's apartment and would stay there for the night, and had a neighbor who could check on their animals. Then he tried his sister again, who still wasn't answering. He went back to Franci's bedroom.

His heart skipped a beat. The lantern cast long shadows over her curvy form. She lay on her bed on her side. Honu curled in front of her.

"Hey." She sent him a guilty smile. "Needed to rest for a bit. Honu agreed."

"Of course you did. And of course he did, too."

There was a reason the dog had never finished assistance training and Archer had been able to get him for a reasonable price. Honu had great instincts but was too damn lazy to be on the job all the time.

Hovering in the doorway didn't feel right when he had some big truth bombs to drop on Franci. He went over to the bed and rotated his prosthetic knee so he could sit on the edge and face her, his other foot planted on the ground.

"What's wrong?" she asked. "Who were you talking to?"

"Rachel. She and Winnie are stuck in Hideaway Wharf. They're going to spend the night at Sam's place."

"They're stuck?"

"Yeah. You feeling steady? When's your next contraction due?"

"A few minutes yet."

"Okay. Deep breath, then." He took her hand. Smaller than his, obviously, but still strong. Soft, except for the cuticle on her left thumb. She'd been chewing on it. He ran his own thumb along the worried edge.

Her eyes widened, but she squeezed his fingers.

It felt like the most natural thing in the world to hold her hand.

To comfort her. Nothing else.

"I ever tell you I delivered a baby once?"

She rolled her eyes. "Every time you did anything notable, it made the local paper, Archer. That one even made the *Seattle Times.*"

Right. A few stories had, not all with happy endings. He ran his teeth over his lips. "The wind was howling. Worse than this. And this couple—why they hadn't found safe harbor and headed inland, I never learned, but it was on me to get them up to the bird with the basket. Pretty sailboat, too. Shame." He shook his head. "When I realized she was in early labor, I nearly sweated through my survival suit. Baby arrived before we made it back to land."

And so long as he used his training, he'd manage this situation, too.

She blinked. "I do *not* want to deliver in a helicopter."

He chuckled. "Doubt anyone does."

"I…" Her mouth tightened as if she tried to smile but couldn't. "They put Dad on a helicopter. Sam went with him. I was in an ambulance. They diverted the ferry for me."

"I remember that," he murmured.

"Do you know how long the ferry ride feels when you don't know if your dad is going to make it?"

He tightened his grip on her hand.

"And then pacing the hall for weeks afterward…" She shook her head. "My delivery is supposed to be joyful, ultimately. And the hospital will never be that for me. I don't want to leave Oyster Island. Not unless there's no other option." She paused. "Am I being illogical?"

No more than I am, avoiding Daniel's attempts to share his dive training with me.

He wholly understood Franci being unable to disentangle the hospital from her dad's injuries in her mind. He was the same, lacking the ability to separate the memories of being underwater with his best friend from the thought of Daniel being underwater *without* Eddy.

"Some things stick with you," he said with a stiff shrug.

Her gaze flicked to his left thigh, where his sweat-pants collapsed around the narrow mechanical joint.

He nodded. "See, I'm talking from experience."

Attention darting back to his face, she winced. "Sorry."

"No need to pretend it isn't noticeable." He sure as hell couldn't forget. But he wasn't going to let his memories get in the way of him keeping Franci and her baby safe tonight. For the time being, he was all she had. He would not let her down.

"I see it, but I don't notice it, if that makes any sense," she said quietly.

Interesting. "I think it does."

"Hard not to see it." She smirked. "You waltz around half-dressed on the boat all the time. But still…" Her amusement faded. "I don't want to remind you of…that time in your life."

She said it as if it wasn't usually on his mind anyway. Eduardo followed him around some days, a shadow, a ghost much like his phantom limb. Throbbing, sparking, aching. Whenever it got really bad, he headed for the tattoo parlor on Wharf Street.

He'd run out of space on his chest and arms, had moved on to his back sometime last year.

He took a deep breath as subtly as he could. "With all we've got going on here, I'm fully distracted from my own crap."

She let out a weak laugh.

"I've got you. And your baby. No matter what."

"Beyond a ride to Violet's, is that, uh, necessary?" She rose on an elbow, the fingers of her other hand idly scratching the dog's tummy.

It was up to him to stay calm. Once she heard the news, she'd be scared enough for both of them.

"Can you trust me to keep you safe, Francine?"

She stared at him, eyes wide, thoughtful. "I—I can, yeah. I mean, I do trust you."

"I'm glad." Maintaining her trust would be a big part of helping her and her baby, which meant honesty. He swallowed. "About that ride to my sister's—it's not going to work. We need a new plan."

Chapter Five

Franci cuddled the dog, Archer's words a jumble in her brain. How could he claim *I've got you* in one sentence and then insist on a new plan in the next?

She rubbed a finger between her eyebrows. "But finding Violet makes the most se— *Unfh.*"

Oh, damn, there was the contraction she'd been waiting for. It burned from between her thighs to the top of her belly and all the way around, meeting in a clash at her spine.

A big hand enveloped her knee and squeezed.

"Why...*ahhh*...why... Twice as bad...each time?"

"Maybe admitting what's happening gave your body permission to give over to the process."

The contraction eased. "Ooh."

The faster she could get to Hideaway Wharf, the better.

"Finished?"

"Yeah." She gave him a sharp look. "The ride. Or lack thereof. What's the deal, Robin Hood?"

His gaze went thoughtful. "Which Robin Hood? *Prince of Thieves*? Russell Crowe?"

"The fox, obviously." She covered his hand with hers. "What are you not telling me?"

He stared at the comforter. "There's no road."

"I'm sorry?" Her throat felt coated in molasses. Sticky, like she was two seconds from choking on her air, which was impossible, obviously, but so was the fact she was in labor and there was no flipping road to take to the hospital. "A road can't just *disappear.*"

"Not technically. But it's covered in debris, live electrical wires and a creek."

Her mind thrashed to make sense of the news, to formulate any other solution. "Take me by boat, then."

His eyes were a bottomless blue, the color of the ocean in the pictures Sam and Kellan had taken in Australia. Beautiful water. Calm water. Why couldn't the water here be like that today?

"You know I can't," he said. "There's no point in drowning trying to get to somewhere with power."

"I see." She went so hot, she shivered. And then numb.

No, calm. Like being fully aware during meditation, or the peace of gliding across the ocean on a rare glassy day.

She knelt, getting into the position that felt the most comfortable. "Okay, then. I'm on my own. I can… I can do this."

"Hey." His hand was a steady anchor at the base of her spine. "You are *not* alone. I will not leave you."

"You're going to deliver my baby." Those words made as much sense as the road being washed out.

"No, I'm going to keep you company until we can get Violet here. You're going to have a long, easy labor. The storm will be calmer in the morning, and she'll be able to dock at my place."

"Your place?" His place was stunning, renovated to allow for easy movement in his wheelchair. It boasted an endless view of the Pacific. Even so, moving anywhere but this bed seemed like a terrible idea. She'd planned on a home birth in *this* house.

He nodded. "I can rig some power with my generator to charge my leg and our phones, in case they pick up a signal. We'll have hot water and food. We can light the fireplace. I've got a landline, too, and a tricked-out first aid kit. Everything we need."

Oh. Yeah. She only had a few of those things here. And figuring it all out…

I don't have to. Archer's got it.

The weight on her chest lightened.

"A regular slumber party," she said dryly.

A smile cracked across his serious face.

She rose to sitting. "I'd rather be in my own space, but all your amenities tip the scales. Let's go to your place before I don't want to move."

They got drenched on the way out of the house. Honu sulked when Archer made the dog ride in the hatch to keep the seats from smelling like wet fur. She settled in the front seat while Archer loaded her bags into the back seat.

Minutes later, he had them crawling along the long driveway. The headlights of his SUV were the only brightness in the world besides the blue glow of the dashboard, stark on his clenched jaw.

"Wow." She panted a little as she came down from another intense wave. "There is really nothing like having a contraction in the front seat of a car."

"Tip the seat back if you need. Or I'll stop. Whatever you need."

"I *need* Violet."

"I know, Franci. We'll try my sister again once we get to my place."

The words could not get gruffer. As much as he was trying to come across as calm, she could see the strain. He was going fifteen miles an hour, tops. Branches scattered across the road and wind buffeted the car. The tendons on the back of his hands looked as tight as her rock-hard stomach.

Finally, he backed the vehicle into the carport of his oceanfront house. Once he cut the engine and the lights turned off, the world went black. Neither of them moved from their seats.

She laughed to herself and then belted out a lyric from one of her dad's favorite Guns N' Roses songs, about nothing lasting and cold November rain.

Archer finally relaxed, cracking up. "Seriously? That's more my era than yours."

"'It's a classic, Francine, like you,'" she said, a passable imitation of her dad's growly praise.

"You're something, all right." Archer shook his head. "Let me come help you out. I don't want you falling."

She opened her door. Frigid pebbles of rain lashed

sideways through the open side of the carport, pelting her face. Rivulets ran off her jacket, threatening to leak through what were supposed to be waterproof seams. He gave her a hand down, his big palms and fingers enveloping her chilly ones. Taking her elbow, he walked her up the short wheelchair ramp to the front door.

And then he was just…everywhere. Getting her a towel to dry off and lighting a fire in the grate. Hooking up the generator, making her tea, heating some simple soup for dinner.

And then finally, *finally* getting through to Violet.

"Holy crap, Franci, you're doing this *tonight*?" her friend shrieked.

"I know."

"Giving birth in a storm! You're such a cliché."

Franci wanted to laugh, but couldn't. "We're stuck here, Vi. And you are *not* here. And I need you."

"Hey. I'll get there. I promise."

"How?"

"Let me worry about that."

She would. She would worry until her friend's face was right at her side, smiling all the encouragement in the world.

"You're with my brother, though," Violet said quietly. "Good. If he needs to, he can—"

"No. Not happening." In her deepest, most secret moments, she didn't mind the thought of Archer seeing her naked, but those moments did *not* include her baby's head crowning.

"How far apart are your contractions?"

"Nine minutes. You always say first babies stall, though, right? Maybe instead of going overdue, I'll just have a super long labor." She'd never thought that would appeal, but facing being without her friend and midwife for the birth, a marathon labor sounded like the best thing in the world. "I'm good here for now. We've got a while."

"Right. Sure." Violet did not sound convinced. "Let me talk to my brother."

She passed the phone over to Archer, who repeated all sorts of medical terminology Franci in no way wanted to contemplate. After a few minutes, he handed her back the phone.

"She wants me to listen to the baby's heartbeat. I'm going to dig out my first aid kit."

He disappeared down the hall.

Huh. He had the supplies and ability to detect a heartbeat? That was...hot.

Reassuring. Don't be immature.

Except his competence...*oof.* How could she *not* consider him hot?

"Franci? Francine, you there?" Violet called.

"Sorry. Distracted."

"Contraction?" Violet said sympathetically.

Franci didn't answer.

Violet ran through a few labor-management techniques they'd previously discussed. "Like I said, I will get there as soon as I can."

Franci's heart sank. "There's a river over the road."

"The Ring Trail is worth checking. Might even be passable by ATV if I can get the keys to the gates."

The rugged terrain of the state park trail filled her vision. "You *cannot* cut through the park in this weather, Violet Frost."

"It's sheltered from the wind. I won't be careless. I promise."

"Violet!"

"Gotta go, sweetie. I'll call when I can."

The dial tone rang in her ear.

"What the *hell*?"

Archer appeared at her side, a large first aid kit in hand, rushing enough that his steps hitched. "What's the problem?"

"Your sister." She wrung her hands. "She wants to get here by trail."

Swearing, Archer took the phone from her and dialed a number. "Let's get you under a blanket, Francine. You're shivering. I'll fix this."

Knowing she was a minute away from her next gift from her uterus, she followed his advice, wanting to get back into the crouch that felt best. How had she been here for an hour already?

As she left the kitchen, she heard him gruffly address their friend Matias before walking around the corner, disappearing into the hall. He couldn't go far—the phone cord was only so long—but she couldn't make out what he was saying.

Violet is smart. She won't do anything dangerous.

But really, like she needed one more thing to worry about tonight?

Ten minutes and one contraction later, Archer rolled his wheelchair into the living room. He had a cribbage board and a deck of cards tucked next to his residual limb. His first aid kit was perched on his other thigh.

"Leg needed a rest," he explained. "Better take it now before things get hairy."

"Things are not going to get hairy."

"You're right. Cool cucumbers. Smooth sailing."

She took in the rain battering the wall of windows. "Not tonight. Rough waters."

He put the cribbage set and aid kit on the table and zipped open the red canvas bag. Once he'd pulled out a stethoscope, he rolled as close to her as he could get. "Let's have a listen, yeah?"

"Violet knows best." She scooted in front of him. One of her knees brushed his whole leg. She bit her lip.

Eyes fixed on his watch, right hand searching for the heartbeat with the bell of the device, he looked as serious as a priest at a funeral.

Agh, stop. Do not think of funerals. This is joyful. Birth. New life.

His jaw dropped.

So did her confidence. "What?"

"There it is." Amazement spread on his face. "That's...*wild.*"

"You didn't hear it when you delivered the helicopter baby?"

"I did, but this is *your* baby. Kinda different," he murmured.

It is?

He was clearly counting, so she stayed quiet until he took out the ear pieces and handed it to her. "Here, you listen."

"This is one of my favorite parts of being pregnant," she admitted, accepting the stethoscope and falling under the meditative rhythm of her baby's heartbeat. "It's fast."

"It's right in the range Violet was hoping for."

Lub dub. Lub dub. Lub dub.

The storm whistling outside made it hard to hear. She glared at the window. "You've probably been out in seas this high a hundred times."

"More than that." He played with his wheels, making the chair roll forward and back, forward and back. "You haven't lived until you've seen a gale in the Arctic."

"Oh, I think I'm good," she said softly. She loved the ocean, refused to live anywhere but Oyster Island, but even she had her limits.

"Yeah, so am I. I'm getting soft."

"You are *not* getting soft. Every part of you is hard."

He stared at her, eyebrow lifted. "Every part?"

"Oh, my God, I didn't mean *that* part." Warmth spread through her. *"Archer."*

He chuckled.

Wow. Two laughs in one night—it seemed like a bigger deal than being in labor.

Of course, a contraction hit right then, proving her inner amusement so, so false.

He rolled in close and reached for one of her hands, tucking it securely between his. "Squeeze."

She did.

"Aw, you can do better than that." His calm, assured gaze was as much of a focus point as his touch.

Clenching harder, she said, "Since when do you make jokes about sex?"

"I'll joke about anything if it'll help distract you, Franci."

Oh. A means to an end, then.

The wave of the contraction crashed, dissipated. So

did her hope he was starting to see her as more than Sam's little sister.

"You are so strong," he said, tightening his grip before letting go to set up the game board. The coffee table was one of those fancy ones where the top lifted, making it more like a desk, easier to reach from his chair.

"Guess I don't have a choice but to believe you." She made a come-and-get-me motion with her hands. "Deal 'em up. I'm thinking—" *hoping* "—we're in for an all-nighter."

An hour later, Archer was spinning circles outside the door of the en suite of his primary bedroom on the main floor of the house. Literally—there wasn't much room in his bedroom to pace in his chair. He had his bed stripped to the fitted sheet and layered with garbage bags over towels in case she needed it.

His hot-water tank was propane, thank God, so Franci had full rein to shower as long as she wanted. The spray hissed on the other side of the closed door.

They'd abandoned their card game twenty minutes ago. Franci's contractions had gone from nine minutes to six minutes.

His heart rate had gone from run to sprint.

"Archer?" she called, her words muffled by the water and the door.

"Yeah?"

"Can you… Can you come in here? I don't… I don't want to be…"

Was she crying? Damn.

He opened the door and rolled through the wide doorway. "What's wrong?"

She had the spray directed at her back. The T-shirt he'd lent her to provide some modesty in case he needed to help her with something hung sodden around her thighs. She had her hair back in a chaotic knot. A few damp auburn strands framed her face. She wiped at her eyes with the heels of her hands. He couldn't tell if the water on her face was from the shower or tears.

Grabbing one of the metal handles attached to the tiled shower wall, she bent over and moaned.

"It hurts," she said simply.

"I bet."

He would do literally anything to take some of her pain from her. He'd blocked off his emotions long ago—to give himself the strength to get through the physical loss of his leg—but body pain was something he'd conquered.

Not that his emotional blockages didn't cause problems—his Reiki practitioner gently pointed them out every time she treated him—but he wasn't about to release all that energy into the world. Grief and guilt. Agony. He'd never recover.

"What do you need?" he asked.

"J-join me?"

A few minutes later, hot water cascaded over them both. He hadn't woken this morning expecting to throw on his surf shorts and shower leg and keep Sam's little sister from collapsing onto the tile floor. Sometimes, life called a guy to do the unexpected.

In another world, another time, another universe, what would it be like to share a shower with her? To be naked instead of clothed, to have the right to explore her lush body?

But I'm in this *world, where I'm too damn old for her and can't offer her anything she really needs.*

"Give me as much of your weight as you need to," he said. "I can take it."

"I'll try anything." Franci's fingers dug into his biceps and her forehead rested against his sternum. "God, *why* did I want to do this without pain medication?"

"There's no right way to give birth." He assumed, anyway. He didn't have a lot of experience with pregnant people or delivery, outside of his first aid coursework and one harrowing night in the middle of a Florida hurricane. His older sister, Sara, had been on the other side of the country when she had her kids. Violet didn't have any and his closest friends were single, or in Sam's and Kellan's cases, both cis guys. And his ex-wife had wanted to, but their many, many attempts hadn't worked. The closest he'd come was when Clara had been pregnant with Daniel. Archer had hung out in the waiting room until Eduardo came out with his precious son wrapped in his arms.

Now the closest I've come is this.

He looped his arms under Franci's, laying his hands on her lower back and keeping his breathing even, encouraging her to follow his lead like Violet had suggested over the phone.

They rode a couple of waves. Franci's body was definitely more relaxed than when he'd first joined her.

"This working for you, Francine?"

"Having your hands on my back feels even better than the water."

Validation built in his chest. "What else do you need?"

She yawned. "A nap."

"Let's try it."

"Yeah, that ship long sailed. I need to sit. No. Maybe hold on to the bar and squat? No. I'll get water in my eyes. I'm tired of the water. The warm is good, but I don't want the water anymore. I'll drain your well. Waste your propane. We should get out of the shower."

She could drain the entire five-hundred-gallon tank for all he cared. "Want me to get out first, or you? My bathrobe is clean, hanging from the back of the door. You can use it if you want."

He hadn't offered a woman his clothes since before his divorce. He'd had relationships here and there, but solely based on sex. He wasn't going to pretend he had anything else to give to a woman beyond conversation and a few orgasms.

So why have I been so reluctant to think of this *woman as my friend?* She'd been justified to call him on it.

Something about her pulled him toward long-buried feelings. Set him on a crash course with the openness he'd denied himself since he'd proven he had no business being truly intimate with anyone.

Christ. What was more intimate than supporting a person through labor?

Delivering their baby.

Yeah, hopefully they'd avoid that.

"Okay, I— *Ohhh.*"

He checked his watch. Three minutes? He swallowed a sharp curse.

"Shower off?" he asked.

"Once it's… Once it's…" She let out a sharp cry, then a long breath. "Done."

He cut the water and guided her over the shower's low lip, then wrapped her in one of his fluffiest towels. "I'll let you deal with the T-shirt and dry yourself off. I'll be on the other side of the door."

He was working on drying himself, taking off his shower leg and getting dressed when she let out a yelp.

Grabbing his crutches from beside the bed, he swung into the bathroom, still only in his underwear. "What is it? What's wrong?"

She clutched the towel between her breasts with one hand and held on to the support bar by the toilet with the other. "I wrecked your bath mat! My…my water broke…and other stuff."

He glanced at the grippy microfiber mat. Nothing a wash cycle wouldn't fix. "I think we both know this might get a little messy. And you're talking to someone who lived in a military hospital for months. Nothing fazes me, promise."

She let out a whimper, color high in her cheeks. "I'm so sorry."

"About the bath mat?"

"About *everything*."

"Hey." He swung closer, balancing on his leg and a crutch and cupping her cheek. "Know what? I'm not sorry at all."

If he let himself dwell on it for a minute, he might even start wondering if everything in his life had led to this, had prepared him for this.

But talk about dangerous thoughts. He might be prepared to deal with Franci's labor and delivery, but he was in no way capable of managing everything else that could come along if he let himself go down the trail of fate and Franci Walker.

She tipped her face into his hand. Her delicate lashes lay on her pale freckled cheeks. The scar near her mouth was a stark pink against her skin. He fought the undeniable urge to kiss it. Goddamn, she was beyond beautiful. Some level of feminine energy, of humbling, primal power.

"Here," he said, snagging his robe off the hook and draping it over her shoulders. "I'll close my eyes and you can tie the belt. Then you can come and have a lie down. We'll see if we can reach Violet and tell her about your water breaking. Ask if we need to consider air transport."

Even though beyond the small frosted window on one wall of his shower the storm raged. It would take a hell of a pilot to navigate this mess.

He gave her a second to deal with the robe and then opened his eyes. Her freckles stood out like pen dots on her too-pale cheeks.

"You okay, Francine?"

"I don't want to fly." Her voice shook, and her brown eyes widened, frantic. "If I have to… But no. That can't be necessary. It c-can't…"

She buried her face in her hands.

Half-naked and with one hand gripping his crutch, he could only give her so much physical support, but he could at least say the right things. He rubbed her shoulder and said, "Violet will have some advice."

"If we can even get a hold of her ag-gain."

"We will. Even if I have to run down the street and borrow my neighbor's satellite phone," he said.

A long breath shuddered from her lips and she dropped her hands to her sides before jamming them in the pockets of his robe. "Give me a minute to put something on under the robe?"

"Of course." He went to finish getting dressed himself. Shorts and prosthesis in place, he left her for a minute to refresh their water glasses and get a better view of the weather. Options swirled in his head, more furious than the storm. It would take time for a medevac to arrive. Plus, going out in a storm like this was risky. If everything with the birth went right, it would be safer to stay put.

But holy shit, if something did go wrong?

He knew what it was like to live with the worst-case scenario.

Sam, this is not *what I had in mind when I agreed to watch over her.*

Shaking his head, he walked back to the bedroom.

"You look so serious," she said.

She looked adorable, snug from neck to calf in his robe. Standing and facing the bed, she had her hands braced on the mattress. She rocked her hips from side to side.

"Your brother'll be choked," he said lightly. "He gave you strict instructions *not* to give birth while he and Kell were away."

"Yeah, well, Sam doesn't run the universe, as much as he'd like to."

"Feels like we're the only people in the universe tonight," he admitted, then winced. He didn't want to put nervous thoughts in her head. "But it'll be fine. We'll stay put as long as it's the safest choice."

"Good. Good plan." She fidgeted with the tie over her bump. "Too hot." The robe landed on the side of the bed. "I'm sorry. So nice of you to lend it to me, and you smell—I mean, *it* smells, *it*—like, the best, but I'm going to pass out if I keep it on."

He swallowed. The nightie she had on was simple, but it cut low in the front and hit her midthigh. Under different circumstances it would have been sexy as hell. "Wear what's comfortable. Anything. Nothing."

Maybe not nothing. Though he'd heard stories from Coastie friends about people not giving two craps if they were buck naked in a room of seventeen people during labor.

"This is better," she said, gritting her teeth. "Oh, my *God*, this would be so much easier if I could yell at you for putting me in this position. I'm missing out on the whole 'you're never touching me again!' thing."

He smiled. "Yell away. You can pretend."

This was, after all, the closest he was going to get to supporting a partner of his own through delivery.

"This is all your fault!" She cracked a smile. "Nah. Doesn't work. As if I'd order you to stop touching me—" Squeezing her eyes shut, she mouthed a curse. "I didn't mean that."

"Of course. People in labor say things they don't mean all the time," he said. "I'm uh… Right, we were going to call Violet."

He had a landline jack in his bedroom, and he'd plugged a phone into it, but Violet wasn't answering. He tried Rachel again, who passed along that the San

Juan fireboat was busy taking a patient suffering a heart attack to Anacortes.

"We're on our own for now, sweetheart," he said, rubbing her back and pressing on either side of her hips and wishing he could do more. "But we've got this."

The time from three minutes between contractions to one passed in a blur of Franci's cries and Archer feeling so helpless, he wanted to throw something. His residual leg throbbed. He gritted his teeth and kept going, knowing he might pay for it later. But Franci was in too much agony to tell her she needed to labor a different way.

"You are amazing," he told her for the thousandth time. She'd asked him to hold her hips somewhere between two minutes and one and a half, and push to counterbalance her pain. A small ask, considering she could demand the moon right now and he'd figure out a way to get it for her.

"This isn't going to work," she croaked.

"It will, Francine. I know it feels unending, but you're getting there." In transition, maybe? Her pain matched the description Violet had given him when she'd run him through the stages of labor earlier. Labor *and* delivery.

No avoiding it now. This baby was on course to arrive before midnight, let alone morning.

The phone rang. He answered. The other end was crackling. "Arch—coming—over the hill—Ma—"

"Violet?"

"You've got this," she said, bracketed by static.

It's what he'd been telling Franci all night.

He wished he believed it.

Franci perked up. "Violet?"

"If you're close, Vi...hurry."

More crackling, and the line went dead.

"Where was she?"

"On her way." How he had no idea. Hopefully Matias had caught his sister before she headed out into the woods alone. He didn't want to mention the hill in case it wasn't the one nearest his house.

"Did I hear her say— *Ahh!*"

He barely caught her in time before her knees gave out. Her death grip dug into one of his arms. Her other hand cupped under her belly, almost between her thighs.

"Hey. Francine. Let's get you on the bed, yeah? I can kneel with you on the mattress easier than the floor."

He'd long ago hit acceptance in the stages of grief over the loss of his leg, but damn, having to deal with adaptive devices when he wanted to fly into action was a pain in the ass some days more than others.

"Ok-k-k-ay," she said.

"You're not getting shocky on me, are you?"

He gently guided her onto the center of the covered mattress and then followed, doing a quick first aid assessment. Everything was normal except for her straining jaw and the hand sandwiched between her legs.

"Not shock," she said. "It's...it's burning. And I can feel— I think—" She gasped and then let out a roar that drowned out the storm.

"Need me to take a look?" he asked.

"Yeah." She took both his hands and squeezed them until his joints ached. Her hips lifted. "Can't push ear-early, but..."

"Hang on, Franci. Let me see what's going on."

He nudged her nightgown to her hips. *Crowning. Crowning is what's going on.*

This baby wasn't waiting for Violet.

Chapter Six

Contractions weren't like waves. They were like running into a brick wall, over and over. What was even happening? She was supposed to be in early labor until the morning when Violet could arrive to catch the baby. She hadn't planned for Archer sweating through his T-shirt and Violet being somewhere in the middle of a flipping forest and her own fingers brushing something that felt like peach skin an hour before midnight.

The contraction eased, but the burning didn't.

Every part of her body was telling her to push.

She stared at his forearms, focusing on the black lines inked into his skin.

"Hang on. Hold. Wait." Soothing, but a command nonetheless.

Orders from someone who wasn't having a watermelon emerge from their body.

"I have to," she said, whimpering.

Archer's gaze fixed on Franci's. Beautiful eyes, so determined.

"You're going to hold your baby—soon," he promised.

Yes. Only that would make this worth it.

She gasped. Tension gathered at her hips, like undertow sucking retreating water over a rocky beach.

Archer's hands were in place. Franci rode the growing intensity, visualizing being in the tide. Every muscle in her body tensed. Oh, God, she was going to break, to shatter, to…

She howled.

A soothing voice muttered platitudes.

And the burning went from an inferno to numb.

The cries shifted from hers to her baby's.

She did shatter then. Sobs racked her as Archer rested the tiny person on her chest—*her* tiny person. He tucked a towel around the baby and was a blur around her, caring for her and her little girl, dealing with all the mess and wielding his stethoscope and blood pressure cuff.

She didn't want the fuss.

She just wanted to hold her baby and for him to hold her.

"She's—" another sob "—she's healthy."

"Sure is."

Her daughter lay on her chest, snuffling, eyes wide.

"She looks surprised," she whispered, regaining her calm with every one of her baby's breaths. "Hey, little one. Welcome. Archer, look at her. She's perfect."

He hitched a hip on the side of the bed. Brushing the

hair from her face, he let out a long sigh. He settled a hand over the towel covering the baby's body. "Yeah, she is. And you... You were incredible."

"Only because you kept me calm," she mumbled.

"No. Your body knew what to do."

Her and her baby. A pair. A team.

Alone.

Emotions welled in her throat.

"Hey," he said. "Easy now."

"We— The cord, and the afterbirth—"

"Not yet. Relax."

"H-hold me."

A strong arm wedged between her and the pillows, his body, too, pressed to her side, the comfort and weight she needed.

Time suspended, hung in that moment, as she was surrounded by Archer's arms and the scent of him on his pillows and sheets and the dim light of the lanterns.

"How can fingers be so tiny? And eyelashes?"

"I don't know." He sounded as awed as she was.

A thump came from outside the room. Then footsteps.

"Someone's here."

It didn't matter, though. Nothing mattered except the dark blue eyes staring at her. Her body was a live wire—hormones, no doubt, held together by the security of Archer's steady hug.

"Oh, my God, I *missed* it." Violet, from the doorway to the bedroom, dripping with rain. A large backpack dangled from one of her hands. A tall shadow lurked behind her. Matias, no doubt. "*Look* at you two. I mean, three. You…you had a *baby*, Franci."

"Yeah, I'm aware," she said, voice raspy from shouting.

Archer eased away. "Violet. Just in time. You can take over."

No, no, no.

"Stay," she pleaded.

His jaw set, and he settled back in. "Okay, Francine. I'm not going anywhere."

"You could name her Noah," Violet suggested, snuggling on Archer's king-size bed next to Franci early the next morning. "Arriving during biblical rains."

Franci laughed. "Not sure I want to be that literal. I don't know what to do about a name."

"No hurry." Violet traced the baby's tiny ski jump nose with a fingertip.

"Don't think we would have made it through the last few hours without you."

"Pfft." Violet stroked the baby's swaddled back. She'd brought all sorts of magical things in her backpack— flannel blankets, sanitary supplies, pain meds, formula. She'd also managed to help Franci latch properly. The baby had fed a couple of times, and they'd managed a few stretches of napping. Having a midwife as a best friend was a lifesaver.

Then again, having a friend trained as a medic had been pretty damn fortunate, too.

"You and my brother had things well in hand," Violet said. "If I didn't know better, coming in last night, seeing you snuggled on the bed, would've given me ideas."

"Oh, noooo. Nope."

Violet's brows crinkled. "Big protest."

"Because it's absurd," Franci insisted.

Sure, a hundred times last night she'd wished she was going through this with Archer as more than her birth attendant. But she wasn't going to let herself hope for real. Besides, as if she'd have time to even think about anything but the baby for the next few months.

A soft knock sounded on the door, and then it creaked open. "Everyone decent?"

"Decent, yeah." She stared at her baby's alert eyes. She wanted to keep staring, never to look away.

She also couldn't keep her own eyes open. Her entire body hurt, and lounging on Archer's mattress was like reclining on marshmallows.

But falling asleep while her daughter was awake… Guilt racked her, making her tender belly sore in a whole other way. "I can't fall sleep until she does."

"Oh, honey, no," Violet said, stroking her hair. "Sleep's good for you."

Archer crutched in and rested the sticks against the nightstand, then perched on the edge of the bed. "You need to rest," he said gruffly. "Best way to heal."

"She's the most amazing human I've ever seen. How can I close my eyes right now?"

"Necessity?" he said.

She let her head tip back on the pillow. "Ugh, it's true. All I want to do is sleep."

"Then listen to your body," he said.

"That's what your best friend is for," Violet pointed out. "I kind of hold babies for a living."

She frowned an apology at Archer. "I'm taking up your bed."

"Stay as long as you want," he said.

"You can't mean that."

"I do." He cleared his throat and looked at his hands. "Need to talk to you about something."

"About staying? I won't. Once I've napped, Vi can take me home and can help me with the generator."

He winced. "Take a breath for me?"

"Why? I'm calm. I—"

"Your basement is flooded, Francine."

Her vision swam. She struggled to process his announcement, one too many pieces of information at the end of a long, long eighteen hours.

The baby stared at her. *Whatcha going to do, Mama?*

Fear choked her. This little being was depending on her entirely, and she didn't have a room for her, or a livable house…

She had to force out her response. "How bad?"

"Not sure. I noticed it last night but didn't want to add one more thing to your plate. Rachel and Winnie are going to assess the damage as soon as they can get around the mudslide. They'll come by boat, once the wind warning's downgraded. But you don't need to worry about any of that."

"How?" The baby startled. More guilt racked Franci. She lowered her voice to a whisper. "How am I supposed to not worry about it?"

Violet snuggled in, a comforting presence. "Your only focus is you and the little one, promise. The rest of us will manage everything else."

"Exactly. You let your landlords fix things up," Archer said.

"And while I wait, what? Where do I live? My dad's house, disturbing him and Charlotte with newborn chaos? Sam and Kellan live in a one-bedroom apartment. So do you, Vi. And my mom... She doesn't have space."

Square footage *or* emotional.

A lump filled her throat. This was supposed to be a happy time—Franci knew in her bones that this baby was the best thing she would have in her life. They all needed to celebrate the precious, surprising arrival, not be concerned about finding a place for Franci and her daughter to live.

Archer crossed his arms over his fitted long-sleeve technical shirt. "I told you—stay here."

She laughed. "I still don't believe you." Though he wasn't one to joke.

He lifted an eyebrow.

"You *are* serious."

Violet squeezed Franci's arm, a silent "He has a point."

"Why would you want a newborn in your house?" Franci asked, sinking farther into the pillows. None of this made sense.

"I want you to be safe," he said, voice as rough as the waves she could see through the bedroom window. "And this little one..." He brushed a finger along the baby's cheek. "She came into the world under my roof. She'll always be welcome here."

It felt like a monumental decision. But time was a

luxury Franci didn't have. She needed somewhere secure to live while Rachel and Winnie fixed the water damage.

Breath shuddered from her lungs. She sent him a weak smile. "Fine. If you insist, roomie."

Chapter Seven

Archer shifted on his makeshift bed on the couch, too restless and keyed up to fall fully asleep.

He stared at a string of unread texts from Clara and Daniel.

Once they heard of his adventures last night, they'd understand why he hadn't had the time to reply.

Time? Keep making excuses, Frost.

He tossed the device onto the coffee table, startling Honu. "Aren't you supposed to be on guard, dog?" he muttered.

The baby was barely twenty-four hours old, and Archer was already on alert for the slightest cry. With the storm waning but still fierce, he needed to strain to hear over the rain lashing the glass of the sunroom off his main living area. He could have slept upstairs in more comfort, but he wanted to stay close by.

Around midnight, a squawk and a thunk jolted him from the briefest of cat naps.

He grabbed his crutches and then rushed to the bedroom. They were alone in the house. After making a trip to Franci's to get her more clothes and baby gear, Matias and Violet had hiked back to town earlier in the afternoon. As soon as Vi had learned the ferry was running again, she'd realized she needed to get over to her client on Orcas. She'd be back tomorrow to see Franci.

For now they were on their own. This time with a baby out in the world, insistent on having her needs met.

He burst through the door to a crescendo of infant wails.

Franci sat on the edge of the bed, rocking the baby in her arms, staring in frustration at her cell phone lying on the floor.

"I dropped it while I was replying to Sam. I'm too sore to bend over," she said. "I feel like I've done a thousand sit-ups."

Leaning on a crutch, he grabbed the device and put it on the bedside table. They were still without power and were conserving their batteries so he didn't have to run the generator all the time, but she'd been texting her brother off and on over the day.

"Still trying to convince Sam not to fly home?"

"He'd better not." She laid the swaddled baby in the middle of the mattress and climbed back onto the bed, nestling into the pillows before picking up her little bundle once more. "But to give him credit, it's more about wanting to meet his niece rather than concern over the shop."

"He knows Kim, Nic and I will have things in hand."

She frowned, disgruntled. "It was supposed to be me."

"Full of surprises as always."

"A good one, at least." She didn't sound like she fully believed her own words.

"The very best, Francine," he said, the truth of the statement washing over him. The little being in her arms would go on to live a whole life, to change the world around her, bringing joy and color and so many laughs.

But right now, she was full of squawks, and the look on her mother's face was closer to tears than happiness. Franci's gaze darted away.

"Hey," he said, leaning his weight on the hand grips of his crutches. "You want me to leave?"

"I just fed her." Her lip wobbled more with every failed shush. "She doesn't want to be in her bassinet. But I keep drooping while I'm holding her. I'm afraid I'll smother her."

He made his way around the bed and hoisted himself onto the opposite side, then leaned against the pillows and headboard. He held out his hands.

Franci looked doubtful but passed him the infant. "You should be sleeping, too."

"Plenty of time for that later." He'd done many a night watch in the Coast Guard. At least with this one, he was warm and dry. The baby was impossibly light. All rosy cheeks and birth-blue eyes, and a serious little mouth screwed into a bud. A tiny beanie was tucked down to her eyebrows. Her cries faded and she stared at him.

"Hey there, jellybean," he said quietly. "Not too sure about this out-of-the-womb business yet?"

"It was miles easier when she was an inside baby," Francine said. Her eyes went wide. "I mean—this is amazing. I'm not complaining."

"You're allowed," he said. "Parenting is the hardest thing a person can do. Or so I've been told."

He'd watched Danny grow up, witnessing the challenges Eduardo and Clara had dealt with raising their son. And he was willing to bet that if Eduardo could have a second chance, he'd grab it, even to be able to relive the very worst days.

His throat tightened.

Franci yawned. Dark smudges marked the skin under her eyes.

"Rest, Franci. I can have a staring contest with the night owl for a bit."

Sighing, she rolled toward him, resting her head on the pillow right beside his shoulder. She laid a hand on the baby's swaddle. "She needs a name. I can't decide."

"It'll come to you."

Franci was sound asleep before he could make a suggestion.

He shushed until the baby's eyes drooped, too.

There was no way to get her in her bassinet without his chair or his prosthesis nearby—he'd jar her awake if he hobbled around with one crutch. He contented himself with counting her wispy eyelashes in the dim lantern light. Franci settled closer to him, clutching his biceps. Eventually, he put his arm around her. He needed to keep his emotional distance, but she needed comfort, and he was the only one who could provide it right now.

Even once they were reconnected with the rest of

the island and Franci's family and friends descended in droves as they surely would, Archer didn't expect the instinct to fade.

He was going to want to protect Franci and her daughter for the rest of their lives.

If only he hadn't proven himself incapable of that long ago.

Well, four days in, and at least I'm standing.

Franci padded into the kitchen, figuring she had at least fifteen minutes before her darling daughter realized she'd been left alone in her bassinet and made her ire known. There was still no electricity, they were stuck accessing town by boat, she was leaking from more parts of her body than she'd ever expected and she was taking up her friend's bed, but she could at least make herself toast.

He'd showed her how to use the warming tray under the propane oven as a makeshift toaster, given his electric one was out of commission for another day or two. She wouldn't even have known what day it was had she not been counting the nights when Archer climbed onto the left side of his bed and held the baby while Franci got three precious hours of sleep in a row.

Four times.

She'd only woken up with her head on his shoulder the one time.

She'd wanted to *every* time.

Postpartum hormones were no joke, and they were confusing her, that was all. Making her needy and indecisive.

She couldn't even get her daughter's name right. How

did people pick them so easily? It wasn't like deciding what color to paint a wall. Her decision would stick with her child her whole life, or at least couldn't be changed without significant effort. And there were so many good names. The squishy little face... How did a person pick a moniker that worked for a bundled baby but could also work for an astronaut or a Supreme Court justice or any of the other wild and wonderful roles her child could play to shake up the world?

Not to mention it would be nice to acknowledge Archer, given he'd literally ushered the baby from her uterus.

She put the kettle on the burner and got the toast in the warming tray. A quiet breakfast—seemed like the biggest luxury in the world. The baby was sleeping, Archer had taken his boat to the wharf and Violet wasn't due for a visit until later.

She dropped a bag of chamomile in one of the many hand-thrown mugs in Archer's cupboard, prepared to snuggle on the couch with one of the name-your-baby books he'd borrowed from the library on his trip to town yesterday.

All of it was Archer, really. That punched her square in the diaphragm.

Every little thing. He paid attention. Saw her.

A woman could get used to that.

The scent of brewing tea and toasting yeast were a giant hug. She pulled the tray out from under the oven and flipped the toast, mouth already watering at the prospect of a few slices of Rachel and Winnie's award-winning sourdough, then took a quick glance outside to see if she could spot Archer's boat. His dock was being used by a number of neighbors who needed a way to commute to and from the harbor until the road finally got cleared, but none of the vessels tied to the long pier was his beauty of an antique wooden Chris-Craft.

He should be back any minute, having worked the morning at the shop and then done a grocery run.

And she *missed* him, and good grief, she couldn't afford to indulge the feeling.

A plaintive cry split the air.

Ack, she'd just go grab the baby quickly.

She raced to the bedroom and picked up her perfect nugget of a child, those blue eyes that would likely darken to brown and the tinge of cinnamon hair on top of her little head. As she slid her hands under her little body, her fingers slicked across wetness.

Dang.

Sighing, she smiled at the unhappy little face. "No wonder you're screaming, hey? Baby's first blowout? No fun, sweet pea."

She sang a little as she changed the sleeper and disastrous diaper. One of many, no doubt.

But the baby was wide-awake now, and would be looking to be fed soon, so Franci didn't bother putting her back in the bassinet. She bobbed and weaved a gentle dance out to the kitchen to get—

My toast.

"Oh, no!"

Needing both hands free, she laid her daughter in her bucket car seat next to the dining room table. She rushed to the oven and yanked out the tray. Smoke rose from the charred slices.

Tears sparked. She only wanted toast. Toast and tea, and fifteen minutes to figure out the perfect name—

A sharp electric wail pierced the air.

The baby followed suit.

The smoke detector's shrill peal severed her ability to think. Her tears full on welled.

The propane. And...and...escape? She turned off the oven. She scooped her daughter from her carrier and cupped the hat-covered head to her chest, protecting the little ears as she darted for the deck to get away from the noise.

The sun was shining, but the wind was fierce, biting her cheeks and fingers. She pulled the bottom of her sweatshirt into a cocoon around the baby and jiggled her enraged bundle, trying to soothe her daughter's wails.

"I'm so sorry," she said, tears dripping off her chin onto the makeshift blanket. A gust cut through her thin T-shirt, a slice of cold against her abdomen. "So loud. Mommy messed up. I tried... I just wanted..."

Damn it. Her little one didn't care. She needed snuggles and not to be subjected to shrill alarms. Taking a breath, Franci tried to find peace. Couldn't ask for a better place than Archer's wide deck overlooking the poststorm beauty of the water, pale winter blues and streaky white clouds and the far-off bumps of other islands to the north.

"Shh. Shh," she soothed.

Heavy steps sounded inside the house. She looked up sharply, through the window and then to the dock. Oh. Archer's boat was in its slip. She whirled, still shushing, and through the sliding glass door caught a flash

of a red survival jacket and a waving motion in the hallway off the kitchen.

The shrieking stopped.

"There," she murmured. "All better."

Hopefully, her daughter would grow to love the
soothing sounds of creaking docks and calling gulls
and lapping waves as Franci had.

The ocean was her constant, her touchstone.

And the man striding toward the sliding door was
the ocean's equal. Comforting and reliable. Vast and
mysterious.

Occasionally devastating.

His mouth was tucked into a concerned frown.

"All okay, Francine?"

Not really—she didn't have a name for her baby and
was ready to eat an entire *loaf* of bread—but he didn't
need to hear about the emotional whirlwind that was
postpartum hormones.

She did her best to smear away her tears one-handed
and forced a grin. "I couldn't go back inside to make it
stop. Didn't want to hurt her ears."

He shucked out of his survival coat and hung the
thick material around her shoulders. Holding the lapels
close in the front, he sheltered the rest of her and the
baby from the wind with his broad back.

Her stomach went to mush.

"Happens to the best of us," he said quietly. "That
oven's life mission is to burn toast."

The wind carried the fresh scent of his bodywash
to her nose. She recognized the smell—every time she
showered, she flipped open the lid and snuck a quick
whiff.

"I just wanted a snack." Fresh tears gathered and she sniffled. "I *always* want a snack. My milk is officially in, and—" She stopped herself before she went into detail. Some things friends didn't need to know.

Even one I'm sharing a bed with.

It wasn't *that* kind of sharing a bed.

She lifted her chin. His serious gaze was enough to take her knees out from under her. "I should move upstairs tonight."

"Whatever you're comfortable with." He frowned. "Harder for me to hear if you need a hand, though."

"I've got it," she said.

I so don't *have it. But I can't handle what might come with staying so close.*

She should avoid even this kind of proximity, standing inches apart with all the wonders of the waterfront around them. But she couldn't bring herself to step back.

His hands, still grasping the sides of his survival coat, were right close to her daughter. He brushed a thumb along a perfect pale-pink cheek.

His blue irises sparkled, the color identical to the surface of the sun-kissed water.

Wait. That's perfect.

"Iris," she said.

He cocked his head.

"For her name. I read that it means rainbow. And she's kind of my rainbow after the storm, you know?"

He smiled. "It's pretty."

"And then maybe Gale for a middle name. Though I was also thinking I could work in something Archer related, given how important you were for her birth. I was doing some research, burning through my data while I was breastfeeding, and Diana's the goddess of the hunt, and is always depicted as an archer with a bow and arrow. So it would be subtle, but still connected to you."

He dropped the sides of the jacket and took a step back. "Stick with Gale."

Oh. "You don't want a namesake?"

"Gale's more meaningful. The storm was more responsible for everything than I was."

She cocked an eyebrow at him. "Uh, try again."

"Fine. The truth? People might get the wrong idea."

Her jaw dropped. "That's just…" *Mean? Sad?* "You don't want to be associated with my baby?" *Or maybe with me.* "Pretty sure everyone on the island knows your heroics by now."

He jammed a hand into his hair, sending the windblown strands into further disarray. "It'll be a fun story for her to tell at parties one day. Not something she needs to live with on every piece of identification forever."

Why was his refusal so crushing?

"Maybe we should get out of your hair, then," she said quietly. "Cut things off before anyone gets the 'wrong idea' about why I'm here."

She turned to go inside. He caught her arm, stilling her. "No. It makes zero sense for you to leave."

"It does if you're worried people are gossiping about us." Realization flashed. "You don't want people to think she's your kid."

"No." Agony slashed across his face. "It's about her. She deserves better than having to carry around the name of some guy who happened to be in the right place at the right time, Franci."

Oh. Damn. Just when she had a good mad going… "You don't think you're *worthy* of being connected to my daughter?"

"Look at her, Franci," he said, voice thick. "She's a damn miracle. And I'm…me."

Yeah, he was. His own kind of a miracle. He nearly hadn't made it out of the ocean alive.

"What do you mean, you're *you*? Because of your leg?"

"No." A defensive staccato syllable.

Not a lie, though. "Then what is it?"

"Nothing worth getting into."

"I doubt that's true." But thanks to him being a flipping vault, she doubted she'd be able to pry out the truth. "She is a miracle. Because of you."

"You did all the work."

"Uh, not quite," she said. "But if the honor would make you uncomfortable, I won't push. Gale it is."

Chapter Eight

Later that night, Archer lay on his bed, Iris in the crook of his arm. The spray of the shower was the only sound to accompany smacking baby lips.

Franci was in his shower. Even though she'd decided to sleep upstairs, he insisted she use his bathroom. She was still moving mighty slow, and the accessible features could only help.

Help *her*, that was.

Employing every fiber of willpower he possessed, he pushed away the tempting image of water sluicing over her lush body.

He stared at Iris's studious expression. Judgmental, almost.

"You know what's going on already, don't you, Iris Gale?"

Her arms jerked to the side, one of those random baby spasms he'd quickly learned were normal. She looked annoyed at the reflex.

"Yeah. No fun when your body does things you don't want it to."

He understood that like nobody's business. Right now, in fact. Holding Iris was helping him ignore the tingling sensation wrapping around his left leg.

"It would be easier to do something about it if it was still there," he told the baby. Energy work lessened the phantom sensations, but some days, he just had to manage.

Those dark blue eyes peered at him. Her pacifier was going a mile a minute.

"Are you going to have brown eyes like your mom?"

They won't ever look like mine.

The thought pinged through his body like lead shot. Ridiculous. He didn't want to be a father. Parenthood would require a willingness to lay himself bare, which he couldn't do.

But with how cute Iris's little face was, it sure was easy to hold her and enjoy their nightly staring contests.

"Your mom's insisting you sleep upstairs tonight," he murmured to the baby. "You think you're up for it?"

He wasn't sure he was. He'd gotten used to listening for any noise from the primary bedroom, to coming in some time between midnight and one every night to hold Iris while Franci slept.

These moments in the low light of the lantern. That dark gaze, fixed on his. Nothing else mattered for a long precious span of minutes.

Tomorrow, the power would be restored. The road would open and life would go back to normal in some ways.

Part of him didn't want it to. Part of him wanted to stay forever in this cocoon with Franci and her baby, pretending he knew how to meet the needs of the people who depended on him.

They'd be doing so for the near future. Word from Rachel and Winnie was the damage to the basement was bigger than they'd predicted, as it had fried the heating system. But still, with road access, people would be coming to visit, to help. Franci wouldn't have to depend on him as much.

Probably for the better.

His phone buzzed. He startled, not realizing he had a cell signal.

He checked the screen.

"Ah," he said to Iris. "Daniel. My godson. You'd like him. He's a good kid. And right now, he's—" he scanned the message "—finished his first pool dive. Good for him."

His chest ached. Eduardo would have been so damn proud. His friend would never know, though. Would never see all the ambitious things his son set out to do in his life.

"You going to let your mom teach you how to dive one day, little one?" he asked Iris.

Her mouth gaped, and the pacifier lolled to the side.

His phone vibrated again. Holy crap, an actual call had gotten through. He answered it even though he wasn't in the mood to talk to anyone who was more than five days old.

Especially not Clara Martinez.

"Clarabelle. Been a while."

"Not because of me, Archer." His buddy's widow sounded like her usual no-nonsense self. She'd moved back to her Oregon hometown after Eduardo's death, and juggled work and being the best mom Daniel could hope for.

Being a good friend, too.

"Called to bust my balls?" His sister would give him grief for using language in front of the baby, but not only was she months too young to understand anything, she was officially sound asleep.

"Did you do something to deserve a ball busting?"

"Oh, probably." She'd no doubt love to hear the story about Franci's delivery and the fact he had houseguests, but he didn't even know where to begin.

"Well, consider it done, but I was more calling to remind you to stop feeling guilty."

"Huh?" Not the first time he'd feigned ignorance when Clara got on his case about his survivor's guilt.

"Dan and I have noticed your messages have been short, and we want you to know—"

"Damn, I'm sorry." He didn't particularly want to hear what they wanted him to know. They could spout off about how they didn't blame him for their loss a thousand times. He knew the truth. "I've had houseguests. A friend of mine and her new baby. You know how infants are—make it hard to keep a schedule."

The line was silent for a few seconds. Had he lost the connection?

"Hello?" he prodded.

"Sorry, I was trying to picture you with a baby. It's been a while since you dangled Dan on your knee. Whose baby?"

"My coworker's."

Hopefully Franci didn't hear that. She didn't seem to like it much when he pointed it out.

"Your coworker is your houseguest? How long is she staying?"

"For a while yet." He explained the storm and the flooding at Franci's. "We had a pretty chaotic time, escaping her place."

"You must have been scared."

"We've both seen worse storms. We were distracted by her contractions."

"Wait, what?" Clara asked. "You need to fill me in."

He gave as brief a description of the night as he could. Somewhere while he was talking, the shower shut off.

"So this baby you're holding is brand-new." Clara's voice was full of longing.

"She has an old soul."

"Aha! You're hooked. I know how it is. You look into those little eyes and see the whole world, and then you want to give it to them."

He did want that. "She's not mine, Clara. And she never will be."

The bathroom door opened. Franci stood in the arch, frowning.

Disappointed?

"Talking to a friend of mine," he explained. A line formed on Franci's brow. She looked huggable—fine, kissable—in her long fleecy robe. Mouth turned down at the corners, she took Iris from him and left the bedroom. Losing the featherweight left a hole the size of a meteor crater. "I'd better go, Clarabelle."

"Of course," she said. "And I'm telling you, the diving is good for Dan. Helps him feel close to his dad."

"Eddy should have gotten the chance to teach him. And thanks to me—"

He hated when he slipped up and voiced his regrets. Clara had enough to recover from.

"Can't live a life built on *should*s, honey." She cleared her throat. "Snuggle that baby. Take care of your *co-worker*. Send me a picture. And trust me—Dan's doing great. He'd love *you* to see him dive."

"I miss you guys," he said. The truth, one that wouldn't set his godson up for disappointment.

"Come see us," she said.

"I need to stick close to home while Franci's staying with me, and then I'm headed to Hawaii with my dad for part of December."

"In the New Year, then," she insisted. "I'm glad you're moving on, Arch."

"This…this isn't that," he sputtered.

"Your voice says otherwise. You're a smitten kitten." *Her* voice was blithe, carefree.

Infuriating.

And he didn't like to have to make excuses.

Nor had he liked Franci's frown. Had something about him talking to Clara bothered her?

He put on his prosthesis and went to find her.

She was in the living room, in the middle of lighting a fire. Iris lay on a plush blanket on the floor, staring at the flames.

He sat next to them, legs outstretched. "If you don't want me to talk about Iris's entry into the world with people, I won't. I didn't think to ask permission."

She scooted a few inches sideways. Away from him. "Tell anyone you want. It's fine."

Nothing was ever fine when a person used those words.

You seem upset. He couldn't get the observation out, though.

Doing things for her, cooking meals, providing her a safe space to hide out, being a second pair of hands with Iris—those things he could do. But if he asked about her emotions, it might dredge up his own. Keeping his assistance to tangible things would be safer for both of them. She had Vi for BFF duty, anyway.

She turned from stoking the fire. Her open robe fell to the side, exposing a creamy white thigh and the edge of her pajama shorts.

Lace trim against skin dotted with cinnamon freckles. One glimpse of those shorts made him hotter than the fire crackling in the hearth.

"Is the scuba tour running tomorrow?" Franci asked.

Huh?

Oh, right. The world beyond their cozy isolation.

"Yeah, it's a go," he said. "Full, too, with a handful of people who rebooked."

"I want to come with you."

"Out on the water?" he asked. She couldn't be serious.

She shot him a disgruntled glare. "To the wharf. I have an appointment with Vi, and I'm going to drop in at the bakery to say hi to Rachel and Winnie. And I owe Nic a coffee for being easy about starting his full-time hours early."

Only her closest family had made the trek out by boat to come visit. Not even her mom had managed.

After five days of having Franci and Iris mostly to

himself to coddle and care for, it chafed to think of sharing them from now on.

She leaned over the baby with an exaggerated smile on her face. "Oh, hello. There's my sweet pea."

She might have been running on too little sleep, but she overflowed with love for her daughter.

Violet had pulled him aside the day after Iris's birth and confessed she was worried Franci would try to do too much, too soon. The lack of a road had helped there. It'd been sweatpants, decaf coffee with lots of cream and lounging on the couch for days. Going from isolation to hours of socializing would be a shock. "You're sure you want to plan so much at once?"

She shook her head and lifted her gaze to the ceiling. "We've been holing up here for almost a week. You've at least made a little bit of contact with the outside world, heading into town on your boat. I've only seen you, Vi, Dad and Charlotte. I can't wait to show Iris off to the world. Everyone's going to love her. Who could resist this face?"

He nodded in concession. *Not me.*

Her cheer dimmed. "Plus, I need to make it easier for my mom to have her first visit with Iris."

"You're dealing with a newborn," he said. "It's not on you to make things easier for anyone else."

She lifted a shoulder. "You know how my mom is. I might have a brand-new baby, but Drake and Jordan are waaaaay more work. She always finds a reason to be busier than whomever she's comparing herself to, especially when my little brothers are concerned."

That had to hurt. He didn't know Franci's mom, Alina, well, but Oyster Island was too small not to run into her from time to time. From the little he saw, she was solely focused on her second family, especially her tween sons, at the expense of her relationship with Franci and Charlotte. He'd never thought much of the woman, to be honest.

"Well, consider me here to make *your* life easier," he said. "And if that's driving you to town tomorrow, you got it."

He tucked a strand of hair behind her ear.

He ached to lean in for a kiss. Just a taste, a nip, a quick test of her pink lips. They were parted, perfect for a stolen taste. An unspoken invitation?

No. No way. She stared at him, frozen in place. Not the posture of a woman eager for a kiss. Franci wasn't interested in him.

More importantly, he needed to protect her from everything he brought with him.

Walk away while you can.

He shifted, ready to stand, but before he could, she knelt, leaned toward him and caught one of his cheeks in her hand.

"Archer, wait."

That. *That* said "kiss me."

Holding in a groan, he covered her hand for a quick second before sliding her fingers from his face. "If I wait, I'm going to do something that we'll regret."

She settled on her heels. Curiosity passed over her pretty face. "You sound awfully certain about *my* feelings."

"I am."

More than anything else going on in his life right now. He couldn't even peek at his grief himself, let alone ask someone else to face it.

"Too bad I disagree," she said, eyes twinkling.

This woman. Goddamn. Shaking his head, he rose to his feet as quickly as his prosthesis would allow and backed away from pure temptation.

Franci chuckled to herself, standing next to Archer's SUV in front of the pastel-painted row of houses on the main drag. Rain dripped off the hood of her jacket, splattering between the adorable bear ears on Iris's tiny winter suit.

He was rushing to get the stroller frame open. This brawny, vital man, panicked about precipitation. Her stomach growled, teased by the savory-sweet smells coming out of Hideaway Bakery. The warmth of the space would be miles better than being on the street, too. November on Oyster Island guaranteed rain over snow. Today's drizzle was miles better than the storm heralding Iris's birth, but it still chilled to the bone.

Archer muttered a curse under his breath.

"Need a hand?" she said lightly.

"Christ, no. It's just a stroller. But it's damn cold out."

"Iris is toasty warm." Only a little pink nose, bow lips and two dark eyes were visible inside the hood. Which was still too much exposure for Archer, apparently.

Unless the stroller had nothing to do with his mood. Change the subject of his stubborn protectiveness from Iris to Franci herself, and his mood wasn't far off the one he'd been in when he'd walked away from her last night. This picture he had of himself, a guardian but behind his own fortress, was heartbreaking.

Then again, most walls weren't impenetrable. And Franci wasn't in a hurry.

Archer, on the other hand, seemed to be, for entirely different reasons. His fingers slipped on the bassinet attachment and he swore again.

"She's a West Coast baby," she assured him. "She was going to get wet eventually."

He was silent, but his stern jaw said, "Not on my watch."

Oof. Her belly warmed.

It had been a few days since she'd been treated to Petty Officer First Class Frost. Any moment when he was sweet around Iris made her soften but something about the ultraprotective streak coming out turned her into the hot fudge sauce served at the ice-cream stand by the ferry terminal.

He yanked the hood of the bassinet forward to stop the rain from getting the base wet, and rolled it in Franci's direction.

"There." He snapped the word, but she could tell he was irritated with himself, not her.

She smiled. "Thanks."

"You look tired," he said.

She felt it, too. Her stubbornness, moving upstairs, meant the stretch between twelve and three o'clock had been spent mostly awake. But the distance was necessary. Otherwise, she'd give in to the feeling that they were a team on this, even though it was only a short-term solution. "I'll be fine. You're diving today. You needed not to be woken up."

"I *want* to help."

Sometimes, looking a gift horse in the mouth was

necessary, and this one needed to be examined down to counting the tastebuds on its tongue. "Why?"

He frowned. "Does it matter?"

She lifted a shoulder. The wind shifted direction, and rain misted her face. "I don't want to take advantage. It's not exactly like I'm a weekend houseguest."

"Stay as long as you need. Please."

Ugh, whenever he pulled out *please*…

"Thank you," she said quietly.

"My tour's done at two."

"I know. I booked a few of those people. I should be on the desk today." But staring at her baby as she laid her in the stroller and buckled her in, she had no compunction to be at work. "Though there isn't an amount you could pay me to be at Otter instead of with Iris right now."

"You deserve every day of leave. And more. This time is precious."

"Especially today. I managed to catch a time my mom was available for coffee." She was *finally* going to get to introduce her mom to her granddaughter. "Then the clinic, and after, we'll see where the wind takes us."

"You're *sure* you want to stick around town that long?"

"I can keep myself occupied for four hours, Archer. Worse comes to worst, I'll go to Sam and Kellan's and steal a nap on their couch."

He gave a curt nod. He reached out as if to brush her cheek but dropped his hand before making contact. His mouth was in a grim line. He turned on a heel and headed for the dive shop next door.

"Have *fun*, Hawkeye!" she called.

He lifted a hand but didn't turn back.

"What's up his ass?" asked a male voice from behind her.

She turned to Matias, Sam's other best friend. She hadn't seen him since he'd hiked out with Violet the night of Iris's arrival. As always, his brown eyes glinted with the promise of giving her an amicable hard time. Matias had her firmly defined as an honorary little sister, which was fine by Franci.

Matias Kahale was not Archer.

A good-looking guy, sure. Broader than Archer, even, with his Hawaiian father's bronze skin and dark hair and the same joie de vivre that his mother, a world-famous Austrian runway model, was known for. When he laughed, it felt like a comforting hug, and any person entering his pub never walked away hungry. But unlike his long-absent parents, who'd left him on Oyster Island for his aunt and uncle to raise, he was a homebody and a fantastic friend. Never the man to catch her eye, though.

His Gore-Tex jacket was unzipped, exposing the logo of his pub, The Cannery, on his T-shirt. She waved at him to join her under the eaves in front of one of the Wharf Street gift shops.

He carried a grocery bag overflowing with what looked like a giant bag of cheese curds in his big hand.

"Ohhh, are you making your goaty goat special?" He got his curds and meat from a farm over by the old ferry dock. His ability to turn any kind of tough cut into the most delicious pulled topping and gravy was unmatched on the island, not even by classically trained Kellan. "I could smash a plate of poutine."

"You know when we open." He pointed down the

strip of stores to Otter Marine. "Seriously, though—Frost looked pissed."

She drew her brows together. "He's worried I'm over-doing it."

"Interesting."

"Not really. He's always protective."

"Not with everyone." Matias leaned over the stroller. "Are you the bee in his bonnet?" He wiggled a gentle finger against Iris's fleece-covered tummy. "Maybe he doesn't know what to do with you, baby girl."

"He knows exactly what to do, actually." And she was growing to depend on it.

It's temporary. Just until after Christmas.

Matias raised a knowing eyebrow. "'Exactly' what to do, strawberry?"

"Oh, God, Matias. Not like *that*."

Sure, she *wished* it was like that. But she didn't want Sam's friend speculating to her brother about something currently nonexistent.

"Well, you take it easy. Let Frost do what he needs to do so you don't have to—" Straightening, he stared over her shoulder.

She turned her head, then grinned. A familiar pair of bouncing braids was coming their way.

Violet wore thick workout gear and a wide smile. She threw her arms around Franci. She clearly hadn't been running long because she smelled like fresh air, not sweat. "You're out and about."

"You knew I would be—I'm coming to see you at noon."

"Can't wait." Violet peeked into the stroller. "Ohhh, she's sleeping."

"She likes the sound of the raindrops," Franci said.

Violet narrowed her eyes at Matias. "If you'd let me bring your ATV, I would have been there to see her born, you know."

Matias raked his free hand through his longish black hair. His bronze cheeks turned ruddy. "The trail was too soft. We would have rolled into a ditch, Vi."

If Violet had made it, it would have been different, and… And Franci didn't want different. Her baby's birth had been perfect. *Archer* had been perfect.

She wouldn't change a minute of it.

But afterward, it had sure been a relief to have Violet there.

"That hike you two did." Franci's throat tightened. "You're part of the reason Iris and I are healthy."

"And I was supposed to *be* there." Violet glared at Matias again, but it seemed like a front.

He groaned. "Wasn't it better to be alive and late?"

"Yes, it was," Franci said, putting a hand on Violet's damp shoulder. "It played out exactly how it was meant to."

Violet sighed. "I suppose. My brother's sure taken with her." Her blue eyes turned on Franci. "I can't blame him at all, but I wonder—"

"Would you look at the time?" Franci didn't want Violet and Matias comparing stories and fabricating some wild speculation.

Not when she so badly wanted for that speculation to be the truth.

Lifting a dark eyebrow, Violet said, "In a hurry?"

"Yeah, we're meeting my mom for coffee." Excitement filled her. "I should go. I need to go grab a good table."

She left Violet to bicker with Matias and headed into the bakery. She grabbed the best table, the one by the window in the front. Her family had good luck at this table. Sam's first date with Kellan happened on these very chairs.

"And you, little miss, are going to meet your grandma for the first time." She rocked the stroller back and forth to lull her sleeping baby and waited.

And waited.

Fifteen minutes later, it felt like they'd said hello to half of Oyster Island. Winnie and Rachel, oozing affection and lamenting how the flooded basement in the cottage was cheating them out of baby time. A parade of people from the cozy-mystery book club who met in the bakery once a week. A few friends she'd grown up with, and a few she'd met over the past few years, transplants from the mainland.

But not her mom.

Iris's eyes flew open and she stretched her arms and legs. Franci took her out of her winter suit and cuddled her close.

"I hope Grandma's okay, Iris Gale," she said, checking her phone yet another time. She should have planned to drive her own car to her mom's house—

A message flashed on the screen. Running late. Drake forgot his lunch and his basketball uniform and I needed to run to the school. Got caught volunteering for reading circles. Be there at 12.

Franci's hand shook. My midwife appt is at 12.

She can't change it?

Her breath hitched in surprise. She couldn't decide if she was hurt or annoyed. No, she's going to Orcas this afternoon.

I have boot camp after lunch. Headed to San Juan for Jordan's volleyball game after school. We'll have to find another day.

Tears welled at the corner of her eyes. She dropped her phone on the table and hugged Iris to her chest. At least her daughter wouldn't remember this.

Rachel rushed over, hands outstretched. She rested a palm on Franci's back. "Hey, now. How can I help?"

Be my mom?

Guilt bolted through her core. How badly would it hurt if Iris ever thought something similar about Franci because of one of Franci's shortcomings?

But when Mom's shortcomings hurt me...

She stood, nestled Iris back in the bassinet and melted into Rachel's offered embrace. "Got stood up," she said, words muffled by the shoulder of the other woman's handknit Fair Isle sweater.

"But didn't you say you were meeting—oh, *honey*." Rachel growled. "This family of ours, we are a mess sometimes. Your dad did wrong by me when we were young, and then Alina did wrong by him... And you kids get the brunt of it, even all these years later."

Franci held Rachel tighter and let the tears fall.

"I know, Franci. And nothing replaces your own

132 *A HIDEAWAY WHARF HOLIDAY*

mother. But if you ever need it, Winnie and I have plenty of Big Mom Energy to surround you with."

Franci nodded, sniffling. "I want to be that for Iris."

"You already are, sweet love." Rachel paused. "Oh! Here's more hugs for you. More love."

Rachel passed her into a pair of muscled arms and for a split-second Franci thought they belonged to Archer, but no. This person was a bit shorter and smelled like an airplane and the peppermint stress-release spray her brother-in-law-to-be liked to spritz everywhere. Part of her sadness eased as she let Sam hold her up.

He gripped her tightly. "Rough morning?"

"Didn't know how much I missed you until this very moment."

"You lied," he teased. "Telling me you'd still be pregnant when I got home."

Nothing he hadn't complained about a hundred times in the few calls they'd managed since Iris's birth.

"And you're supposed to be on the Irish coast today," Franci said. "Why are you home?"

Another hand landed on her back. "We couldn't stay away a moment longer, love." The lilt in Kellan's words was a hug in and of itself.

And for the people who were here, surrounding her, she could smile and introduce them to Iris and make sure they weren't worried about her brief spate of tears.

"I can't believe you changed your flight, but now that you're here…" She pulled away from her brother and lifted Iris from her stroller. "One niece, ready for snuggles."

"Jesus, she's perfect." Kellan's gray eyes looked a little damp.

Sam didn't say anything. His jaw gaped and he held out his hands.

Iris fixed him with her Very Serious Stare as he took her from Franci and brought her into a careful embrace. Kellan stood close to her brother, the two of them forming a little circle of love around her daughter.

Their smiles were soft, and she watched as two more men she loved fell under the spell of a seven-pound infant.

"You did good, Franci," Sam said.

She grinned, even around the lingering ache in her heart. This was why she'd done this, insisted on continuing with a pregnancy that had rocked her world. Babies brought so much love with them, brought people together, and it would only continue to grow as Iris grew herself. A little sprite, bringing joy wherever she went.

Sam passed the baby to Kellan, who accepted the offered bundle with a murmured endearment.

"Uncle duty is looking better and better," her brother said.

Rachel, who'd gone back to busing tables, clearly overheard him. "You know what's better than being an uncle? Being a da—"

"Not happening!" Sam corrected his mom and gave Franci another hug. "But I'm so glad *you're* getting to be a parent. Now, what the hell is going on with your house? Mom? Status of the repairs on the cottage?"

It was on the tip of her tongue to tell Sam to mind his own business, but her brain was already swimming with Iris-related things, so getting an assist with the house was great.

Rachel made a face. "Supply delays," she said. "It'll

be a while. Between Christmas and New Year's at the earliest."

Sam returned his mom's apologetic grimace with a frown of his own. "What are we going to do with you, Franci? I wonder if there's a vacation space in town we could get for you, so that you're close to Kell and me."

He didn't mean it in a negative way. She did need somewhere to go. But she had a place at Archer's. Yeah, she spent a whole lot of energy not looking at him and trying not to let her emotions get to her when he got a fond smile on his face talking to some Clara person, but... "I'm comfortable at Archer's. So is Iris."

"He likes his space, though," Sam said, confused.

"He's been nothing but welcoming." *And is cool with me having moments where I'm not a shining Franci light, which I would feel obligated to be if I were at Dad's.* "I don't want some random rental. I like the company."

Granted, her nights in the upstairs bedroom hadn't gone as well as when she was sharing his massive king bed and had his assistance two seconds after Iris cried out. She kept hoping the distance from the flight of stairs would help with all that not-staring energy.

Kellan was too busy counting Iris's tiny fingers over and over to be paying attention to Franci's admittedly odd plan, but Sam didn't look convinced.

"Tell you what," she said. "With you home early, we can have Thanksgiving dinner on time. Archer and I will cook it at his place."

And Sam would see she and Archer had everything well in hand.

"Oh, love, that's a lot to take on," Kellan said. "If you want to celebrate tomorrow, Sam and I can host."

The plan had been to have a big family spread in the Forest + Brine space above Otter Marine the weekend after Thanksgiving instead, but now that Franci thought of it, hosting at Archer's on the actual holiday would be even better. "You won't be fine—you'll be jet-lagged all to hell. Plus, if we're at Archer's, I won't have to haul around any of Iris's stuff."

Sam touched a knuckle to her cheek. "If you're sure."

"I want the time with our family, Sam," she said.

Maybe a night surrounded by them would be a Band-Aid over the scrapes from being stood up by her mom.

Chapter Nine

Hours later, Franci maneuvered the stroller into Otter Marine. The expansive basket underneath the bassinet holding her dozing infant was overflowing with the groceries they'd need for Thanksgiving dinner.

At least, she hoped she'd remembered everything. She had a fresh turkey that cost a mortgage payment, potatoes, enough whipping cream to make the potatoes worth eating and a rainbow of vegetables. No marshmallows for the yams—Charlotte considered them an abomination unto God—but some pancetta, because surely that would make something taste better. Maybe the yams. She'd decide later. And pecans and sage, and—

If I forgot something, we'll make do.

Nic stood behind the counter. He had the reputation on the island of being a bit of a heartbreaker, though he'd only had eyes for Franci's little sister since the spring. Any time Nic wasn't working and Charlotte wasn't busy with her online college courses, the pair was attached at the hip.

He looked up from the point-of-sale system, his expression brightening. "You brought the kid to say hi?"

"She's not saying much yet," she joked. "And yeah, I've been showing her around. Also, Archer's my ride home."

"He's finished his tour." Nic came around the desk to peer into the stroller. "Getting dressed, I think."

"All done, in fact," Archer said, emerging from the staff change room. He was in a T-shirt and shorts and was toweling off his hair. His biceps flexed, shifting the black outlines of his tattoos. Why was it that everything he did made it feel like the ambient room temperature was set for a hot-yoga class?

Holding herself back from fanning her face, Franci said, "Ready to hit the road? I have perishables that need a fridge."

He stilled his toweling. His gaze dropped to the stroller basket and quickly turned confused. "I went grocery shopping yesterday, you know."

"Yeah, uh… I might have invited a few people over for dinner tomorrow night."

"I thought we were going to Violet's for Thanksgiving."

"But Sam and Kellan are home."

"What?" he said, clearly taken aback.

"Yeah, I was surprised, too. So Violet's coming our way. With my family, and Dad's bringing Alice. Oh, and I invited Rachel and Winnie."

"Charlotte's going?" Nic added hopefully.

"She is," she said. "You can join us, if you aren't eating with your folks."

"I'd rather be with Char."

She couldn't blame him for being eager to spend every available minute with her younger sister. She kept catching herself having similar feelings about Archer.

Archer held up a hand. "Whoa, whoa, whoa. That's… eleven, including us?"

Us. Sigh.

She nodded.

"Franci," he said gently. "I get you want to celebrate with your family. And I do have the day off. But be reasonable—by six o'clock every night this week, you've been ready for bed, not for a party."

Her cheeks heated. "I have a mountain of things to be thankful for this year." *And you are one of them.* "I want to have my family over for a proper meal. The ones I can count on."

He studied her, gaze more knowing than she'd like. "How was coffee today?"

"Didn't happen." She tried to keep the bitterness from her tone, but didn't entirely succeed.

He nodded, as if she'd confirmed something he'd been expecting.

He was smart to expect her mom not to follow through. Maybe one day, Franci would fully clue in herself.

"Come on, Archer. It's just dinner."

Whether Nic's presence gave him caution, or he was being kind, he didn't call her on her underestimation.

He blew out a breath. "If it's really what you want, then I'll be happy to host with you."

I really want you.

Talk about a Thanksgiving wish that wasn't about to be granted.

"You're sure you're okay with this?" Sam asked Archer. He was leaning against the kitchen counter, nursing a beer and eyeing Archer's Sweet and a Little Salty apron. The black cotton number had shown up on a wall hook in Archer's kitchen around the time Franci informed him they were making dinner for a crowd. Didn't take much to deduce she'd been the one to get it for him.

She was too eager to please everyone around her, and he was too eager to please her. There was no way he would have refused to wear it.

"I'm cooking a turkey, am I not?" Archer said.

"Yeah, since when do you roast entire birds on demand?"

"Your fiancé cooks for a crowd for a living. Do you give him the third degree over it?"

Sam took another drink. His throat worked for longer than was necessary to swallow a mouthful of beer. "She's my little sister."

Sam and Archer had spent thousands of hours together over the course of their lives. Building beach forts as kids. Obsessing over *StarCraft* in high school. Exploring every underwater nook and cranny Oyster Island had to offer the minute they got their dive licenses. But Sam's tone suggested none of their shared history mattered when it came to one Francine Walker.

Archer rose to his full height. "You don't trust me to look out for her?"

"No, I do." Sam's baffled expression matched Archer's own confusion. "It's just... She's here. For weeks. And it's you, and... Shit, I don't know."

Snorting, Archer nodded. As soon as he made sense of it himself, he'd fill Sam in.

"So you're grinding my gears for no reason, then," he said.

"She's my little sister," Sam repeated.

"I'm aware." Archer reached into the oven to pull out the glistening golden bird Franci had carted home yesterday. He didn't mind changes in plans so much when they put a smile on her face. She'd looked sad as hell over her coffee date with her mom getting canceled. Archer was of a mind to drive to Alina's house and shake some sense into her, but it wasn't his place to get involved.

Sam put his beer on the counter. "Are you into her?"

Archer nearly dropped the roasting pan.

"Damn it, are you trying to cause me to start a grease fire?" He carefully placed it on the stove top and put the trays of par-cooked yams and brussels sprouts with pancetta in the oven to finish.

"Answer the question."

Once the oven door was closed, Archer turned, barely keeping himself from chucking the oven mitts at Sam's face. Franci was in the living room with her family, but they could still see through the pass-through into the kitchen, and more importantly, they'd hear any raised voices. So Archer moderated his tone. Barely. "Why would you think I am?"

"You tell me."

"I'd like to think you're asking out of genuine curiosity rather than 'what the hell are you doing with my sister,' because the second is insulting to Franci and me both."

Even if Archer knew he was too damn old for her.

Not so much in literal years, but in experience. They were like the candleholder he'd yanked out of a drawer earlier to center the table. Her, the flickering flame drawing the eye and lighting the room. Him, the tarnished base. He was stable, useful, but nothing about him glowed anymore. They weren't a match.

He yawned, the cumulative effect of making a big dinner after a string of disjointed sleeps. It'd been years since he'd put in sixteen-hour days like he often had during emergencies with the Coast Guard. He'd lost his stamina.

Sam ran a hand down his face. "I don't get why she wouldn't stay with Dad and Charlotte."

Because you all count on her to smile all the time and that's exhausting?

He had a feeling she wouldn't want him to fill her brother in on that truth. If she even fully saw it as truth herself. Maybe she wasn't aware of her forced cheer. He hoped she never felt she had to put on a facade around him.

"She landed here out of necessity, and it's easier to stay." Not a lie.

Sam studied Archer like he was trying to see through to his marrow. "It's not your age difference, you know."

What? Had he read Archer's mind?

"You're talking out of your ass," Archer said, covering the resting turkey with a sheet of foil.

"You know I love you, man."

Archer grunted and gave Sam a quick slap on the shoulder before pulling plates from the cupboard over the counter.

"Franci being younger than you doesn't matter," Sam continued. "You not letting anyone in does."

Archer froze. He gripped the edge of the shelf holding the plates.

"Sam." He didn't turn. Couldn't look at his friend. "We are on the exact same page. Believe me."

Though if anyone could get past Archer's walls, it was Franci and Iris. Good thing he'd been reinforcing the damn things for years and years. The only wall that had ever crumbled on him was the one that had taken Eduardo and him out underwater the day he lost his leg. Never again would he let his guard down and get crushed under the weight of his own failures.

Franci's heart filled as she looked around the dining room. Charlotte and Nic were helping Archer clear the dishes, dodging Honu as he followed each promising platter from the table to the sink. Rachel and Winnie were busy serving the delicious sugar-dusted cranberry-pecan pies they'd brought from the bakery. Sam had finally relaxed after whatever discussion he'd been having with Archer in the kitchen and was holding hands with Kellan as they poured everyone a dram from the bottle of scotch they'd brought back from Edinburgh.

Their dad was enjoying a finger of it, as was Alice. He took a sip, then leaned over to give Ali a kiss. Franci smiled, until he winced while straightening.

Something wobbled in her chest. His pain hung on her conscience like a fishing weight. She'd do anything to go back and take two more seconds to look both ways. If she had, maybe she would have seen the truck careening toward them…

She shook her head. Out of her control, and not the kind of mental trail she needed to go down at a joyful family dinner, aside from being thankful they'd both survived.

Today, her thanks started and ended with the man in the kitchen.

Archer was impossible to ignore, no matter how hard she tried to keep her gaze off his powerful frame. Once he'd served the meal, he'd taken off the silly apron she'd bought for him at the touristy store next to Hideaway Bakery. He *had* worn it while he was cooking, though, which meant something.

She'd asked a lot of him by hosting such a big event on short notice. But she was also proud of having pulled him into the family fold. His parents had sold Archer this house and moved off island when they retired, so Archer and Violet were often on their own for big occasions. And it warmed her heart to know she'd been the instigator here, the person who'd brought everyone together.

Actually, the tiny person tucked into Kellan's embrace was the unifying force.

Even though her mom hadn't found time to meet Iris yet, so many people were eager and brimming with love.

She focused on that for the rest of the gathering, reveling in all the smiles and laughs.

By the time their last guests left, with Violet catching a ride back to the wharf with Sam and Kellan, Franci was yawning, and Iris was demanding her nighttime snack. Archer headed for his room, mumbling that he was going to take a shower, so she relaxed on the couch and fed her daughter.

A little while later, the shower was still running and Iris's mouth was slack, happy milk-drunk. A thrill ran through Franci—finally a chance to read a chapter or two of the rom-com she'd been neglecting for a month. Where had she left her e-reader again?

In Archer's bedroom. Dang it.

After resting her drooping baby in the bassinet she'd brought into the living room, she left the dog on guard.

Well, sort of. Honu was sacked out by the coffee table, paws twitching. But Iris wasn't going anywhere any time fast.

She knocked on the door to Archer's bedroom. "Hey, you decent?"

No response.

Sneaking the door open, she peeked into the low-lit space. Empty. No half-naked warriors to be found.

She couldn't decide whether or not she was disappointed.

The bathroom door was closed. She ducked in, rushed to what had been her side of the bed for a few days and grabbed her e-reader.

The bathroom door opened.

"Oh, sorry, I—"

She didn't bother finishing. He didn't look surprised to find her there. Just contemplative.

Soft pants encased his legs, the left pant leg hemmed so it didn't hang empty under his residual leg. He gripped his crutches. Arms bare, his biceps flexed.

Not the first time she'd seen him shirtless this week.

It caught her in a different way this time, low in her belly.

She wanted to trace every line of his body art. And God, the flannel of his pants looked strokable.

Keep it platonic.

He did deserve thanks, though. He'd carried the lion's share of dinner prep.

"You were so generous today. Thank you." Three steps, and she was right in front of him. Giving into impulse, she brushed a kiss on his cheek.

It burned her lips.

Gaze smoldering, mouth parted, he tossed one of his crutches on the bed and caught her cheek with his freed hand, his big palm infinitely tender on her skin. "You light up my home."

She froze. "I do?"

"Yeah."

Leaning a little nearer, she waited for his reaction. Unlike last night, he didn't pull away. She closed the distance, kissing his mouth this time.

Mmph, he was delicious. Hints of tart cranberry and sweet Chantilly clung to his lips. Even more, it was him. She could taste the flavors of their dessert on a hundred other men and it wouldn't be as good.

His soft acceptance turned to hunger, owning her with a hand on her face, his mouth devouring her.

Hot seconds, moments, stretching into minutes of only feeling him and the way her body demanded close, closer, closest.

Her hands were on his bare pecs, one palm over a simple outline of a plumeria entwined with a lupine and a snapdragon, one over the intricate sketch of a clock.

None of the designs had color. She could put on lipstick and fill in the blank spaces with kiss prints.

Deep pleasure rumbled from his chest, the vibration tantalizing on her lips.

She rose on her toes to deepen it more, stroking her hands up taut neck muscles. She delved her fingers into his soft hair. Tugged a little.

He stumbled back with an awkward crutch and hop. "Whoa, now."

The blood rushed from her face. "Crap, I didn't mean—"

"It's okay."

"No, it's not. You didn't like it."

He blinked at her. "How'd you figure?"

"Well… We're not still kissing? You're an arm's length away?" And that was only physical distance. Emotionally, they were miles apart.

"Whether or not I liked it isn't the point. Shouldn't have done it."

"No?"

"You just had a baby."

True. The last thing she'd expected so soon after pushing seven pounds of baby out of her body was to be interested in any sort of intimacy.

Unless… Maybe he didn't find her attractive in all her postpartum glory.

"I get it," she said quietly, an ache building in her chest, dousing the heat of their kiss. "The brand-new-mom look isn't for everyone." She tugged at her less-than-flattering nursing shirt.

His face fell. "Francine, no. You— Christ, you're always… You made *life*. No, it's—"

"It's okay. I get it. You're not into me. No need to feel bad." Her smile wobbled, but she kept it in place.

"That's not it," he grumbled. "We work together. You're my guest."

She laughed, one of those nervous laughs she didn't like to let loose but were too weighty to hold in. "Which makes it complicated enough?"

"More than."

She went to move past him. He caught her arm with his free hand. "Wait."

Lifting an eyebrow, she paused.

A featherlight touch rasped across her cheek. "I don't want to distract you from everything going on in your life right now."

"You wouldn't be."

He kissed her again. "And this is as good as it could ever get."

"Because you're too old for me? Because you're Sam's friend? Why?"

"Yeah." His gaze darted sideways. "Those exact things."

Try again, Archer Frost. You're so lying.

But she wasn't going to push. *Yet.*

Smiling gently, she backed away a step. "You let me know when you're ready to tell the truth."

Chapter Ten

Two weeks later, and Franci's invitation still dragged at Archer like he was trying to walk around strapped into the heavy-duty weight belt he'd worn on salvage missions.

She thought she wanted the truth. He didn't want to go there. No one needed to be weighed down by his decision to wall off from love. Knowing her, she'd want to fix it, and he was as fixed as he was going to get.

But every time she smiled at him as they ate together or he took Iris from her so she could have some rest, he wondered what life would be like if he laid himself bare before her.

He might find relief.

In doing so, she'd be burdened beyond measure.

So instead, his leg was aching from him running so much and he was getting professional-level good at the complicated finger picking of "Blackbird."

He came in from today's run, panting harder than Honu from the long distance. Heading through the front door, he was greeted by wails. Iris was finding her lungs more and more.

After letting Honu off the leash, he hitched toward the cries, off-kilter on his running blade but not wanting to take the time to switch it out.

Franci had the plastic bath on a towel on the dining room table and was gently scooping water over the baby's hair.

Iris was red faced, having none of it.

The strain around Franci's eyes suggested she was having none of it, too. She had on leggings and a long T-shirt sporting a milk stain on the shoulder. Her bun was off-center and her mouth was tight, throat working.

Honu got to the pair before Archer did and stuck his big furry nose onto the tabletop with a concerned look in his eyes.

"Iris likes her bath about as much as you like yours, doggo," Franci joked weakly.

Archer joined them, chuckling. "For a dog who loves water, I've never been able to figure out why he looks at me like I've betrayed him when I take him into the shower." He leaned in, hoping his postrun sweat wasn't too bad. "Hey, there, jellybean—why the shouting?"

Iris quieted. Her gaze latched on to his face. Her frown relaxed and the angry pink faded. Warmth spread along his limbs, along with the urge to scoop her up and never let anything bad happen to her. Damn, she was an incredible little human.

"Oh, sure, smile for Archer." Franci's words faltered. Her hand shook a little as she trailed a cloth over the wiggly little body. "She's been nothing but complaints all morning. And I—I'm tired." She winced. "It's fine, I mean. She's going to cry. It's unavoidable. And we had some nice snuggles, so—"

"Hey." He rubbed a gentle palm over her back. "It's okay to admit you've had a rough morning."

"Mmm." She sounded unconvinced. She rested her head on his shoulder for a second. "Can you hold out the towel for me?"

"Sure." He did as asked, accepting the bundle of baby and wrapping the snuggly cloth around her teeny body. "You better get your mama to hold you tight, not me—no one wants a part of me after I put on fifteen K. I need a bath, too."

Franci's gaze dipped over his body, and for a second, he could have sworn heat flared in her gaze.

"What's your pleasure? A nap, or fresh air and a fancy coffee?" he asked.

She screwed her mouth up. "The second, I think."

Mind whirling, he nodded. Franci had to miss being on the water. He could fix that.

A week ago, he'd ordered three different infant life jackets for Iris. His Coast Guard roots ran deep, and he'd wanted to follow the policy of testing the safety gear in water to the letter. They'd filled up the bathtub and took Iris for a float, and he was confident one of the three options was safe.

"Let's take the boat into town." He threw out the words. "Clear out the cobwebs. Grab you one of Rachel's lavender lattes, harass Matias…" Anything that forced him to keep his distance and stopped him from leaning in for another kiss. A few more days and he'd be on his holiday. He didn't like leaving her or Iris, but he would at least welcome the break from the temptation.

"Could we?"

"You bet." He'd take her on a thousand spins around the island if it put that glow on her face.

An hour later, he slowly cruised into the harbor and pulled into the *Oyster Queen*'s empty slip. Sam had a dive tour out for most of the day, so the spot would be open for a few hours.

Franci looked more than perfect in the passenger seat of his Chris-Craft. The sun glinted off her hair, the reddish tones matching some of the varnished wood inlay in the dash. A peaceful smile softened some of the earlier stress and exhaustion from her face. Iris was bundled in layers and her yellow life jacket, and was staring at him and gurgling.

He tied up, dealt with the stroller and held out a hand to help Franci out. "I swear this contraption is fancier than my first car."

She nodded. "Dad and Alice spoiled us."

As they should. And it was good they did. Franci's mom had managed two half-hour visits since Thanksgiving, a piss-poor effort in comparison to what Franci deserved.

They made their way off the dock and onto the sidewalk on the street side of the wharf. Archer waved a hand with a flourish at the various food options. "Fish and chips? Coffee and a doughnut? Poutine special at The Cannery?"

"All of it. I'm starved." Her face brightened as she took in the evergreen swags and bows adorning the lampposts, and the strings of white antique-style bulbs crossing back and forth across Wharf Street. "How did I miss the decorations going up?"

"Well—"

"Don't answer that. Rhetorical question. I've been lost in InfantLand."

He frowned. "Are you going to feel too isolated while I'm on my trip?"

She shook her head. "Violet said she'd sleep over a bunch. And now that the road's fully passable, I can drive into town when I need to. I just haven't much because… Well, I've felt cozy at your house. And everyone's come to me. But I won't want to miss out on all the preholiday festivities."

And he'd be missing seeing Franci squire Iris around to all the island's mid-December activities.

His heart panged, only half mollified by getting to join them for the annual boat parade before he left.

Franci sniffed the air. Pleasure skimmed across her face. "That french fry smell… Matias officially wins snack choice of the day."

She took off, past the pastel front of Otter Marine Tours. He caught himself reaching to put a hand on her back. What was he thinking? He jammed his hands in his pockets.

The Cannery was on the waterfront, past the stretch of businesses nestled in the heritage houses. It took up part of an old fish-processing warehouse that his parents still owned, despite them having sold their other assets when they moved to La Conner. His sister's office and apartment were in part of the top floor of the two-story building, and she kept an eye on the multipurpose space for their parents in exchange for virtually non-existent rent. Archer was happy to leave any management details up to Violet—he had no interest in being a landlord.

He held the door open for Franci so that she could push the stroller through. Matias's pub had a rustic-industrial feel to it, but still managed to be cozy and welcoming. The lunch rush was approaching, and most of the tables were filled.

It didn't take long to find a familiar face.

Kellan waved at them from a table. "Over here, love! I've plenty of space."

Franci squealed, left the stroller in a nook near the door and carried her daughter toward the Irishman.

From behind the bar, Matias was eyeing Archer and Franci with a dangerous level of curiosity. Archer headed in his friend's direction first.

"What?" he said, not bothering with a greeting.

Matias smirked and wiped his hands on the denim apron he wore over a white T-shirt and jeans. "You put the *Sunday* in *Sunday drive* today, man. Cruising around the corner like a snail."

"Nosy much?" Archer hadn't thought anyone would notice their arrival by water. He leaned an arm on the aluminum bar.

"Hard to miss."

True. The Cannery had a heck of a view of the entirety of the cove.

"Wasn't about to jar the stuffing out of Iris," he explained.

Still wanted to be careful with Franci, too. She didn't talk about it often, but she wasn't even a month post-delivery. She had to still be healing. He glanced over to where she was settling in at Kellan's table. Sam's fiancé already had the baby out of her travel sack, and was depositing kisses on her cheeks. If nothing else, she would be loved by many.

"Gone much?" Matias murmured. He pulled a pint of the seasonal ale and handed it to Archer.

"Huh?"

"You, man. Ass over teakettle gone. You should see yourself right now."

"What, see me doing this?" He flipped Matias a middle finger.

Matias hooted. "Yup, snagged worse than the crab pot I lost out by Lighthouse Point last weekend."

"Babies are cute."

"It's not the baby who hooked you."

Archer gripped the edge of the bar and glared.

His friend shook his head and layered ingredients into a cocktail shaker. "You like to think you're a lone wolf, Frost, but you're lying to yourself."

"What the hell would you know about it?" Matias had a string of failed relationships behind him. Most recently, a potter who'd left him pining during the summer when she'd moved to Vermont. And every once in a while, he looked at Violet with a fondness that had Archer wondering.

A bottle of vodka landed on the bar with a clunk. "At least I've tried."

"I did try." And failed.

He'd never forget the agony of coming home to the lacy camisole he'd bought his wife for her previous birthday puddled on the floor of the hallway next to a pair of men's suit pants. And the closed bedroom

door, and that goddamn headboard he'd been mean-
ing to tighten squeaking like it needed an entire can
of WD-40.

Argh. Why was he letting himself go there? And
especially not to the events that followed. Distraction
and the slip of a hand. Something like magma cours-
ing from his hip to his foot. Eddy's face above him.
Bubbles everywhere.

Darkness.

He swore, then took a sip of beer.

"So try again," Matias said. "You deserve more than
one shot."

Ha. It wasn't about taking a shot. The gaping void
his losses had left, deep at his core, meant any attempt
would fail.

His gaze drifted to Franci. She deserved to be loved
wholeheartedly, and Archer's heart was torn beyond
repair.

He set his jaw and glanced at the chalk menu behind
the bar. "Franci wants fries. We'll take a sampler platter, heavy on the cheese."

"It'll cost you. The advice is free, though."

"Better be—I didn't order any."

Matias chuckled. "I'm the gift that keeps on giving."

No, Franci was.

But he'd have to leave that particular package
wrapped under the proverbial tree.

A few days after their impromptu boat trip, Franci
strolled into Archer's house, feeling the glow from the
yoga class she'd been to with Violet. Archer had been
out for a dive that morning. When he'd gotten back

midafternoon, he insisted she get out of the house for an hour without Iris.

A person didn't realize what time to herself was like until she'd been with one tiny human nonstop for a month.

Rejuvenated, she left her shoes in the mudroom and went into the empty kitchen. A quiet guitar melody filled her ears. She peeked through to the living room. Archer was sitting sideways on the couch with his legs outstretched and splayed open, playing a soft lullaby. He had Iris on a blanket between his knees.

Oh. *Oh.*

Her emotions puddled in her belly.

She rushed out of the kitchen, not wanting to miss a minute of this.

Her baby's eyes were wide, and her mouth…

"Archer, she's *smiling.*" She nearly tripped over the coffee table trying to get a picture.

His lips curved. "Looks like a real smile."

"She's young, but it's gotta be!" She knelt in front of them. "Do you like the music, Iris Gale? I know. I could listen to it for hours, too."

Archer's hands stilled on the strings. "Yeah?"

She scoffed. "You know how good you are." She pulled up the picture on her phone and held it out for him to see.

"Wow." His voice was soft. He cupped her cheek with a big palm. "Prettiest smile I've ever seen."

His eyes were on Franci's for each word.

Her breath caught in her throat. *Her smile or mine?*

She rose on her knees, bringing their faces closer together.

He licked his lips.

She let out a noise close enough to a whimper that heat rose on her cheeks.

"Francine..."

The way her name sounded when he was reduced to growling...

Need razed her. Their mouths were inches apart.

But no, he'd said he didn't want this, and she wasn't going to throw herself at him.

She jumped to her feet and rushed from the room.

"Franci!" he called.

"I need a shower," she said.

I need you. All of you.

Maybe the shower could rinse the craving away.

Chapter Eleven

Archer was lying on the living room floor stretching and doing energy work when Franci stomped down the stairs. She'd been touchy with him since their almost kiss earlier today. Made a man want to claim her mouth and feast until he kissed her fears away.

He got it, though. His skin was electric and he'd been walking around half-hard all day. The mere thought of kissing her again pushed him close to making the poorest of decisions.

She tromped into the kitchen and started opening and closing drawers, each one with a louder *bang* than the last.

So much for fitting in a bit of self-administered Reiki. He liked to do it daily but hadn't had the chance yet today between work and hanging out with Iris. He wouldn't be able to finish so long as he knew Franci was unhappy. He stood and went into the kitchen.

"What do you need?" he asked, leaning a hip against the counter.

"Batteries," she said sharply.

"What for?"

She paused, eyes flashing. *"Things."*

Oh, Christ.

Things.

"My hand would work as well as a vibrator."

He said it at, like, 1 percent volume. Couldn't even call it a whisper. But her spine went as straight as the flagpole by the walkway to his dock. *Damn.*

"Valuable information if you were, in fact, offering." She nearly spat the words. "You're being a tease."

Closing his eyes, he groaned. "No, I'm being reasonable."

She poked him in the chest, and he blinked them open, soaking in her frustration—the pink blush on her cheeks, the deep brown of her eyes.

"I'll show you *reasonable*, Archer."

He caught her wrist before she could poke him again and lifted an eyebrow.

"*Reasonable* would be having a supply of triple-As in the house!" Her chest rose and fell and with it, her lush breasts, full and tantalizing.

"Your *things* still take triple-As?"

"My backup does," she seethed.

Had she run out of juice with her other one, or forgotten to charge it?

The skin on the inside of her wrist was so smooth. Her pulse thrummed against the pad of his thumb. The rhythm called to him, stoking the flame between them.

The tangible tattoo of her need, the teeth biting the inside of her lip, the pinch of worry at the corners of her eyes.

He could ease her plight.

Not anything permanent, or ongoing, even, but... right now.

Her pink plush mouth begged silently for relief.

His own lips—his entire being—craved the same.

He curved her body into his, backing her against the counter. Digging his fingers into her hips, he dropped his mouth to hers. Coaxing, teasing until she opened, until she gasped and clutched at his shoulders.

"I thought you didn't want..." Her words dissolved into a soft whimper.

"Of course I do." Another long sip at her mouth, savoring the sweetness of her tongue, her taste. "I think— I know—it'll go sideways on us, but, Franci..."

"Yeah?"

"Can't talk myself out of it right now."

"Mmm, 'bout time." Her fingers trailed up his neck and delved into his hair, pulling his face closer to hers. Her kiss threw him off-kilter, tilting his world until he felt less balanced than if he had one foot on his dock and one on his boat. Liable to tip in at any minute, to splash into frigid reality.

She pulled back. Erratic breaths kissed his neck as she sucked in air. Flushed cheeks, reckless eyes.

He'd flustered her. The knowledge was addictive.

Could he do more than overwhelm her? Could he satisfy her?

Shifting, he brought his right leg between her thighs and pulled her closer. Her breath caught.

So did his. The heat of her core singed his skin, even

through their clothes. He didn't want to assume what felt good, so he paused, waiting for her.

She rocked against his thigh, slowly, gently. Testing, maybe.

With one hand anchored on her hip to keep her close, he splayed the other under her T-shirt until his palm met smooth heated skin. He traced the edge of her rib cage with his thumb, a test of his own, of how delicate she felt under his hand.

"Archer..."

He stilled. "Not what you want?"

"I don't understand what I want. This isn't supposed to be remotely on my mind right now. I'm supposed to be exhausted and overwhelmed and focused on Iris... And I am all those things, more than, but also—"

She dropped her head back, exposing the pale line of her throat, and let out a needy, throaty moan.

He pressed a kiss between her collarbones. Nibbled and tongued a line along pretty freckled skin to the base of her ear. "Also?"

"Yeah. Also. Also this." Mouth parted, slack with desire, she circled her hips. "It's good. It's so good."

Christ, he was weak.

"I could make it even better." A plea of his own as much as a promise.

He didn't want to get turned on. Damn impossible, of course. With every wiggle of her hips, he got harder. Not surprising. In no world could he keep from responding when someone as sensual as Franci was letting him turn her on. But his heart, torn and cracked—it clamored to get in on the action, too.

Teasing him. Taunting him.

This one was special, this wildflower. She could be the one. The one who could mend those tears, fill those cracks—

Impossible.

His cracks were unfillable.

But he wasn't going to push her away. Not when it felt like his life depended on learning what glorious expression crossed her face when she came.

Maybe, *maybe* if he focused on her pleasure alone, he could keep from tipping too close to needing more than release. Inching his hand up, he stroked the underside of her breast through the soft fabric of her bra.

"Not there," she said. "Lower. God, lower. Make me..." She splayed her hands on his hips and pulled, riding his leg harder. "If you get me off, just once, I promise I won't mention this again. It won't go sideways. It won't."

"It's been long enough since you delivered?"

She nodded. "Not for everything, but for touching. Please. One little release."

He hooked a finger in the waistband of her leggings. "Francine. I can make you come. But it won't be little."

"So you say."

He crooked a smile. "So I *know.*"

"I'll believe it when—"

Growling, he thrust his hand between soft skin and stretchy underwear to cup her slick sex. His fingertips kissed her center, not pressing farther. Just enough to tantalize, to feel her muscles clench. With the heel of his palm, he circled lightly.

He could drive her wild, he knew it.

Every raspy breath, the disappearing space between

them as she clutched and keened and shifted, her slickness on his fingers—

His body was like cement, straining for release.

Her hand shifted, seeking, nearly landing on pay dirt.

"No," he said roughly. "I'm not done with you, yet."

And he wasn't going to be able to do right by her with his hand alone. Not enough, anyway.

He nipped at her earlobe. "Can I kiss you?"

"You already have," she mumbled, grinding against his hand.

"Not here, I haven't." He tapped his fingertips against her sex.

Her eyes went wide. "I—"

He cursed silently. "It's too soon. Should've known that."

She shook her head. "I just hadn't expected…"

"Forget I asked." He swirled his fingers, trying to put the hazy, spacey look back on her face.

"Oh, no. You don't get to offer and then renege, Archer Frost."

He grinned, slow and easy.

Tucking his hands under her lush ass, he lifted.

She squealed. "Ohmigod, what are you doing?"

"Following through on a promise." He placed her on the wide countertop, scooting her back so he could taste her without kneeling.

"But…"

"Shh." He slid her leggings and panties off, and groaned as he spread her legs. Before him, she was everything feminine and strong. One gentle kiss, and she moaned. Goddamn, her sultry lust. Any more, and he'd lose control.

She was salt and honey, heat and need. Her desire melted on his tongue, hips lifting as she panted and begged. She weaved a hand into his hair, the other slapping the counter in an erratic, needy rhythm.

Stroking his tongue over her center, he fell further under her spell, enrapt in the softness, the pulse of her muscles as she responded.

Her grip tightened in his hair.

One more circle of his tongue, a gentle trace of his fingers and she cried out.

He glanced up, catching her eyes fluttering closed and her mouth curving into bliss.

"Archer."

Oh, hell. His control spun away like he was caught in a whirlpool.

"Archer," she repeated, barely a breath this time.

He tried to pull himself together, to ride the edge and hop out the other side. He'd done it a hundred times in the eddies off Buoy Point, letting his boat curve with the pull before gunning the engine and escaping to safety.

Not today.

Not with Franci.

He was lost. Lost to her smile, her sweetness, his name on her lips.

Groaning in release, he braced his elbows on the counter on either side of her and tried to keep his sound knee from giving out. He buried his face in one hand and palmed her belly with the other. Heat chased up his neck, the lingering rush of his orgasm. Some embarrassment, too, because he was thirty-seven, not seventeen, and should be able to control himself.

Featherlight fingers brushed his cheek. She rose on her elbow. "Hey. Uh… You put me up here. Want to help me down?"

Her blasé tone was a jolt back to normal. He straightened, flattening a palm on the counter and helping her sit.

He pressed a kiss to her forehead.

She was smiling, her cheeks flushed.

But she looked happy, not wrecked.

He blinked at her in confusion. His insides were a twisted knot of posthurricane debris, and she was… unaffected?

All right, then.

He helped her get off the counter.

She fixed her leggings, rose on her toes and kissed his cheek. "Thanks, Fox Robin."

He gripped the edge of the granite slab, still shaky. "But—"

"You followed through. I concede, that wasn't small." She backed up a step. "And now it's my turn—never mention it again."

Jerking his head, he watched her stroll toward the stairs to the second floor, as if she hadn't a care in the world.

Once she was out of sight, he stumbled to his bathroom to clean up.

Less straightforward? Figuring out how he was going to keep moving forward after Franci Walker had blown his path all to hell.

The key to functioning after being sent to the heavens and back by Archer Frost's clever tongue and fingers was to stay busy. To stay out of his way, too. She'd hidden in her room upstairs for the rest of the night. As he'd gotten ready for work the next morning, she'd been feeding Iris on the couch and had held her finger to her lips, as if silence had been necessary for the baby.

He'd been out on a tour all day—underwater visibility was apparently spectacular this week, and they'd added an extra dive.

She'd taken off to town in her own car. Anything to avoid the kitchen. Looking at the smooth cold counter made her blush. It had been icy on her back, the opposite of his hot mouth.

She was surprised they hadn't shorted out the nearby toaster and coffee maker from their sparks alone.

"Are you *sure* you're okay?" Violet asked as they ended Iris's appointment. They were in the comfortably appointed exam room of Violet's office, sitting in a nest of pillows on the couch. Cross-legged with a blanket in her lap, Violet had Iris in the well of her knees and was checking the baby over.

Act cool, act cool.

"Happy as a clam," Franci said.

"Which makes no sense, because clams aren't sentient." Her friend narrowed her blue eyes.

Ugh, why did Violet have to have the same color irises as her brother? Franci couldn't see that particular shade of cobalt without remembering his smoldering gaze staring at her from between her thighs.

Think about something else, anything else—

"In high water," she blurted.

A dark brow lifted. "Huh?"

"That's the rest of the phrase. Happy as a clam in high water."

"Still makes no sense."

Not much does about the last twenty-four hours.

And she couldn't even talk to her best friend about it.

"Come ride on the *Oyster Queen* tonight," she said. "Iris's first holiday boat parade."

Violet winced. "I... I have a date. Sort of. I'm going out on one of the other boats. No big deal."

"With who? Have I been so out of touch that I missed someone new coming to town?"

"Not exactly."

"Vague much?"

"I don't want to make a big deal about it." Violet tugged on the end of her French braid.

"You're talking to me. We tell each other everything." *Until last night, anyway.*

"I'm going out with Kim," Violet blurted.

"*Kim* Kim? As in my temporary coworker?" The woman was one of Archer's Coast Guard friends, and had come to town in the spring to pick up any slack Archer couldn't with Franci unable to dive. Then again, with Sam getting busier and busier with Forest + Brine bookings, maybe there would be enough hours for Kim to stick around longer than the agreed-upon year.

Violet groaned. *"Yes."*

"Hey, that's great. A date. I'm happy for you."

And jealous. *Definitely* jealous. What would it be like to be interested in someone who had no qualms about going on a date?

"Thanks. You know what it's like to start a relationship on the island, though. And she's my brother's friend. He's going to give me such a hard time. I know it."

Franci laughed. "Maybe he won't."

If he does, he's a hypocrite.

Archer tightened a zip tie on one of the metal rails holding up the *Oyster Queen*'s fiberglass bimini. A string of colored lights ran in a precise row, the bulbs all sticking in the same direction. The boat was lit up enough to put Clark Griswold to shame. As was tradition, Sam had dressed one of the store mannequins in a red wet suit, dive gear and a Santa hat, and had fixed it in place on the front of the boat. The world's silliest bowsprit.

Sam was grumbling at the stern, fighting with a tangled string. "Hate leaving this so late."

"We've been busy." Archer wrapped another plastic strip around the pole. "Everyone would have forgiven us if we passed on the parade this year. They know you were away and are missing Franci's helpful hands."

Sam scoffed. "Skip my favorite holiday event? No way. Especially not Kellan's first. I want to see his face under the lights. He's seen pictures from past parades, but you know how it is—gotta experience it to get the magic of it."

"I wonder if Franci will bring Iris."

Sam straightened. "You'd know best, given she's living at your house."

The edge wasn't gone from his friend's voice yet.

"She was going to make a game-time decision," Archer said, "but she hasn't told me what it is."

Too busy letting me make her moan on my kitchen counter. And then avoiding me this morning.

"Is she okay?" Sam asked.

Sure was last night.

His gut roiled over what he'd done with Franci. Not because she was his friend's sister, or even his coworker, but because he knew there was no chance of it going anywhere.

Yeah, she'd seemed okay with the temporary caveat last night, and had promised not to mention their shenanigans again.

But had she expected it to be that good? Or maybe she hadn't been rocked like he had. She'd been steady as she'd walked away. Happy, not ruined.

Maybe she was following through on her vow to wipe the memory away.

He couldn't seem to put it behind him. How could he forget her taste, her moans, the elation when she'd dissolved?

It was hot, yeah, but also…tender.

Way, way too close to feelings. No damn way could he let the affection he felt for her deepen. If he dug down, found the part of himself that used to be able to create the kind of intense bond Franci deserved to find, who knows what the hell he'd unearth in the process.

His vacation couldn't come at a better time. They needed space.

He'd dive away the urge to have Franci in his bed. Ditch his need on the ocean floor among the coral and fish off Hawaii's shores.

By the time he got home on the twenty-third, the repairs on Franci's house would almost be done. He'd wander around his house alone again. No baby gurgles to lighten his heart, no smiling redhead to set him aflame.

The *Oyster Queen* was a popular gathering spot come six o'clock that night, when the long procession of boats mustered at Hideaway Wharf for the trip. The colorful spectacle was scheduled to meander past the foreshore walk, the public beach in the next bay over and end at the public dock past Lighthouse Point. A loose line of all the watercraft Oyster Island had to offer left the harbor, one vessel at a time. Sailboats with red, white and green lights twirled around their masts to give them the appearance of candy canes. The Silvermans had strapped their glistening homemade ten-foot-tall menorah to the boom of their thirty-eight-foot Catalina. One trawler had gone all out with a new design, the industrious fisher making an arced rainbow along the splayed arms. Some smaller boats were done up with a few glowing strands, or with a single inflatable snow globe or Santa on the bow, people out less to win the competition than to share community spirit and to have a water view of all the festive beauty.

Much like Sam, Archer thought it was the best sight of all December. Or at least he had until tonight. Franci had made a little nest on the bench seat centering the *Queen*.

She outshone any light display, bundled in a thick survival jacket and holding her life jacket–clad and down-ensconced daughter.

Looking at Franci made his heart ache. So why couldn't he tear away his gaze?

Thankfully, the other two couples on the boat were

too wrapped up in each other to pay attention to Archer's wandering focus. Sam and Kellan were snuggled at the helm, sharing captain duties. Nic was dressed in a reindeer suit and, joined by Honu in his best light-up antlers and bow tie, was hamming it up for both the people on shore and Charlotte next to him.

Archer sat on the bench. Was the foot of space he left between Franci's crossed legs and his hip fooling anyone? Sure wasn't quelling his need to hold her.

"I feel like I've forgotten to tell you something about the house," he said.

"If there's something Violet and I can't fix, then Sam or Dad will be able to take care of it," she said calmly.

Coolly, almost.

"I should have put up a Christmas tree for you. Want me to grab you one from the tree farm? I have time before my flight."

She shrugged. "I can find one."

His gut churned. She would throw herself into selecting the perfect evergreen. Probably loved making a mess with tinsel, too. God, he hated the thought of missing out on Franci in tree-decorating mode. If he was home, they could wind garland around branches, and then lie together on the floor, gazing at the sparkle and shine. Much like the lights on the bimini were kissing her cheeks, the ones on a tree would glow on her skin as he slowly stripped her of her clothes.

He'd never made love underneath a Christmas tree before, but—

Something screeched in his head, like a poorly pitched propeller. *Making love?*

Where the hell had that come from?

From wanting Franci to look at me with any emotion except placid neutrality.

From plain wanting Franci.

He shifted closer and rested a hand on Iris's blanket. "She's sleeping through her first parade."

"Dad said I always conked out in the family boat when I was small. The hum and the vibration did me in. She's just taking after her mommy."

"Lucky girl," he said gruffly, tracing a finger along the baby's impossibly soft cheek.

Something flickered in Franci's eyes. Her mouth drew into a frustrated pout.

He had a clear view of Sam and Kellan, who had their backs to the bench. Checking over his shoulder, he confirmed Nic and Charlotte were turned around, too, waving and trying to talk to Kim and Violet. His sister and her date were in the Otter Marine Zodiac, following in the *Queen*'s wake.

Chances were none of them would turn in the next ten seconds.

"Hey," he said, cupping Franci's cheek. "You still okay with last night?"

"What about last night? We agreed to forget last night."

"We did." He leaned in and stole the quickest kiss he could risk. Her lips were sweet with Kellan's secret-recipe peppermint hot cocoa. He savored the hint of chocolate long enough to feel her gasp before pulling away. "Except… I can't."

Chapter Twelve

"*Archer.*" Franci spat out the warning and darted a look at Kellan and Sam behind her, making sure they hadn't witnessed Archer's spontaneity. Kissing this man was so easy. Between the soft lighting and the notes of "The Christmas Waltz" playing over the speakers, the night was made for snuggling close to someone. But *not* in front of half her family.

He swore. "Sorry. Won't happen again."

He moved to stand, and she caught his arm, keeping him near.

"What do you mean, you can't? Can't forget?"

A dry laugh. "It's more than that, wildflower."

"Start with part of it, then."

Frustration twisted on his face. "Last night. I can't stop thinking about it."

"Why do we need to?"

Shaking his head, he leaned his elbows on his thighs and stared at the deck.

"What? If you're going to pivot on me, kiss me in front of my brother and sister, you at least could explain why."

"You don't want…" He fixed her with an anguished gaze. "Let it go."

"You don't know what I want." Right now, her sole desire was to help him manage whatever was putting that look on his face.

"Well, it can't be me," he said.

Too late there, Hawkeye.

"I'm going to take a turn at the wheel." He stood. She didn't try to stop him this time.

They said an awkward goodbye the morning after the boat parade. A whole lot of him rubbing the back of his neck and wincing, and Franci holding back from throwing herself into his arms. She had to grip the kitchen counter to stop herself giving him a goodbye he wouldn't forget.

The damn counter.

She could still feel the chill of the stone surface against her back.

She blushed and stared into her coffee. "Text me pictures?"

"If you want."

I want more than pictures.

She wasn't going to point that out again. She couldn't bear another *It can't be me.*

His throat worked. "Let me know if you run into problems with the house."

All my problems are with you, Archer Frost.

"I'll manage."

"You should stay in my room while I'm gone," he said.

"I want to stay in your room while you're *here.*"

She couldn't regret saying it, not when her heart clamored for honesty.

Eyes flashing molten blue, he let out a frustrated grumble and dropped his bags. "Goddamn it, Francine."

And like two nights ago, his hands were in her hair and he pinned her against the counter. He devoured her lips, feasted. In danger of being bowled over by the intensity of being someone's entire focus for a brief, precious moment, she locked her knees.

She couldn't remember the last time she'd done anything that brought her close to this rush. Archer's hands tormented her skin, teasing under the hem of her shirt, coaxing her to rock against his hard frame.

He was there. He was overwhelming.

He was everything.

And then he was gone. Bags in hand, a cursory scratch for the dog, a grumbled goodbye, the click of the front door.

The dog came over to her and whined.

She scratched Honu's ears, still humming from the heat of the goodbye kiss.

"I'll manage," she repeated.

Somehow.

She did move in to his room. Who could resist a bathroom with a fancy showerhead? Which she took complete advantage of later that night, thank you very much. She hardly felt guilty at all for having his face on her mind, the growl of his voice in her ears, when she took herself over the edge. The smooth tile wall was cool on her back, so easy to drift into the memory of him kissing her into oblivion.

The spray was a poor substitute for his fingers, his tongue.

And staying in his house without him was a poor substitute for having him close.

Wrapped in her best holiday jammies, with Iris tucked into her bassinet, she bounced into the living room full of false cheer, ready for a girls' night in with her best friend.

"First of many sleepovers!" She did the running man for Violet and winked. "Unless you're going to be crashing at Kim's at some point."

"We'll see." Violet lifted her chin. "Are you going to explain the kiss I saw from the Zodiac last night?"

Franci froze mid dance move.

"What, you thought you were subtle?" Violet said.

"I didn't think anything. That was all your brother," she said defensively.

Damn it. It had been Archer, but she'd made it sound too much like he was actually interested.

Vi frowned. "He better not be jerking you around."

"Why would you jump to that conclusion?" Franci stole Violet's tea and sat on the other end of the couch.

"He's never healed from his accident."

She bristled on his behalf. "He runs half marathons, and still pulls off bananas technical dives—"

"Emotionally, Franci." Violet's smile was fond, but cautious. "And you, babe—you're one giant feeling, sometimes."

She stiffened but couldn't deny it. "You don't think I'd be good for him?"

Pulling a blanket to her throat, her friend chewed her lip for a few seconds. "I need to think about it. I haven't before. You two never seemed interested in each other."

"We weren't. Or at least, I wasn't. Not until recently. Flipping pregnancy hormones."

"You're not pregnant anymore," Violet pointed out.

"Flipping nursing hormones."

Violet laughed.

"I don't know what to do," she griped.

"I want to believe he hasn't closed himself off forever. And given you're my two favorite people in the world, I'd like to believe you could beat the odds and be happy together." Vi scrubbed her hands over her face. "You have some time to think, at least."

Franci did, and she tried to use it wisely. The next week and a half passed in baby snuggles and family gatherings, and with exactly one picture per day from Archer's travels, usually a shot of the palm tree off his lanai, texted at 9:00 p.m. Oyster Island time on the dot.

She didn't want to think about him every second he was gone. She wanted to soak in the lead-up to Iris's first Christmas and to enjoy one of her favorite parts of the year with her family. But how was she supposed to think about anything else when she was living in his home, sleeping in his bed, for God's sake? Walking his dog, and drinking out of his favorite mug in the mornings…

Okay, she didn't *have to* use that specific piece of pottery, but it was gorgeous. Painted with a beautiful mix of ocean blues, it fit an extra-large serving of coffee and had the exact right handle placement for sliding three fingers through the loop and cupping the rounded bowl. She'd seen him holding it and staring out the window a dozen times since she'd moved in. She couldn't blame him for the habit. She loved standing at the kitchen sink and sipping her coffee, watching his tarpaulin-covered boat bob off the dock as morning light broke through stars and dark. Only Archer sliding in behind her, stealing a sip of her drink and laying a teasing kiss on the side of her neck could make it better.

Holding the mug in front of the window, she snapped a picture and texted it to him before she could talk herself out of it.

A few seconds later, a selfie popped up on her screen. A luxurious-looking pillow cradled Archer's sleep-mussed head. He had his arm across his eyes and his mouth was open as if he was in the middle of swearing. A text followed. It's 6:00 in the morning, beautiful.

I said hello to 6:00 two hours ago. Was up at 5:18, in fact.

Iris had already roused, eaten and gone back to bed. Franci was tempted to follow, but she didn't think she'd be able to get to sleep. Especially not if Archer was in a chatty mood. Would it be wrong to make the selfie he'd sent her the wallpaper for her cell? He was too sexy, stubble thick like he was getting lazy with shaving on his holiday. An adorable pillow crease marked his cheek.

Is our jellybean not respecting your beauty rest?

Our jellybean?

She was still staring at his words on the screen when another selfie appeared. He was face-palming, and under his big hand, his expression was a regretful scrunch.

Too early. Late night with Dad and some mai tais. Misspoke.

MisTYPED

I'm going to shut up, now

Her heart lurched and she shot back, Please don't. No reply.

Ugh, she should not have sent that. Her thumbs slipped a few times as she typed. Sorry. That was weird.

Her pulse thrummed. It was just honesty. And in taking emotional risks, she might inspire him to do the same. I miss you.

Another image loaded. No, a video. She quickly hit Play.

His handsome face filled the screen. Serious, as usual. "Miss you, too. Three more days."

He was counting?

She hit Play again.

Once. Twice.

Fine, five times. The video was short, after all.

Violet, who'd slept over again last night, came into the kitchen, stretching and yawning. "Do you have my brother on speaker? I need to talk to him about Mom and Dad's Christmas present."

"Not exactly."

Her friend leaned over Franci's shoulder. "What is it? What did he send you?"

"Never mind."

"I know your password. I could look later."

She elbowed Vi. "You wouldn't."

"Do you want to put it to the test, though?"

Sighing, Franci queued up the video. Was treated to the little twitch of a smile at the corner of Archer's mouth one more time.

"Oh, my God." Violet whipped out her own phone and stuck it in front of their faces. She pressed Record. "She misses you, too. And you better find something good to bring her home as a souvenir."

"Don't!" Franci protested. "Just come home safe."

Violet cut the recording and sent the video. Her phone buzzed not too long after. She flashed Franci the screen. Already ahead of you. Christmas is coming, after all.

Her friend's brown eyes lit with curiosity. "Ohhh. I wonder what he's getting you."

Franci's stomach flipped. "More importantly—what am *I* going to get *him*."

And after all he'd done for her these past months, it needed to be perfect.

Determined to find the right gift—and spurred to finish the rest of her shopping list, too—she left Iris with her dad and Alice for a few hours and headed for the shops at the wharf.

One year, she'd get all her Christmas shopping taken care of early. This year was not that year.

Charlotte had been easy—a gift card to an online

clothing store—and her dad always appreciated a gift certificate to the local hardware store, but the rest of the men in her life were proving difficult. She poked through the eclectic gift shop next to Hideaway Bakery, praying something would surface.

The store smelled of local goat-milk soap and the wax used to polish the hand-carved arbutus bowls that rarely stayed long on the shelf. She spotted a scarf she thought her mom might like... *Nah.*

They'd fallen into the habit of Franci buying her mom wine and her mom getting her the same day planner ever since Franci had turned sixteen. Franci didn't use a day planner, mind you, but her mom did pick out a beautiful one, at least. They sat in a row on the bottom shelf of the bookcase in her living room, a row of nine sage green spines below her collection of memoirs and biographies. She imagined she'd be adding a tenth this year, and she'd make sure to get her mom a nice bottle of red to serve with the crown roast she made every Christmas. Franci wouldn't be there to eat—she and Charlotte had long ago gotten the message that Christmas dinner was easier without blending families—but maybe her mom thought of her when she popped the cork on the bottle.

Except... This felt like a special year. Her mom was a grandma for the first time. Was it time to switch things up? She grabbed the scarf off the shelf, and then spotted a set of salt and pepper mills, each painted with a whimsical harbor seal, which would be perfect for Sam and Kellan. And a bracelet for Violet, which left her...

Archer.

Something that would make him laugh, maybe. For more days than Christmas.

"An Advent calendar!" she said, earning a contemptuous glare from the store clerk, who happened to be one of her mom's friends. One of the elementary school mom crew. Franci had always gotten the feeling her mom was self-conscious about her age, having had Franci's half brothers in her early forties. She tried so hard to fit in with the younger set. She'd clearly collected some kind of loyalty, though. The clerk, Maureen, had already been eyeing Franci with curiosity and was now downright staring.

"Sorry," Franci said. "Just came up with an idea. January Advent. Jan-vent."

Maureen picked at a cuticle. "Could be cute, I guess."

Cute didn't cut it. It was perfect. Exactly what she wanted to do. Once she'd moved out, she'd know that every morning, Archer was opening a little something to bring him joy.

"Where's your baby?" Said differently, those words could have been a lament for not getting to meet Iris. But Maureen's tone was all judgment.

"With my dad," Franci explained, not sure why she was bothering. "Why?"

"She's young for you to leave her."

Anger built at the base of her spine. Violet had warned her she'd inevitably come across mommy pressure and would have to ignore it and find her own path, but facing it for the first time was jarring. "No, she isn't. My dad's happy to have Iris for a bit."

"Hmm." The clerk's gaze landed on the scarf. "Is that for your mom? She already has one."

Franci gritted her teeth. "Thanks for the warning."

She put the scarf back, and the salt and pepper mills, too. One of those bars of soap would have filled a day in Archer's present nicely, but she wasn't going to buy it here. She'd find one at the grocery store. She could get many items to fill his calendar there. They carried all sorts of local products and knickknack type things.

She'd start at Otter Marine, though. There was a pair of silly socks with cartoon sea lions on them that would be just right.

After nodding a goodbye to the clerk, she made her way two stores over.

Sam was behind the counter. His face lit. "A niece visit?" His grin tempered. "Oh, she's not with you."

She threw up her hands. "I'm batting a thousand all over town today."

"Huh?"

"Oh, Maureen was being judgy about my style of motherhood."

"That sucks. Came to be reassured you're an all-star, then?"

"Wouldn't say no," she grumbled. She made her way through the racks and found the socks. They made her chuckle—hopefully they'd do the same for Archer on the day he opened them. She grabbed a new set of waterproof wet bags, too, because he was always complaining his set leaked. And she'd noticed his floating key chain for his boat keys was on its last legs, so she grabbed one off the rack of ten-dollars-or-less items Sam kept near the register.

Her brother eyed her pile with suspicion. "What's this all about?"

"You're not supposed to ask questions about purchases close to Christmas."

"I don't see you buying things for me *from* me."

She tried to look nonchalant.

"Who's it for?" he pressed.

"I'm making Archer a thank-you gift."

He leaned forward on the high half of the counter. "Not a present for under the tree?"

"I don't think we'll do a real Christmas morning."

Though her heart warmed at the possibility of sharing one with him. Hot chocolate with extra marshmallows, a roaring fire, snuggling in blankets on the couch and being thankful for everything the year brought.

"Are you going to be at Dad's for pancakes, then?" Sam asked.

Their dad had an everyone-welcome policy on Christmas morning, though in recent years, she and Sam had done their own things for breakfast and headed over for family time in the early afternoon.

She lifted a shoulder. "We'll see."

"Well, make sure you aren't alone."

"I'll never be alone again." She fiddled with the key chain float. "I have Iris."

Sam shot her an exasperated look. "But this year, make sure you're with other people who are capable of talking."

"I'll be fine. You enjoy whatever romantic brunch Kellan is planning for you and don't worry about me."

Maybe Archer would be willing to share a romantic brunch of his own with her, one last shared moment before she moved back home.

A long shot, no doubt, but at least there *was* a shot. Those text messages renewed her hope in something she'd assumed was impossible.

Chapter Thirteen

After a red-eye into Seattle, Archer dropped his dad off in La Conner and had lunch with his parents, and then headed for the ferry.

The water was reasonably calm.

He was not.

Coming home to Franci was something else. He was used to the aches and pains of travel, the annoyance of dealing with his prosthesis on an overnight flight. He wasn't going to say no to a long soak in the claw-foot tub of his upstairs bathroom at some point this evening. But something hard to define muted his usual travel fatigue.

By the time his tires bumped over the Hideaway Wharf ferry ramp, his stomach was twitching.

Not nerves, exactly.

Plain excitement.

Where would Franci be when he walked in the door? Would Iris be awake? Would she have learned something new while he was gone? The twenty-minute drive home was interminable.

He left his luggage in his SUV and headed for the house, keys rattling as he fumbled to unlock the door. It didn't smell the same as it had before Franci moved in. A hint of vanilla kissed the air, and the scent of Christmas drifted in from the living area.

The farther he got into the house, the more the scent of tree boughs and cookies got overpowered by the umami and spice coming from the kitchen. A small tree centered the front window of the living room, covered with unfamiliar ornaments and, naturally, glittering tinsel. His dog lay on the carpet next to the festive display. Honu opened one eye, grinned in his doggy way and thumped his tail on the floor. Didn't bother getting up, though.

"What, no greeting?" he said to the canine.

"Of course you get a greeting," Franci said, two seconds before a pair of arms wrapped around him from behind, pinning his arms to his sides. She rested a cheek on his back.

Warmth rolled through him.

He was home, and not only because he was standing in his own living room.

Untangling himself from her grip, he turned and brushed a thumb along her cheek. She was in leggings and a loose-necked sweatshirt. An oversize wool scarf pooled around her shoulders. "Hello, wildflower."

"Hello, Hawkeye." The lights from the tree danced in her rich brown eyes.

Listening to the short video she'd sent him was not the same as his ears filling with her cheery, warm voice.

He pressed a kiss to her forehead and then yawned. She narrowed her eyes. "You're tired."

"Always a long travel day. You know how it is."

She shuffled him over to the couch. "Sit. Take the weight off. Give your leg a break. We can eat on TV trays. I hope you're hungry—I made stew."

"Yes please to the stew." His stomach growled. "The smell of it has me drooling. But I can wait a minute."

He settled into the corner seat, pulling her with him. She folded into his embrace.

His hunger could wait. All he needed right now was this, holding Franci, burying his nose in her soft loose curls and inhaling her shampoo. The vanilla drifting around the house, plus a hint of cherries. He'd first noticed it on his sheets, weeks ago.

He never wanted his sheets to smell like anything else.

She burrowed her face into the crook of his neck. "What was the best thing you saw in Hawaii?"

Your face on my phone screen.

"Tough call," he said. "Hard to go wrong with turtles."

"Oh, right. But you're biased with it being Honu's name," she said.

"True." He'd originally thought to name the dog Turtle, but Matias had suggested the Hawaiian translation of the word, and it stuck.

A cooing noise came from a baby monitor set up on the dining room table.

"Oh! Iris's awake," she said. "I can't wait for you to see how much she grew."

She went to rise, but he stopped her with a gentle hand to her elbow.

"Wait," he said.

She frowned. "You don't want to see Iris?"

"Of course I do. In a minute." He cleared his throat. "I missed you."

And then he held her so close it felt like they were going to fuse together. He nuzzled behind her ear, dropping tiny kisses and inhaling another heady rush of her scent.

"I missed you, too," she said with a gasp. "I'm so happy you're home."

Happy.

He'd talked to Clara while he was in Hawaii. She'd tried to get him to admit to things he would never be ready to say out loud. She'd repeated one thing, over and over—*you deserve to be happy.*

Enough times he couldn't shake the message.

You deserve to be happy.

Maybe he did.

And maybe it meant not being alone.

Being away had made him realize how attached he could get to Franci, but the time hadn't produced any magical solutions.

She was precious. She deserved to be with someone who wasn't afraid to feel, and right now, the intensity of the connection between them was making his pulse trip double time. He was breathing too fast.

She gave him a gentle closed-mouth kiss and scooted out from his arms. "Stay here. Rest. I'll go change Iris and bring her out here. And then I'll take care of you for a few hours. Return the favor for all the amazing things you did for me after she was born."

He sat on the couch and finally took off his prosthesis. Honu deigned to pick his lazy ass up and come for a proper scratch. Archer obliged, though he was quick to give his dog grief for having forgotten him so soon.

"Or maybe you didn't forget me. Maybe being with Franci is so good, you barely missed me," he said quietly. Staring at the tree and listening to her sing "Silent Night" over the monitor, he didn't blame the dog's shifting loyalties one bit. He rested his head on the back of the couch and tried to remember what his house was like before Franci had made it a home.

Something wet dragged across Archer's face. *What the—*

"Gross, dog," he complained, opening his eyes.

All the lights were off except an ambient glow from the front hall. The kitchen was dark and empty, and the air in the living room held the chill and stillness of not having been moved for hours. He checked his watch. *Damn, 2:00 a.m.* And his limbs were still heavy, like he could sleep for another day and not be sated. He must have fallen asleep when Franci was changing Iris.

The hall light glinted off his crutches, which lay on the coffee table in front of him. He had Franci to thank for the thoughtful gesture. Also for the blanket across the lower half of his body. Once he'd slid his arms into the cuffs, he hitched to the door. He let Honu out for a quick pee and then made his way into the bedroom.

He knew she was there, on the other side of the bed. So she *had* switched beds while he was gone. Good. At least the hours of sleep he'd lost, picturing her snuggled between his sheets while he was away, hadn't been for naught.

He clenched the grips of his crutches, knowing he

should go upstairs and sleep in one of the spare rooms, or even back out to the couch. But damn, he was wiped.

It wasn't like they were going to get up to no good while he was so tired.

Plus, he'd finally be able to help her with Iris again in the night. He'd missed the routine.

He hadn't even *seen* Iris yet.

It made total sense to get in his own bed. He'd explain to Franci in the morning. He leaned his crutches in their spot between his bedside table and the bed frame, shucked down to his boxers and T-shirt, and crawled between the covers.

She murmured in her sleep and rolled over, throwing a leg over his and settling a hand on his chest.

Oh, Christ. Work with me, Francine.

A bolt of lust ripped through him, and he took a few slow breaths, trying to savor her sweet smell without letting his body react.

Those cherries and sugar, like the irresistible aroma that drifted from Hideaway Bakery over to Otter Marine when Winnie put cherry turnovers on the daily specials list. The scent cocooned around him, coaxing him into sleep. Or maybe he was the cocoon *around* the turnover, because all the warmth was in his arms. Wait. Not dessert, but the woman of his literal dreams. She danced in and out of his consciousness all night, teasing him, delighting him, loving him.

Waking with Franci spooned in front of him was the best Christmas Eve gift he could ask for. Her smooth cheek tucked against his biceps, using it as a pillow. His other hand rested over her stomach. Soft curves pressed against his aroused—

Damn it.

He needed to jump in a cold shower and get a hold of himself. Besides, the clock on Franci's side of the bed read 7:45—he was on deck to work the half-day Christmas Eve shift at the shop so Nic could go for a holiday hike with Charlotte.

He kissed the top of her head and went to roll away, but she caught both his hands. Her hips wiggled. Chances were she was either realizing he was as hard as a rock, or noticing how spooning with someone missing more than half a leg was different.

"Ignore that," he whispered in case it was the former. "Sorry."

"Why are you apologizing?" she asked, voice a bare hum. She reached back and palmed his butt, pulling him closer and rocking her hips again.

His eyes nearly rolled back in his head. *Stay still. Do not move.* He'd done a ton of training on basic-needs deprivation, but "A" school hadn't dealt with waking up with a warm, pliable woman in his embrace.

"You didn't invite me into bed," he explained.

"Consider this your hand-lettered, hand-delivered card stock."

Swallowing a groan, he rocked his pelvis forward. The friction of her curves against his aching length was almost more than he could take. "You're irresistible, Franci."

"Good."

"But we're not alone."

She groaned softly. "I forgot about my tiny roommate for a second. Am I a terrible mother?"

"You're an amazing mom." He kissed her hair again,

and then the side of her neck. "Did she seriously sleep for six hours?"

"No, she woke at five. You were passed out, though."

"Damn, I wanted to help."

"You did."

"How? I slept through it," he said.

"But you give excellent snuggle." She released his hip and laid her hand over the one he had resting on her warm T-shirt-covered abdomen. "I figured if you were joining me, you were okay with this. So I took advantage."

She'd snuggled in on purpose, then. Not a sleepy instinct. Something primal rose in him. Why did he want to be her comfort so badly? Her pleasure, too. Her solace.

"Mmm, I *do* feel taken advantage of," he teased.

"You should. If it wasn't for my infant alarm clock, you'd be naked right now."

"Would I?" Any minute now. Any minute he'd stop pretending he could have her. He was being selfish, and one of them, maybe both, was going to get hurt.

"I was hoping so."

"Not sure you should."

"Oh." Her tone fell from amused to disappointed. "Maybe I read the situation wrong."

She scooted away from him and sat on the edge of the bed, head hanging low.

"You didn't." He scrambled to sit next to her.

She peered at him in the dim light. "What else do I need to do, Archer? To be the one you *want* to wake up with?"

He scrubbed his face in his hands. "It's not about you doing anything."

"What is it, then?" Her cheeks were bright red. "I was hoping your time away would, I dunno, make you want me more."

He took her hand and squeezed. "It did. Promise." He was going to spend all of Christmas Eve hiding his bulging fly behind a pillow if he didn't get a hold of himself. "Every night in Hawaii, I fell asleep wanting you."

"So...have me."

What would it be like to be able to offer himself the way Franci did, without artifice, without reservation?

If he tried, he'd pull her into the bottomless pit within him. Pain and guilt he had no clue how to process. He didn't want to touch her with any of that.

He stared at her, not knowing what to say.

Iris let out a cry.

"Do you want to feed her a bottle?" Franci asked. "I usually breastfeed first thing, but I could pump instead."

"No. Do what you usually do." And because it all felt too intimate, he escaped to his frigid shower like the coward he was.

Franci stared at the bread pudding recipe and cursed. "Oh, no! I brought the wrong kind of chocolate."

"There's a variety in the pantry," Kellan said calmly, managing to braise short ribs, chop carrots and sauté shallots all while she couldn't even manage one dessert. He moved through the Forest + Brine kitchen like he was born to cook meals in the cozy space. Unsurprisingly, given he had handpicked every item, from the practical to the frivolous. The gorgeous blue enamel stove, the velvet couches over by the window. And tonight, the table her dad had painstakingly crafted would be full of Christmas Eve revelers.

They were making dinner for the same crew as their impromptu Thanksgiving feast, with a few additions. Violet, who'd had stars and hearts in her eyes since the boat parade, was bringing Kim. Matias had promised he'd stop by if he managed to get the pub closed up early. And Nic was coming with Charlotte like he had for Thanksgiving, since Nic's parents were visiting family on the East Coast. He'd passed on the offer to go with them in order to cover Franci's shifts, and she still felt bad he'd had to do that.

It would be more than a full house. So no matter how distracted she was by Archer coming home seeming more conflicted than he had been before he'd left, she needed to come through on this dessert.

She could have sworn her list was complete when she'd done her shopping yesterday, but she'd been thinking about finishing the last few items for Archer's Advent calendar and must not have read the ingredients closely enough. She looked farther down the recipe and groaned.

"And dried cherries."

"I have frozen ones I pilfered from Alice's backyard during the summer," Kellan offered.

"Will they work in a bread pudding?" She'd been flipping through the cookbooks on one of Archer's shelves while he was gone, and thought the recipe sounded delicious. Of course, it helped to buy cherries and the right kind of chocolate in order to make a chocolate-and-cherry dessert.

"Can't screw up bread pudding, love, as long as you have the right number of eggs."

Panicked, she checked the total. Eight yolks plus four whole. She *had* bought a dozen. At least she'd gotten one thing right.

"Thank you." Her face was hot, and she couldn't blame the warmth of the kitchen.

She was up to her elbows in cubed brioche when Iris let out a wail. Franci hurried over to the baby swing she'd positioned by the street-side window and picked up her daughter.

"Shh, jellybean."

She wasn't hungry, was she? Franci had fed her forty-five minutes ago. Her diaper was dry, the room was warm, there were no loud noises...

"What's the matter, Iris Gale?"

Iris squalled louder.

She shot Kellan an apologetic look.

He responded with the same calm smile he'd given her when she'd discovered her shopping errors. "Babies don't always make sense."

"She sure doesn't understand a clock yet." Some of the people in her family would probably point out *Franci* didn't understand clocks, either, but Kellan earned his nicest-guy-in-the-world title by merely grinning. She relaxed a little and danced around the room, cheerily pointing out the Christmas decorations.

Iris eventually calmed and burrowed against Franci's neck. Great for their eardrums, but not for her ability to finish the dessert.

"I'm sorry. Maybe she'll let me put her down in a second."

Kellan waved off the apology. "I'll have a few spare minutes once I get the veg in. I can throw the dessert together if your hands are still full."

Throw it together. Like it was that easy.

Well, sure, for him it was.

A knock sounded on the front door.

Franci went to open it, but before she could reach the knob, the door swung open. Archer entered. An Otter Marine hoodie covered his broad chest. Concern darkened his expression, and he examined both her and Iris. "You two okay?"

"Not really."

"Figured. I was pulling in the T-shirt rack downstairs and heard her." He reached for Iris and tucked her angry little face into his neck. His big hands spanned her diaper-padded bum and her whole back.

"And you ran to my rescue," she said. It didn't land as right as it had weeks ago. Jumping to save people was easy for him. But she wanted to be able to do the same when he needed it, and he seemed no more willing to open up about his needs and weak spots than before his holiday.

"I knew you were on a timeline," he said, sounding puzzled. "Want me to take her with me while I finish closing? I can deal with the cash-out one-handed."

"Sure," she said, feeling oddly hollow. She forced a smile. "Thanks."

Still looking confused, he snagged Iris's blanket, tucked it around her, brushed a hand on Franci's cheek and disappeared out the way he'd come.

She frowned at the closed door, took a deep breath and summoned the will to finish her dessert. Turning, she caught Kellan gaping in the same direction she'd been a moment prior.

"Mother of God. How do you not get pregnant again every time he holds your baby? I swear I just did myself, despite the impossibilities." His lilt was stronger than usual. He blinked, shaking his head. "Sorry. I only have eyes for your brother, promise."

"I get it. Archer's…intense." And she had a month and a half of restless daydreams as proof.

Kellan tilted his head. "You look upset."

Shoot, she didn't want anyone to think she was less than thrilled today. "It's Iris's first Christmas! How can it be anything but magical?"

Hands braced on the counter, Kellan studied her. "You don't have to smile if you're not feeling it."

"Why would I not be feeling it?"

All those holidays, thinking if she smiled a little harder or behaved a little better, her mom might be happy. But every time, Francine would screw something up—burning cookies because she lost track of time, or tying the ribbons wrong because she'd been too busy playing fairies to remember the exact way her mom wanted them curled. Each little mistake meant having to spend the rest of the day trying to make her mom feel better. Didn't matter that the rest of her family loved her despite her faults—what kind of person was she if she didn't get her mom's unconditional love?

Part of her had always wondered if all her messiness meant she didn't deserve it. But as she thought about the little girl downstairs, Franci's well of love overflowed to brimming. Nothing would empty that well. Especially not burnt cookies or faulty knots or Iris getting lost in her imagination.

Iris didn't need to *do* anything to deserve Franci's love, including putting on a happy face all the time.

A good reminder that Franci didn't need to pretend to be happy for her mom, or for anyone else she loved in her life.

And given how much she knew it hurt to deal with her mom's flaky rejections, why was she pushing so hard to make sure Iris had a relationship with her grandmother? Unless Alina showed she was willing to change, Franci was inviting pain into her daughter's life. Instead of protecting Iris and making sure she created a soft circle of love for her to live in, she'd be guaranteeing disappointment and self-doubt.

Is it the same with Archer? If I keep hoping he'll change his mind, am I setting Iris up to get hurt?

Or setting myself *up for heartbreak?*

She didn't let herself answer. Didn't want to give validity to the *yes* stewing in her gut.

"What's got you tied in knots?" Kellan asked.

"I don't know what to do about Archer," she blurted.

Nodding knowingly, Kellan said, "It's bloody hard to love someone who's scared to love you back."

He might as well have jammed one of his deadly sharp chef's knives between her ribs. Tears pricked the corners of her eyes.

"Wait, wait," he said. "I didn't mean he *doesn't* love you, Francine. It's like Sam and me. I could tell he was having feelings. He was scared." He wiped his hands on a towel before wrapping her in a hug.

"It's always hard to think of Sam being scared," she said. "Hard to think of him without you, too." Kellan had only been in town nine months, but he was so much a part of their lives now. And her lonely brother wasn't so lonely anymore. "He looks at you like you're more vital than air."

Kellan's mouth twitched. "I love that look. And if I saw things right, it was also on the face of the man who just stole away your baby."

She didn't have the energy to pretend she didn't want to be that important to Archer.

Except she had to. "He doesn't owe me his feelings. It's fine. Really."

"Hey." Kellan stroked her hair. "It's not. And you don't have to pretend it is."

Her knee-jerk reaction was to disagree. But she was too tired, too heartsore to stick to her old habits.

"You're right," she said. "It sucks. And maybe it's about time I give up."

Kellan sighed. "Sometimes you need to guard your heart."

"You didn't," Franci said. "You walked away from your plan to run your dream kitchen in London long before Sam got his head out of his ass."

"Well, I made the change for me more than for him," Kellan said thoughtfully. "But I do think me taking a chance inspired him to take one of his own."

"Archer has a ton to work through, I think." She stepped away from her soon-to-be brother-in-law and went back to her dessert, carefully carving the crusts off a second loaf of bread.

Kellan returned to his own station. "Does he want to work through it?"

"I don't know," she admitted.

"Might want to figure that out sooner rather than later," he said, a sympathetic smile on his face.

"Those smarts are why you're engaged and I'm not." The knife slipped, nearly taking off her fingertip. *Oops.*

"Yet," he said, winking.

"Thought I was supposed to figure out where his head was at."

"You are." He laid his knife on the cutting board and lifted his gaze. "But I didn't tell you to stop hoping in the meantime."

Chapter Fourteen

Forest + Brine's cozy entertaining space smelled like a dream when Archer returned with Iris an hour later. She was sound asleep, tucked in her blanket.

"There she is." Franci's frown softened. She was putting the finishing touches on some delicious-looking dish, and looked ready to keel over. "Next year, you'll get to try a few of the good things Uncle Kellan makes."

"She's sleeping," Archer explained. He wasn't quite ready to give Iris up. Wasn't like he'd get to hold her on the daily once Franci was back to her own place. Taking a seat on one of the velvet couches, he settled in.

According to Rachel and Winnie, Franci could move back home on the thirtieth.

His life would be back to normal.

A cherry-turnover-free bed.

An empty house.

An empty life.

The thought dug its teeth in. He tried to rip it out and throw it to the side like he had so often before, but it was harder now that the possibility had a face on it. Two faces.

His cell buzzed in his pocket, jarring him from the persistent ache in his chest. A call, not a text. Pulling it out, he saw Clara's number on the screen. Damn. Couldn't avoid the call, not on Christmas Eve. One of these days, Daniel would finish his dive training and Archer could stop feeling guilty about not taking part.

He answered, keeping his voice low. "Clarabelle. Merry Christmas."

"It is here," she said. "Is it for you?"

"I've got people feeding me—what more do I need?"

She guffawed. "You don't really want me to answer that."

No, he didn't. "Just called to bust my chops?"

"I wanted to let you know Dan's open water tests are scheduled for the twenty-ninth and thirtieth," she said.

"Good for him. Is he still enjoying it?"

"Loves it."

"I'll make sure to text him good luck those days."

"He'd like that." She cleared her throat. "He'd like it more if you administered the test."

Whoa, now. "In Portland?"

At least the distance would make it easy to decline.

"No, we'd come to you."

His stomach turned. "Our boats are booked for the next while, Clara," he said.

Franci caught his eye. "Otter's boats? The Zodiac's free most of this week. And the *Queen*'s only booked mornings."

He cringed. Hopefully Clara hadn't heard that.

"Oh, too bad," his friend's widow lamented. "Dan was hoping for it as a late Christmas present."

"The AirPods I sent him didn't fit the bill?" He kept his tone light.

"No technology can mean as much as time with you, Arch. Especially time doing something he knows his dad loved."

His head swam, and he put Iris on the couch next to him. He was used to his walls affecting his own life. But with those boundaries hurting Franci, and now Daniel... He hated that. He couldn't get his head wrapped around a way to keep from hurting them. Continue to shut them out? Devastate them by letting them into his grief and guilt? There was no winning.

Teaching Daniel would be a privilege.

Diving safely with Eddy's son would be impossible. If he thought too hard when he was teaching people how to share regulators and making sure they didn't lose their buddy, he wouldn't be able to do his job. And if he was underwater with Daniel, all he'd be able to do was think.

Bubbles. Eddy's face. Darkness...

Hours later, the images still haunted him. He should have been able to distract himself, given he was in the middle of the giant Christmas hug that was the Walker family and their closest friends celebrating around a damn feast for the ages. Kellan had festooned the place with evergreen swags everywhere there was space to hang them, from the for-show fireplace to above the curtains. He had a tree up, too. Blue and silver ornaments crowded the bushy fir.

Archer preferred all the personalized ones Franci had hung on the small tree in his living room. He wanted to sit with her while she pointed each one out, soaking her in as she shared each special story.

It was simple. He hadn't had enough time with her. She was at the other end of the table between her dad and Alice Wong, lighting their world much like she had Archer's for the past six weeks.

Nope, not nearly enough time.

"So." His sister's nosy voice came from beside him. "What's Santa bringing you tonight?"

"Coal, no doubt."

Her intrigued gaze traveled between him and Franci. "Have you actually been naughty?"

He fixed a bland expression on his face and took another bite of the delectable dessert Franci had made. Cherries and chocolate, sweet like her skin. Had Iris not been sharing a room with them this morning…

Argh. Now was not the time to travel that road.

"And here I thought you were too stubborn to go for it," Violet said.

He frowned at her.

"Or maybe you are."

"I'm not stubborn. I'm being reasonable."

"Pfft." She poked her fork in his direction, and he had to weave to the side to avoid tines to the biceps. "When is love ever reasonable?"

"I need to protect her, Vi."

"From love?"

No, from me.

He stabbed a cherry.

"I don't buy it," she said. "Love isn't something to

avoid. Just because you feel the need to bury your heart deeper than the Mariana Trench doesn't mean the rest of us want to. Look what Sam and Kellan found."

"Sam and Kellan didn't…" Why was he getting into this? Christmas dinner didn't need to be seasoned with the dregs of his divorce and his friend's death.

She rested her head on his shoulder. "I know you're trying not to hurt her. Thing is, you already are by not trying to love her. Say you give it a shot and it falls apart? She's not going to hold that against you. But if you keep holding back, you might send the message she's not worth it."

"She's worth the world," he said in a growl he barely recognized.

"Then show her."

"As if it's that easy." Unburying his grief… Where would he even begin?

Start by loving her. By giving her what she wants.

The intimacy she'd been asking for.

"No, it's not easy," Violet said, lifting her head from his shoulder and straightening. "But since when did you shy away from hard things?"

"Maybe I always did with love," he said quietly. "Why else would Tamara have gone elsewhere to look for what she needed?"

Violet put her fork down and stared at her plate for a long moment. "Who knows? You got married young, and then she changed? Or she made a shitty, toxic decision? If she wasn't getting what she needed from your marriage, she needed to talk to you. She owed you honesty, at least."

"And I owe the same to Franci."

She shot him a no-kidding look. "So open your mouth and make words come out. About all of it. What you want. What you don't want. What you're scared about. What you're excited about."

"Right. Merry Christmas, baby. Here's all my emotional baggage for you to unwrap."

"Maybe that's exactly what she wants, Arch," Violet said softly. "Not for you to expect her to fix it—that's your job—but for you to be open about what hurts. And what doesn't, too. When you're around her, you get this look on your face. And I want that look for you. You deserve it."

Believing his sister was hard, but she wasn't one to lie.

"Follow her lead," she continued. "If I know anything about her, she'll take you on the best adventure of your life. Consider it *my* Christmas present from you."

"Seriously? That's what you want?"

"For you to be at peace, and loved? Yeah, it is."

He put an arm around her and squeezed. "Love you, Vi."

His sister kissed his cheek. "Love you, too. And I'm pretty sure Franci does as well. So let her," she said.

He let out a long breath. "I'll try. Promise."

A night of being surrounded by family buoyed Franci to the point where she was almost ready to follow Kellan's advice. It did seem the time of year to be hopeful, to believe in the return of the light. Of love. Taking a deep breath, Franci linked her fingers through Archer's and tugged him up the ramp on the front of his house.

"I can't wait any longer to give you your present,"

she said. "We were never a family who opened gifts on Christmas Eve, but tonight I'm making an exception."

He rested Iris's car seat on the stoop and dug in his jacket pocket for the keys, still holding Franci's hand all the while. "I hope you didn't go overboard."

"I did exactly what was needed." She was happy with her collection of little gifts. But it wasn't about the dive accessories or Butterfingers or a copy of the most recent *Pacific Yachting*. She wanted him to know what he meant to her. That she knew things about him, both less significant and critically important.

Wanted him to open something every day for the next twenty-five days and think of her, too.

He held the door open for her. She picked up the car seat and then entered the house. Seconds later, a Labrador insisting on scritches greeted them.

She gave the dog a cursory pat. Fixing her gaze on Archer, she said, "First, though… Can I kiss you? I've wanted to all night."

"'All night,' huh?" Archer said softly before laying a long kiss on her mouth, the kind she'd been craving. The kind that said he craved her, too.

The dog nosed his way between them.

She laughed, but pressed closer, returning the kiss until her head got light. Could tonight possibly be the night they kept kissing and didn't find a reason to stop?

After a minute, Archer pulled away. "Let me take Honu out for a minute, and then we'll talk." He motioned for the dog to head outside to do his business and shut the door behind them.

Talk.

That could mean all manner of things, but the way

he'd just kissed her was pretty clear. Had he had a change of heart over dinner?

An urge rose to set the scene just right. She transferred a conked-out sleeper-clad Iris into her bassinet and headed for the living room. The small tree she'd decorated with her own ornaments dialed up the festive ambience to eleven. Oh! Music, of course. She connected her phone to the small speaker he had on a shelf by the fireplace and selected a lo-fi holiday playlist. What else... Something to drink? She twisted her hands.

The front door opened before she was able to make a decision. A low command for Honu to go to his bed came from the entryway.

She was still standing by the tree, frozen over something so silly as soda versus tea.

A second passed, and then Archer stood in the archway to the front hall. He leaned a shoulder against the barrier, all casual, too-hot swagger. His sweater hugged his chest, a delicious invitation to snuggle close and enjoy the soft fabric.

"Maybe I need to unwrap *you*," she blurted, knowing the joke was corny, but unable to care.

Amusement flickered at the corner of his lips. "Maybe I'll let you."

Her mouth went dry. "For real?"

He strode toward her. "You're better than anything under the tree, Francine."

His hands landed on her hips. His mouth on hers, promising a longer, lingering kiss than the one they'd shared by the door. Heat rose so fast, fueled by weeks and weeks of being close but not close enough.

"Now that we've canceled out each other's cheesy jokes…" She sucked in a deep breath. "Speak plainly."

"I want you."

"I hoped you did." Every one of his scorching glances, quickly banked but impossible to miss, had hinted at his desire.

His hesitance had been equally clear, too.

Soft lips landed on her temple, her jaw. Quick blitzes of warmth, spreading through her limbs.

"Good," he said. "Wouldn't be much fun if you didn't feel the same way."

"I do. Kind of came out of nowhere this year, though," she said.

"Oh, yeah?"

"I mean, I've always thought you were hot. All my high-school friends were so jealous that you and Matias were Sam's close buddies."

He groaned. "I was almost twice your age then."

"A crush on an older guy is a rite of passage. And whenever you came home in your uniform—forget about it. But that was only teenage admiration. Until you moved home after your accident—suddenly I wasn't a teenager anymore, and we were working together. And you were so driven. To navigate life with your prosthesis, to dive, to explore. I loved seeing you meet those goals. I loved just being with you. Out on the boat. Underwater. In the shop, trying to make you smile and feeling like a million dollars when I succeeded." Cheeks hot, she closed her eyes. "Maybe it wasn't *just* this year."

His thumb trailed from the inside of her wrist to the back of her hand, a kiss with his touch. "My favorite part of checking the weekly schedule was discovering how many days I'd get to start the day listening to your laugh."

"It was?" she squeaked.

"You were the best part of my week. And when you told me you were pregnant, I'd never felt so protective of someone. Had to hold back."

His openness caught her off guard.

She gripped his biceps, needing a bit of space to voice the question niggling at her. The one preventing her from launching into him and stripping him to his socks.

"Do you *want* to want me?"

He paused. His brows knit as he drew away. Her skin chilled, no longer warmed by his kisses, and she wanted them back more than anything.

"What do you mean?" he asked.

"You seem uncertain sometimes."

Self-awareness laced his low "ha."

"Want to talk about it?" she asked.

His fingers traced from her jaw to her throat, along her collarbone. The lightest touch.

"It's okay." She took his hands in hers. "Don't rush. We can open presents, enjoy the lights on the tree, figure out the rest later." Would they ever, though? If a month and a half of living together hadn't brought clarity, what would?

"I don't need more time," he said gruffly, his words alarmingly close to her own thoughts. "I want to try, Franci. To be close to you. More than close. *That* part, I figured out when I was eating your dessert earlier and realized it tasted like you. I still remembered it exactly, even though I made you come weeks ago."

Self-consciousness flooded into her cheeks.

"Presents can wait for tomorrow." Fingers spread wide, he threaded them into her hair. His thumbs drew slow lines on her cheekbones.

"Are you sure?"

He took one of her hands and laid it on his chest. His heart beat under her palm, wild and uncontrolled. "Yes."

Her own raced in response. Was there anything better than being that desired?

So much seemed unanswered still. It wasn't the first time she'd dive into something without all the information, though. Sometimes the best things in life came from the unknown.

And she'd take the rapid beat of his pulse as enough certainty for now.

"Iris is still in your bedroom," she said.

"You set the mood out here, anyway." He tugged her back to the couch, sat on the end of the wide chaise section and pulled her onto his lap.

"Oh!" She collapsed into him, then laughed. Surrounded by him, she straddled his thighs and let herself relax. That night in the kitchen, they'd only been close like this for a few minutes before he'd lifted her onto the counter and made it about her pleasure alone.

Tonight, it was about both of them.

"Hey," she said, running a hand over his cheek. His gaze held her as securely as his grip on her hips. Firm. She wanted to call it *safe*, but it wasn't. Tempting heat flickered between her legs. She rocked forward, teasing them both. She bit her lip, holding back from going from zero to needy in a flash. The edge in his gaze hinted at something more reckless than safety, solidity. That sort of intensity could either cement a forever bond or incinerate, leaving an empty void.

And she was ready to take the chance.

She tilted her hips, grinning as his eyes darkened to liquid sapphire. "I think I forget how this works."

"I doubt it."

"It's been a while." Wouldn't be hard for him to guess who her last partner had been—the man she could thank for Iris's existence—and it made her cheeks burn.

"I loved making you feel good before. This will be just as incredible." His fingers dug into her flesh, kneading her, coaxing her forward. The plastic of his socket, under the soft material of his trousers, rubbed the back of her leg. Hmm. She wasn't super sure how his prosthesis would impact sex. She'd have to follow his lead.

She tipped against his length and kissed him softly, tasting the bit of coffee and chocolate lingering on his lips from dessert. She played with his mouth, testing a hard kiss, a long one. Short nibbles and tender strokes with her tongue. Only a fraction of the ways to enjoy Archer Frost.

"One thing about a dress…" He teased the knit hem to her hips. "It's either on, or it's off."

"Off," she whispered.

"Good answer."

She raised her arms over her head and he swooshed off the material, leaving her exposed in her stretchy bra and high-waisted tights. She'd expected to feel self-conscious about her postpartum body, the ways her shape had changed, softened, rounded even more than before… But in this moment, there wasn't space for

anything but bliss. She felt like the victor here, strad-
dling this gorgeous man and soaking in the awe on his
face. The anticipation written in his tilted smile sent a
ripple of excitement through her veins.

Being physically bare didn't make her vulnerable
with Archer. All the uncertainty came from not knowing whether he'd be able to step off the proverbial cliff
with her. And that she could ignore.

His hands skimmed up her thighs to her waist. He
cupped one of her breasts, running a thumb over her
sensitive skin. "Bra on or off?"

"On."

"Touching okay?"

"Mmm-hmm."

She couldn't handle it if he stopped. His thumb cast a
spell over her tightening nipple before his mouth landed
on the other through the cup of her bra. She fought with
the waistband of her tights. "I guess I need to stand—"

"Nah." He rolled them to their sides and somehow
got rid of the stretchy prison.

Fingers shaking, she tried to deal with his belt, but
he took over, unfastening the buckle.

Thump. Thump.

His shoes.

Then his sweater, exposing the dress shirt underneath.

"All that, and you're still fully clothed," she complained.

The slow striptease was the ultimate in torture.
Her core pulsed at the promise of getting as close as it
was possible to get. Speeding up seemed impossible,
though. How could she rush through any of these moments? Reaching for his chest, she plucked open his
shirt buttons. The cotton was thick enough for him not

to wear an undershirt, and the planes of his chest were downright edible, golden in the dim light from the tree, sketched with bold black lines. She kissed him there, once, twice. Teased with her tongue, tasting his warm skin.

"You didn't finish taking off your pants," she murmured, making one of his pectorals flinch.

"I usually ditch my prosthesis," he said quietly. "No one needs plastic and metal when they're trying to be intimate. Not this kind of plastic, anyway."

She wouldn't have been surprised if he'd winked, given his tone, but the expression on his face was the opposite.

"Of course," she said. "Whatever feels best."

He sat on the edge of the couch and shucked his pants, then carefully unrolled silicone and fabric. He set his prosthesis to the side and shifted closer. After palming her knee, he ran his hand up her thigh until his thumb teased the edge of her panties.

Leaning over, he kissed the line his fingers had traced. "This feels best." The gravel in his voice rasped against her skin.

She shivered. His head was so close to her center, his mouth tasting in sweet, open licks along her belly.

"That—oh, that is…"

She squirmed under his touch. She wanted his lips in eight places at once. On her mouth, her neck. Those kisses trailing along her breasts, yes, they worked. But then how good had it been when he blazed a downward path?

"I can't decide what I want tonight," she said. "I want it all."

All. Not just pleasure, but time. His nights. His mornings. His Christmas Eves and New Year's Days. and every lazy Tuesday when they were off and could lounge around in sweatpants, snuggling on the couch and staring at the ocean.

"We have time." His tongue tickled the edge of her bra. One wide palm cupped under her breast, sending sparks along her skin. Achy, restless, craving fulfillment but not wanting to rush, she rolled onto her side to face him. "I don't think clocks exist on December twenty-fourth. There's too much magic in the air."

He lifted his gaze. The happy glint in his eye stole her breath.

Catching a hand under his chin, she nudged, a wordless plea for him to scoot higher. With parted lips, she drew his mouth to hers.

He claimed her, resting on an elbow and palming her cheek. His kiss matched the flames flickering in the hearth.

She wrapped a knee around his hips, craving the friction of hard muscles.

Curious fingers tugged at her underwear and then slid them down like the act of undressing her was a gift itself.

"I—" he faltered. "This way, okay?"

One quick roll, and he was on his back with her over him.

Rubbing against his thigh had been heavenly.

But having her core snug against his arousal, even with his underwear still on, transcended anything she'd felt before. She let out a moan. Rocked, a primal rhythm as familiar as her pulse.

"This…this is what it should feel like," she said.

"You like that?" He reached between them and palmed her sex, grinding the heel of his hand against her sensitive nerve endings. His fingertips pressed lower, teasing her entrance.

"Mmm, your touch. It's—"

"Tell me what you like."

"Well, to start, not these," she said lightly, hooking her thumbs in the waist of his boxer briefs. She slid down his legs, taking the shorts with her, off his residual leg and then his sound one.

She slipped the condom from where she had tucked it in a pocket of her dress.

"And people tease you about not being a planner," he said with a playful smile.

She gasped in mock outrage, then perched by his knee. "What people don't realize… It's not about planning or not planning." She palmed his thighs, the thick muscle and scar tissue—she kissed it all, then nibbled a path to his erection.

He gasped. "What's it about?"

"Enjoyment. Savoring every last minute, every opportunity life presents. Including you."

One long lick of his tip, and she had him groaning. Salt and heat spread on her tongue.

His breath was coming fast. "Save that for another day, okay?"

"What's today, then?"

The foil packet crinkled in her hand, and she tore it open and rolled the condom on, holding his thick penis and earning another low, sexy complaint.

Not complaint. Abandon.

He was usually wound so tight. But naked, sprawled under her, raw energy charged his every sound, every move.

"Today's for being inside you," he elaborated, voice a growly whisper.

"In my mouth?" she teased.

He sat without effort. She might have to spend some time admiring that move later, but for now he had her hips in his demanding grip and was dragging her closer. Teeth scraped her neck. His tongue soothed the sting, and he lifted her above his length.

"'In my mouth,' she says. Cheeky." He lay back against a pillow and gently traced his hands from her hips, along the thin lines on her belly, the marks of her body's hard work. "And so damn beautiful. So damn *right*. This. *Us*."

Us.

Whimpering at his words, she sank onto him.

He tilted his hips, driving deep, sending sparks through every part of her body.

She rocked, keened, tumbled.

How was it even possible to be in a haze, but also to feel every inch of her skin? The parts he was touching. The parts he wasn't.

Hungry kisses pelted her neck. She was on top, but he set the pace. Long, commanding strokes, lifting her higher into brilliant need.

"Make that noise again." Not a request. Begging.

"What noise?" she asked, with barely enough air to get the question out.

"When I do this—" He snapped his hips.

She cried out.

"—then you do that."

"Archer…" She was close. But no. "I don't want it to end."

Time vanished as he kissed her. "It's okay, wildflower. Let go."

Another stroke, more, more, and she shattered over him, safe in his embrace. Lost to the world for a long space of stars and heat and everything.

Everything.

His hips slowed, tender thrusts. He hadn't finished, and was teasing out the last tendrils of her pleasure.

His mouth, soft by her ear. "That wasn't the end," he murmured. "We're only just beginning."

Chapter Fifteen

Archer had loved the enchantment of Christmas morning when he was small. He and Violet always stumbled downstairs, eager to see what Santa had brought them. His parents were there waiting on the love seat, drinking their coffees with their clunker of a digital camera at the ready.

Around when he turned nine, it had become more about family than the actual belief in a jolly gift giver.

But rousing this still-dark morning, stretched out on the wide chaise part of the couch with Franci tucked to his chest, he couldn't shake the feeling that magic still existed.

Franci's tree glittered in the exact spot his family's Douglas fir had always gone, between the two expansive front windows. The dash of freckles across her nose was muted in the glowing white lights.

In truth, this was everything he'd wished for.

He flashed forward a few years, to him and Franci rising early to sit on the couch with their own coffees, waiting for Iris to shuffle into the living room, rubbing the sleep from her eyes and grinning when she realized her heart's desire had been met. Maybe a brother or sister to join her, too. Or both.

Franci shifted, nuzzling closer, clearly awake.

"Morning, beautiful."

"Merry Christmas." She pulled the fuzzy blanket higher over them. "Gotta admit, when we left family dinner last night, I did not have 'sleep with Archer on the couch' on my Christmas bingo card."

"And here I thought you knew I was a sure thing."

She let out a quick laugh. "I was assuming we'd be in your bed."

"We can spend some nights there, too," he said.

She shook her head. "The ambience of the tree and the fireplace is too good. I'm ruined for bedrooms."

I'm ruined, period.

The second he'd had her over him, he'd been lost.

Vulnerable.

Pressure built in his chest, under her idly stroking hand. Violet and her "she's not going to hold it against you if you fail" was patently wrong.

He'd clung to the possibility of it being easier to face his feelings after having sex—making love—with Franci.

A lump clogged his throat. A hint of light tinged the far horizon. Not the actual sunrise, given they faced west, but the hopeful rim of lavender blue on the edges of the sky. He wanted to believe that light was a promise, a guarantee he'd find the answers he needed to face the aching void in his gut. Being here, with this woman, it should have been enough. But how could he let her anywhere near anything so ugly?

"Hey." Her hand crept to his jaw, then stilled over his stubble-roughened cheek. "You sound like you just ran a marathon. What's going on?"

"Huh?"

"Your heartbeat. Your breathing." Humor flickered through the concern in her gaze. "And here I thought sex was supposed to be relaxing."

"I don't—" Maybe he was breathing too hard. "Sex with you is everything I hoped it would be."

It was more than everything, and yeah, that was exactly why his heart was racing. He couldn't love her properly without facing what he'd buried. But how could he do that and remain intact?

Once he'd extracted himself from their tangle of limbs and blankets, he sat on the end of the chaise with his back to her.

The two presents under the tree caught his eye. "We should open those."

He snatched the simply wrapped box holding the gift he'd agonized over. Turning a bit, he made space for her between his thighs. Sitting sideways to his chest, she crossed her legs. He put the present in her lap and his hand on her lower back.

"It's heavy," she said, tone curious.

"I looked at a million rings and necklaces. But you barely ever wear jewelry, and then I saw this." He shrugged.

She tore into the wrapping, the box, the packing material, revealing an irregular resin and wood sculpture.

She gasped. "Two divers. It's like they're actually in water."

"Yeah." He rubbed the back of his neck. "It lights up, too, from the bottom, so the resin glows. And the wood shapes on the side reminded me of the wall off Lighthouse Point. Of seeing it with you."

"Archer, it's gorgeous," she whispered.

"You're gorgeous," he said.

"Cheeseball." She nudged his abs with her elbow.

"Nah. Just a lucky bastard."

Her mouth tilted and her eyes lit. "Your turn."

She grabbed the larger box and put it where she'd just been sitting, then stood in front of him, restless on her toes. Hands woven together, she covered her mouth. "I hope you like it."

Inside the box lay… "More presents?"

None was the same size as the next, and they were numbered.

He lifted an eyebrow. "That's…a lot of gifts, Franci."

"Exactly the point," she said cautiously, kneeling next to him and lifting out a small present numbered with a one. "It's an Advent calendar. For next month, though. One thing every day. Seriously, small things. But I wanted to make you smile. And with January being so rainy and me moving back to my cottage, I thought it could be a bright spot for your morning—"

"Francine." A kiss was not enough for this woman. It didn't matter what was wrapped in each of the packages. Rocks, for all he cared. How much time had she spent putting it together? He pressed his mouth to hers, slowly tasting her, earning a gasp.

She smiled softly. "Open the first one."

He did, revealing a small bottle of champagne.

"It's tradition to do mimosas in the morning at my dad's. I thought we could copy him. I'll feed Iris a bottle so that I can have a drink with you." Her cheeks turned scarlet. "Not that I'm expecting to make it an annual thing or anything, but for today."

"I don't know the last time anyone gave me something this thoughtful." Nothing he'd exchanged with his ex-wife came close.

Every day with Franci was a revelation. He wanted to give her the world.

Instead, he'd be saddling her with a metric ton of his grief and pain.

Nearly choking on the cold wash of reality, he said, "I don't know how to be who I was."

She moved the box containing his gifts and sat between his legs again. She took one of his hands in both of hers. Her skin on his was like the shock of a hot shower after being in the ocean too long.

"Why would you think I would want you to be anything than who you are in this exact moment?" she said.

Who would want me as I am right now, on the verge of breaking?

"Not an easy question to answer." He tried to clear his throat, but the muscles were too tight.

"Take your time. And you can be honest."

He could. She was the safest and most dangerous person in the world to him, all at once.

Best to start at the beginning. "When I found Tamara cheating on me, I didn't handle it well."

"By whose definition?" She sounded ready to wield a sword and shield and stand between him and an advancing army. "How is someone supposed to handle such a severe violation of their trust?"

He sighed. "I was taught to compartmentalize. So I did."

"And it didn't work?"

He shook his head.

She made a sympathetic noise and kissed him softly. "I'm sorry that all happened to you."

A breath shuddered from his lungs as he fought the spin back in time. He'd shuffled through his days like an automaton, depending on the routine of the Coast Guard. Pretending to be unaffected, burying how devastating his wife's betrayal had been.

"Eduardo and I were underwater," he choked out. "I should have been laser focused, given the possibility of live munitions and the garbage visibility. But Tamara and I had argued about who was getting to keep the dogs the night before, and I let that through for a fraction of a second. My hand slipped. And then it was just a wall of noise and pain and Ed looking at me like I was a ghost. But I wasn't. And he stayed with me too long. *I* woke up. *He* was the ghost. He paid the price for my mistake."

"Oh, Archer… No…"

"Uh, yeah."

It came out more harshly than he'd wanted. But it was that, or cry. As if he had the right to cry.

She didn't flinch. Just kissed him again. "Are you sure costs and prices are the right way to frame it? I mean—you lost so much."

"Not as much as he did. As his family did."

She enveloped him in a hug.

The comfort fell short.

He couldn't make a similar mistake again. He hadn't needed his VA therapist to identify his survivor's guilt or his unwillingness to properly process his grief.

Trying to love Franci wasn't him finding courage. More like being selfish, asking her to face everything he'd gone through.

The baby let out a cry from the bedroom.

Iris. Would he hurt her, too?

It sucked the breath from his lungs, as if he'd fallen flat on his back with no warning.

Franci stroked his cheek as she unwound her arms and stood. "We're not done here."

"You seem so sure."

"Because I am."

Holy hell. He wanted even a fraction of her deep belief that things would work out. But as much as he didn't want to ruin her Christmas, he didn't even know where to begin to find a way to heal.

Franci fed and dressed Iris in enough layers to handle venturing outside on a morning chilly enough to frost the windows. She was glad for the pause in conversation, for the opportunity to consider what to do next. The look on Archer's face when she'd left the living room had been a fist to the sternum.

Seeing defeat play on his features made her skin feel a size too tight. Itchy, chafing.

She needed to show him hope. To assure him she didn't care if he was fearless. It mattered more that he was willing to face his fears with her.

Once Iris was dry and cooing, Franci headed for the living room and announced, "Let's get some fresh air."

Archer, who was staring out the front window off into the distance, arms crossed over his broad chest, startled. "Outside?"

"Yeah. Boat? Trail? Beach?" She was always in favor of him being at the wheel of his boat—nothing was sexier than him with a casual wrist on top of the wheel and the wind in his thick hair—but she didn't want him to feel trapped, either.

She could see the tradition of this. Spending part of their Christmas out on the water or next to the waves.

He jammed a hand into his hair. "Let's go for a spin past Kettle Beach."

After getting dressed in outdoor gear, they made their way to the dock, with Iris strapped into her yellow life jacket and wearing the little red and white hat Winnie had knit for her. The tiniest of elves.

"So festive," Franci said. Once in the boat, she had Archer take their picture to send around. "Here, get in with us."

He clutched his phone in both hands. "I don't know—"

Her chest ached. "No matter what, it's a good memory, Archer."

He dipped his head for a second and then got in close, stretching his arm out to get all three of them in the frame. He focused on her and Iris more than the phone's camera lens.

They looked like a trio. She wanted that so badly.

She waited until they were out past Buoy Point before getting back to their conversation.

Might as well be blunt about it. "I still don't get why

28 of

your divorce and your accident means we can't be together."

Archer yanked the wheel enough to jerk the boat.

Sitting sideways in the passenger seat, she had to grab the dash to stay stable, clutching Iris to her chest with her other arm. The baby stayed sleeping. At least the change of course didn't bother her.

Archer swore and righted the wheel. "I'm sorry."

"My fault. I surprised you."

He pulled back on the throttle and the boat slowed until they drifted with the tide. He cut the engine. Water slapped the hull, rocking them gently. "You always surprise me, Franci."

"Is that good or bad?" She pulled her knees to her chest.

His smile was wry. "Some days, I'm not sure."

"Ouch."

"No, it's not against you. It's all me. You challenge me. Have me thinking of things and hoping for things I know aren't smart."

Her lip stung.

Because you're biting it, genius.

She released it from between her teeth. "Why?"

"Because you're you."

She didn't know what that meant, but it wasn't what she'd asked. "No, what's not smart?"

He turned to face her, leaning forward and bracing his elbows on his knees. He linked his fingers together and stared at them. "Thinking I could be in any way the partner you need."

She sighed. "There you go again, making guesses at what I need."

"You need someone whole, Francine."

Her jaw ached to drop. She let it, squeaking out, "You mean, physically? Have I not been clear that I lo...like every part of you?"

He palmed his face. "I'm not talking about my leg."

"I'm confused." Her heart ached for him. She scooted to the edge of her seat and took one of his hands. "Is it because you still blame yourself?"

"I always will."

"Quite the life sentence you've self-imposed," she said gently.

"Wouldn't you?"

"I don't know. I wasn't there." She sighed. "I do know it took some talking it out with my own therapist to make sure I didn't feel responsible for the car accident. For my dad's injuries."

He looked up sharply. "It's not the same."

"I know. Survivor's guilt is powerful, though." Throat thick, she swallowed. "One thing. If it was your fault—don't you think the Coast Guard would have made that ruling after their investigation? But they said it was an accident. The way you described it—your hand slipped. That's a pretty human mistake. And your friend's widow didn't seem to blame you."

He narrowed his eyes.

"She was quoted in a few articles," Franci said softly. "That she didn't hold you responsible."

"Because she's too forgiving. But if I hadn't gotten hurt, Eduardo would still be alive."

"Oh, Archer..." She squeezed his hands. "If you don't deal with the guilt, you'll never be able to properly grieve."

He blinked at her.

"Unless you don't *want* to properly grieve." She lifted one of his hands to her lips and kissed the fleshy base of his thumb. So impervious to the cold he didn't even have gloves on, but in no way impervious to the emotions he was clearly trying to hide from.

"I feel…" His breath was as choppy as the waves hitting the fiberglass. "There's something in me I'll never be able to fill."

She pressed a kiss to his other hand. "I just want… *need*…to love you. All of you. The ragged bits, the wounded bits, strong, fragile—all your smarts and your brawn—"

"'Brawn'?" The word shook, a failed attempt at humor.

"Oh, sure, fixate on that part." Caressing his stubbled cheeks, she leaned in and claimed his mouth. She really wanted this mouth to be hers for as long as she was able.

"I was fixating on 'love,'" he choked out, claiming her back for a long, heated moment.

"I always knew I'd have to say it first. I've fallen in love with you. *All* of you."

"I don't know…" His gaze was bereft. Not the reaction she'd hoped for after confessing her feelings.

"I didn't expect you to answer—promise," she said.

The truth. Still, his uncertainty pounced on her like a cougar, claws raking her back, taking her to the ground.

He shook his head rapidly. "No, it's not what you think. *I* need to think. I'm so… Shit, I don't even know if there's a word for it, but…"

She could offer a few—*emotionally broken*, for a start—but wasn't going to do so uninvited. She'd already said too much.

He wasn't the one trapped out on this boat. She was. She glanced back at the shore.

His hand squeezed around hers. "Time to go home?"

"I think so," she said quietly. "I should get out of your hair."

Resignation crossed his face, making it even more haggard. "Today?"

"Yeah. It makes total sense you need to think. But it'll be easier for you to do that if I'm not in your space." Giving him time to figure out where he stood was important. So was guarding her heart while she waited for him to find some clarity. And not her alone—she needed to protect Iris, too. Franci couldn't bring someone into their lives who was afraid to fully connect, fully love.

She'd experienced her mom's inability to connect too often. She would never, ever make choices to bring people into their lives who might treat either of them in a similar way. And Archer had the power to hurt them by pushing them away, even if he didn't intend to.

Her heart ached, acknowledging the possibility. She loved him, and wanted to keep loving him. Desperately wanted him to love her back, and Iris, too. But if he couldn't…

Well, space was necessary.

"Now who's making assumptions about who needs what?" he said, finally breaking the silence.

"You're right." Her stomach was heavy. "But trust me—my friendship isn't going anywhere. You need to talk, call. You need company for a walk, I'll be there. Need a dive buddy, I'll be on the dock. But not intimacy or partnership. Not while you're in flux. And for now, that means heading back to my own house before the finishing touches are in place."

"On Christmas?"

"Especially today. It's all about family." She gave him a watery smile. "Mine will have me packed in an hour if I call them."

"No. If it's really what you want, we can load your car and mine. I'll help you." He squeezed her hand. "But your basement's still a work zone."

"Good thing I live upstairs." She sighed. "I want to support you, Archer. You deserve time to work through your feelings. To figure out if you're willing to be loved, emotional scars and all. Because I will. And I can. I'm strong like that—promise. You don't need to be 'whole' to deserve and receive love. But you do need to be *willing* to receive it to have any chance of a successful relationship, and you're not right now."

Something flared in his eyes. Not hope, not love. But determination. "I will figure it out, Francine. I promise."

Chapter Sixteen

Two days after Christmas, Archer sat in his wheelchair behind the lower half of the Otter Marine counter and cursed the pit in his gut. Sticky, tar-like guilt coated the sides. He'd told Franci he was going to find some answer, but all he'd done was stare at the ocean—or through the water on the dives he went on yesterday—and come up with jack.

Sam strolled in from the office. "I'm thinking of asking Franci if she's interested in taking over the management of the shop full-time."

Thank Christ he was sitting, because all the microchip technology in the world wouldn't have kept him balanced had Sam dropped that while Archer was standing.

"Uh, what?" Not that Sam would have doubted Franci's capabilities, but that he'd want to let go of control like that.

"Do you think she'd go for it?" Sam asked, clearly assuming Archer's question was rhetorical. "Kellan and

I are going to be busier than I thought with Forest + Brine. And if Franci's salaried as a manager, it'll mean financial stability for her. I want to give her more security."

Archer's chest ached. He wanted to give her stability, security, too. More than that, he wanted to bring joy into her life. Both moments of brilliant excitement and understated connection. And the fact he was struggling to get his crap together had kept him awake at night since the minute she left with her suitcases and all Iris's gear. With Iris, too. He'd been so damn empty the past couple of days. No Franci laughs. No baby snuggles. Him and his dog, alone like he thought he'd be.

He'd had a fraction of the possibility of life with Franci, and the memory of it needled him.

Desperate for something to center himself, Archer gripped the hand rims on his chair. "Since when are you good with letting go of control?"

Sam laughed. "Since when are you one to talk?"

Archer frowned at his friend.

"Look," Sam said. "I'm intending to make this change, but I wanted to give you the heads-up. I know something's been going on between the two of you. Do you think that'll get in the way of the two of you working together?"

He shook his head.

Sam rested his elbows on the taller half of the counter. "What happened, Archer?"

"She made me see…" *That I want to love her. That I don't want to live the way I've been living since I came home.* He groaned.

Sam's gaze was knowing. "Yeah, she's got a certain

something about her. I've waited for her to find the one who finally saw how special she is. Who can direct some of it back at her. Never thought it would be you, but I'm not mad it is."

"Except I'm not!" The back of his neck was hot enough to light tinder.

"Sure you are. If you put the work in, anyway." Sam's mouth pinched. "She hasn't been herself since she left your place, though. She's missing her smile."

"You all focus too much on her being happy."

"You don't think she should be happy?" Sam said disbelievingly.

"As much as anyone can be, of course, but I don't think she should be pressured to fake it. Or to think she needs to make the rest of you happy."

His thoughts kept looping back to her talking about the accident she'd been in with her dad, and how quick he'd been to slough off her experience because it hadn't been the same type of loss.

But really, it was more similar than he'd given it credit. *What* they'd lost hadn't been the same, but the lack of control over the outcome was.

She'd accepted the uncertainty. Did he need to do the same?

"I have to get *me* back," he said. "Or to figure out who I am now, before I can be there for her. But what that looks like…?"

Sam tore a corner off a dive apparel catalog and scribbled a number on it. "Contact info for the counselor who helped me figure out my own issues before I could go chase Kellan down under."

He nodded. His friend had managed to address his

problems from his own divorce to be able to commit
to Kellan, and Archer would always be proud of him.
The trip Sam had taken to meet Kellan halfway around
the world and prove his love was just icing on their relationship cake.

"I've got a therapist." Lifting the next words from
him took as much effort as deadlifting his own body
weight. "I'm not sure he's got the tools to fix what's
inside me."

Or, more to the point, what *wasn't*.

Sam eyed him thoughtfully. "You literally learned
how to walk again, man."

"And?"

"You don't think the tools exist to help you find your
emotional balance, too?" Sam crossed his arms. "Because my sister's worth trying."

Archer nodded. "She is."

He picked up the phone and made the call.

Franci stumbled through the door of Hideaway
Bakery, checking the time on her phone one last time.
Eighteen minutes late. Not terrible, considering how
unhappy Iris had been with everything they'd needed
to do to get ready to come into town. So much squawk-
ing on the heels of a long night. Four wake ups? Five?
Somewhere around there. Of course, Iris was now sleeping soundly in her car seat, and Franci was left to get
through the morning when all she wanted to do was
go back to bed. Around three o'clock, she'd been close
to texting Archer for some sort of support, but she'd
stopped herself. They both needed the distance.

She took a deep breath of sugar-laden air. The

warmth of Rachel and Winnie's storefront never failed to feel like a hug.

Perfect timing, since Franci desperately missed being held by a certain pair of strong, tattooed arms.

She scanned the space, looking for her mom, but came up empty. *Seriously? Again?*

She reminded herself not to make assumptions. She was late herself. Surely her mom was on her way.

Maneuvering the stroller into the line, she decided on her order. When she got to the till, she added on her mom's usual sugar-free vanilla latte with almond milk.

"How are you, honey?" Rachel asked. She looked harried but happy, a blur of Fair Isle knit and a messy gray-blond bun as she served her customers. But, as always, she slowed to talk to Franci. She really looked at a person, really listened. Something Franci didn't expect to fully get from her mom today—she never did—and she always had to gird herself to prevent it from hurting.

"I'm okay. Thirsty," Franci said jokingly.

And lonely.

Not joking there.

"I thought I'd come to town for some company, and to give the work crew a wide berth since they're doing drywall today," she continued.

Rachel made a face and put a cookie in a paper bag and handed it to Franci. "So sorry the work's delayed. Cookies are on the house until it's done."

"No need." But she took the cookie anyway, because only a fool passed on Winnie's salad-plate-sized chocolate-chip creations.

"For a bit there, we thought you weren't planning on moving out of Archer's." Rachel's eyes glinted.

"He was more than generous."

"Mmm, yes. 'Generous.'"

Franci lifted an eyebrow.

"She means 'in love with you,'" Winnie added from her post at the elaborate espresso maker.

"We were going to be subtle," Rachel hissed at her wife, coming around the counter to coo at the sleeping baby.

Franci lost her hold on her smile. "You don't need to 'be' anything."

Archer did all the things he put his mind to. But he'd focused on not falling in love for so long, she didn't know if he could change.

I just need to have faith in him.

Her belief was small. Kind of battered. But still there.

She wheeled the stroller over to a table, put her cookie down and went back to retrieve the coffees she'd ordered for her and her mom.

This time, unlike the last attempt at a coffee date, her mom bustled in. "Thanks for your patience, Francine. You know how it is."

"Do I?"

Alina peered into the car seat. "Sound asleep."

Usually, nap time was precious, but Iris got so little time with her grandma. This was only their third visit.

"You can take her out," Franci said.

"I don't want to wake her."

"She'll be fine."

Her mom toyed with the strap of her purse. "No, I'm good."

Pressure built in Franci's stomach. "You don't want to hold her?"

"Francine."

"What? You're her grandma. I would have thought you'd want a snuggle."

Alina made a face. "I guess I'm not feeling much like a grandma yet. I'm still raising my own kids."

"You can't do both? Dad manages with Char—"

"Oh, of course. Always making this about your father. A college student is *not* the same as two tween boys."

"Sure, but…" The pressure grew to a full-on twist. "Your choice sucks."

Her mom frowned. "Why are you being so selfish?"

"I'm sor—" Her knee-jerk response was to apologize, but…*no*. No flipping way was she accepting responsibility for her mom's awful perspective. "I'm *not* being selfish. It's completely reasonable for me to think you might be pleased to have a granddaughter to love."

Even though Franci didn't need to apologize to her mom, she could cop to having hoped for something she should have known wouldn't happen.

"I was expecting you to know how I felt," her mom said, making a prim face and sipping from the coffee Franci had ordered for her. "Becoming a mom surprised you—why wouldn't it surprise me, too?"

"Sure, it surprised me. But I was still excited. Still am, despite the hard days."

Lifting a shoulder, her mom said, "You're being silly. I can't help my reaction. You put me in a hard place."

The message was a gut punch. No different than some of the things thrown at her over the years.

Chin up, Franci. People like a girl who enters a room with a smile.

Or, *What do* you *have to cry about?*
You're upset? What about me?

Franci should have anticipated this. Nothing about
her mom's recent behavior should have given Franci
the idea she'd change for Iris. Really, she needed to expect the same from Archer, too. He'd never shown her
otherwise. Why would she expect him to be different?
She needed to stop fooling herself. She couldn't smile
this one into existence.

He never asks that of me.

True. He didn't. One of the best things about Archer
was she didn't have to force her feelings. He might not
want to access his own dark places, but he wasn't in-
timidated by her own.

Unlike her mom. Alina might never be okay with
being a grandma, as was her right, but her asking Franci
to be okay with that was awful.

And Franci couldn't put her own daughter in a situation where she'd have to wade through mountains of BS.

She stood. "I'm going to make peace with your feelings, but I'll never agree with them. If you're putting
limits on your relationship with Iris like you have on
your relationship with Charlotte and me, I'm going to
create some boundaries. I won't let you hurt my daughter like you have us. She'll already have to deal with
having an absent father. She doesn't need one more
person to hold back on her." She glanced at the pair of
women behind the counter, always willing to support
her and love her. "Good thing family doesn't have to
be limited to blood."

Leaving her coffee untouched, she pulled the hood

of the stroller as low as she could get it and pushed it out to the boardwalk side of the building.

Banners decorated with local sea creatures buffeted in the wind. The fabric flapped like luffing sails, as if she'd made the wrong turn at the helm and was at the wrong angle to catch the wind.

Tears stung her eyes. More than anything, she needed a hug. The *Oyster Queen*'s slip was empty. She couldn't remember if her brother had been on the schedule for today's dive. Or he might be out on the Zodiac with Kellan and one of the foraging tours. Worth checking his office, though. She took the ramp at the back, then knocked.

Archer answered.

A few day's beard growth darkened his jaw. His blue eyes were as stormy as the threatening clouds on the horizon.

Looking at him made her chest ache.

"Aren't you diving today?" she blurted.

"Had an appointment. Switched with Sam." His brows furrowed. "What's wrong?"

She wanted to pretend it was nothing but couldn't. "My mom…"

"Christ, what did she do now?" Archer opened his arms wide.

So much for distance. This was the only place she could imagine being right now. She flipped the brake on the stroller and nestled in his embrace, taking some of his strength. The stinging in her eyes shifted to tears.

Tears to messy crying.

"Hey," he said, stroking her back for what must have been minutes. "Shh."

"I'm sorry," she said, words muffled by the thick

fleece of his sweatshirt. Damp splotches marked the gray fabric.

He cupped a hand under her chin and brushed a tear away with his thumb. "Why are you apologizing?"

A complicated answer. "You have enough to worry about."

"I do. Got a bit of it out at my counseling appointment this morning. But I have space to listen, too."

"You're right," she said. "I shouldn't apologize. I need to cry."

He wrapped his arms around her again, holding her even tighter this time. "What are you feeling?"

"Sad. I wish my mom wasn't so self-absorbed. She's going to miss out on Iris if she doesn't change. A mistake. But we can't stop people from making mistakes, right? Not even by trying to be exactly who we think they want us to be."

Admitting the truth just made her cry harder.

It took a few minutes for her to get her breath back.

He tilted her face up with a finger. His eyes were so somber, the saddest.

"Which is why it's good you put a healthy boundary between us," he said. "I know you're not trying to be someone who you think I need."

"I *want* to be someone you need." She tugged her lips between her teeth, trying to figure out how to word things right. "But it's different with you, Archer. You've always taken me as I am."

One of the reasons it hurt so damn much when he wasn't willing to trust her.

Unless... "It's about trusting yourself, isn't it?"

He stroked her hair away from her face. Something

infinite swirled in his eyes. "You need a partner who can match your strength."

He thought he wasn't strong? Had he not been watching himself his whole life like she had?

Maybe he hasn't.

"Well, I'm willing to be strong when you can't be. And I know you'd do the same for me."

"You have more faith in me than I do."

"I know." She caressed his cheek and smiled. "But you went to a counselor today. Proves you don't *actually* think you're incapable of progress. I hope it brought you some peace."

"Not yet," he grumbled. "More made me realize how much work I have to do."

"Still, I see you doing it."

"Yes. For me." He stepped back. "And for you."

Chapter Seventeen

A few hours later, Archer was doing the day's cash-out, still contemplating the look on Franci's face when she'd left him earlier. Almost pleased. Not quite, though. Usually, he could read her like a book, but not today.

She tied him in knots big enough to secure the *Queen* to the dock.

And as he'd explained to his therapist earlier today, he never wanted to untangle himself from Franci Walker. Not if there was a way for him to be a safe space for her, too.

His therapist had cautioned him about the ebbs and flows of grief, but had pointed out how millions of people managed to move on, to make a good life after tragedy.

Optimism, at least.

The bell jingled at the front door, and Kellan strolled in, his curly hair windblown and his cheeks reddened.

Sam's fiancé was friendly as anything, but right now he looked like a man on a mission.

"No *Queen* yet? Thought they'd be back by now." Kellan's words were a little more accented than usual.

"Trip's delayed," Archer said.

Concern crossed the Irishman's face.

"Nothing serious," Archer assured him quickly. "One of the clients had an equipment issue, so they got a late start. They'll be in any minute."

"Better be. It's almost dark."

"You know Sam. He doesn't take chances."

Kellan smiled. "Except on me."

"Scariest chance of all," he muttered.

Damn. Shouldn't have let that out.

"I think you and I are the opposite, Archer," Kellan said. "Diving—not Sam—scared me. Unless you *were* scared of the water, and worked past it?"

He assumed Kellan was talking about diving after his amputation. Sometimes people asked, sometimes they didn't. But today, still feeling raw from the conversation with the counselor, he didn't feel like explaining how he felt most comfortable underwater.

"Sam's still so proud of you for passing the dive course," Archer said.

Unbidden, his mind shifted to Daniel and his upcoming licensing test.

Glancing at the ceiling, he counted ceiling tiles instead of picturing Daniel suited up, grinning like Eddy had every time he'd had the chance to dive.

"The test was hard," Kellan said.

"I bet." The man had overcome his fear of the ocean

to check diving off his sister's bucket list, which had included a variety of climbs and dives all over the world.

"Sam made it easier," Kellan added.

For a second it made him think of Franci. Facing all the frightening things out there was easier when he had her support. It wasn't exactly the same, though. Sam and Kellan's relationship hadn't been contingent on Kellan learning how to dive. Had Kellan failed, the two still could have found a way to be together. If Archer failed, there would be no way to be with Franci.

"Sam's solid," Archer said. "I thought I was, too. Except…" *Christ.* Exactly where he *hadn't* wanted to go. "Ignore that. Unrelated."

"Is it?" Kellan's gaze was knowing. "You seem like one of the more solid people I know. Sam sure depends on you."

Not the way Franci would need to.

"Going through a big loss can make us hesitant, like," the other man said cautiously.

"That's one way to put it," he mumbled.

"Sure, and if you need to talk…"

He cleared his throat. His counselor had encouraged him to admit his feelings in safe spaces, and Kellan counted as safe. But still, putting his own inadequacies into words was damn hard. "How long did it take you to feel like yourself after your sister died?"

"Like myself?" Kellan snorted, seemingly laughing at himself. "I still don't. I take it you don't, either? Losing your friend?"

Archer stared at him. "Heard about that, did you?"

Kellan flushed. "Sam explained what happened, once. I hope that was okay."

"Saves me from having to tell it," he said. "And no, I don't feel like myself."

"Did you expect to?"

"I didn't know what to expect." And unwilling to face the uncertainty, he'd blocked off all his feelings instead of sorting them out.

"Everyone's different, but I found it wasn't just grieving my sister. Parts of me… Aoife took them with her. I doubt I'll ever get them back." Kellan winced, and his gaze dipped to Archer's knees, the metal of his prosthesis exposed by the shorts and custom-hemmed leggings he tended to wear at work. "Figurative parts. Insensitive metaphor. Apologies."

Archer waved it off. "Focusing on how I was missing a literal part of me was easier than wading through feelings. Concrete goals, you know? Manage pain. Find the right tech. Learn it. Run. Swim. Dive."

Escape.

"And grieving requires a whole lot of sitting with something." Sympathy bled into Kellan's tone.

"Yeah, I'm no good at that."

"Not something for which anyone's handing out medals."

"Not for me. Eduardo got one." *Posthumously.*

Kellan's mouth gaped.

Way to slaughter a mood, Frost.

"I get what you mean, though," he said.

"Maybe I'm clueless, not having military service," Kellan offered. "Everything I said might be the opposite of what you needed to hear."

Archer gripped the counter. "Loss is loss."

But a civilian might have a tough time understanding the sense of responsibility, of being the team lead and not only losing one of the people under his command, but having planned the mission that led to the loss. Kellan seemed to get the divide.

Seemed to get a lot of things.

"Feel free not to answer, but…those parts of you that slipped away when your sister passed—" Archer took a deep breath "—doesn't it feel wrong to be with someone when you feel like something's missing? I don't know how to ask Fr—*someone* to fill the gaps I don't know how to fill myself."

"So don't," Kellan said gently.

"You found Sam, though."

"Yeah. But only because he loved me as is." Kellan winced. "You want to get figurative? The hollowness is still there. I've just added to my life enough that I don't have to spend so much time with my grief. A lot of which has to do with wanting to be with Sam."

Archer blinked. Franci had said something similar— she'd fallen in love with everything about him, even the shattered parts of him.

"I need to take a page from your book," he said to Kellan.

Kellan shot him a puzzled look. "Have you developed a phobia like I did?"

"No." Though he'd sure as hell been struggling with an aversion to the thought of being underwater with his godson. "I've been putting something off, though."

He needed to see if he could face his worst moments before he took on love.

Once he was home that night, kicked back in his painfully empty living room with only his dog for company, he picked up his phone. His leg was throbbing worse than it had in a while, as if the phantom pain wanted to remind him he'd be hurting until he faced the sludge in his gut.

Rubbing the muscle above his socket, he pressed Clara's number.

She answered on the second ring. "*You're* calling *me*. Finally."

"I've been avoiding you," he admitted.

"I noticed."

"I'm sorry."

"Thank you." Her voice was softer than usual. "I'm sorry you felt you needed to."

He dug his fingers into Honu's scruffy neck, searching for courage. "Well, you've always been more forgiving than I deserved."

"I know you feel that way."

He sighed. "I'm working on it."

"Good. Finally. It keeps me up at night." She coughed. "Well, that and Dan safely passing his diving tests."

"Has watching him dive been hard?" He bet the kid was good. Eduardo had been a veritable dolphin underwater.

"Yeah," she said softly. "But necessary."

A lump filled his throat. "Proud of him. He's like Ed, through and through."

"Yeah, he is. Generous. Funny. Smart, but daring enough to keep me on my toes."

The last glimpse he'd had of his friend's face flashed across his vision. He'd been nearly blinded by pain, and still stuck under the crumbled wall, his ears ringing from the unexpected blast. Eduardo had been right there. So brave, he'd compromised his own safety to rescue Archer.

"Smart and daring." Archer let out a dry laugh and dropped his head back on the couch cushion. "Maybe it'd be better if he didn't have those particular traits. If Eddy'd had any sense of self-preservation, he would have left me and surfaced earlier. He'd still be here."

"And you're insulting him by suggesting he'd leave you behind."

The breath whooshed from his lungs. "Shit, Clara…"

"You know it's true. And you would have done the same thing had you been in his shoes. Dry suit. Whatever." She cleared her throat, a sharp cough on the other end of the connection. "He couldn't have lived with himself if he picked his own survival over you."

They'd had this argument before, but it was landing a little differently this time.

"You deserve to have him around," he said, his voice cracking around his regret. "So does Danny."

"Archer, you can't play that game." Clara sounded like she was fighting tears herself. Damn it, he hadn't wanted to upset her. She sniffled. "He knew he'd been under too long. He stayed anyway. And I need to honor his choice. And also, accepting fate. I don't believe Eduardo's death was meant to be or anything. But his heart attack was no one's fault. It could have happened after any of your dives. Awful things happen sometimes, and I've learned I'm strong enough to deal with them. I need to instill some sort of hope in my son, after all."

She was strong, for sure. Willing to stay optimistic, to see the possibilities even after life dished out a tragedy.

"You got any New Year's plans this weekend?" he asked.

"Nope. And school's not back in until Tuesday."

He ran a hand down his face. He knew what he needed to do next, and it took everything he had not to disconnect the call. "Want to come visit?"

"Yes," she said. "Feel up for testing my son?"

"No," he said honestly. "But I'll do it anyway."

He'd need a boat assistant.

Only one person would do.

Franci stared at Archer's text. She didn't know what to make of it.

Taking a friend of mine out for a few dives on the 1st and 2nd. Will you be my assistant?

The invitation had arrived as she was getting Iris into the crib for what would hopefully be a four- or five-hour stretch of sleep. She stared at her wide-eyed baby and laughed at her own sleep-deprived naivety.

"You're not the least bit tired, are you, night owl?"

Iris gurgled and kicked out of her swaddle. Her arms flailed, and she looked at her hands as if she were half amazed and half annoyed. She smacked her lips and sucked on her fist.

Franci shook her head. "Still hungry?"

Another gurgle.

Capitulating, she carefully lifted her cozily bundled daughter from the mattress and took her over to the gliding chair in the corner of the cheery yellow room. "He painted these walls for you, you know. Put your bed together, too. And your shelf."

Iris looked unimpressed.

"And he's been on my mind ever since."

Sighing, she got her daughter to latch on. Those dark eyes closed a half a second later as Iris suckled greedily.

Franci slid her phone from the pocket of her sweats and examined Archer's text again.

They hadn't gone diving together since before Iris was born. He knew she hadn't gone underwater since the birth, too. So why now? She typed out a quick message.

This sounds important

It is

His short response seemed significant.

She'd told him they'd still support each other as friends, even though the thought of being out on the boat with him, seeing his eyes glint with excitement right before they put their masks on and descended below the waves, made her throat tighten and dry out.

Iris, naturally, only replied with happy don't-even-try-to-disturb-my-meal lips.

Then I'll be there, Franci typed. Before she could second-guess her gut reaction, she pressed Send.

"I don't know what he's getting at, jellybean," she said, stroking her daughter's petal-soft cheek, "but something tells me I should be there."

Of course, she couldn't impulsively do anything anymore, not with the precious girl in her arms, peaceful and trusting as she drooped into sleep. This would take some planning.

The next day, she begged Charlotte and their dad to take Iris. It was a big chunk of time to be away from her still-so-new daughter, but Archer was well aware of that, and had still asked. He wouldn't have if he didn't actually need her there. Thankfully, her family was only too willing to lend a hand so she could do the same for the man she loved.

Early on the first, after a quiet night playing the New Year's Eve fifth wheel to Violet and Kim and Kellan and Sam, she made her way along the dock. Archer had invited her to come over to his place to watch the ball drop—apparently his friends were visiting for the weekend—but it hadn't felt right to crash their party by bringing an infant.

Being out now without Iris was odd.

She clutched the handles of her dive bag—Archer hadn't been clear if she'd need her gear, but she wanted to be prepared—and reminded herself to enjoy the time when she could just be Franci for a few moments instead of Iris's mom.

The creaking rafts and clunking hulls soothed like a heartbeat. An eagle perched in the giant nest out on the breakwater, peering at her.

"Go be judgy with someone else," she told it as she approached the boat. "You try getting ready on time when you're trying to collect equipment you haven't used in ten months at the same time a tiny dictator is screaming for something, but they don't know what that thing is."

She'd tried everything. Breastfeeding, diaper, swing, nap... Iris had still been squalling when Charlotte and Dad had arrived for their babysitting date. She'd felt like pretty much the worst mom in the world, until Dad had told a story about Sam falling off the change table when he was five months old, and assured her he and Charlotte would walk Iris up and down the driveway until she stopped crying.

She'd already gotten a text reassuring her that Iris had only taken ten minutes to fall asleep, at least.

The eagle let out a screech.

"Oh, as if you don't fly off and desert your eaglets on a daily basis," she said, dropping her dive bag on the dock. "This is not the same thing."

Archer's head poked out from inside the bimini.

He was wearing the cobalt blue beanie from day four of the Advent calendar, the one she'd figured would bring out the color of his eyes.

It did.

And he clearly liked it. Her heart went a little mushy.

"Were you talking to me?" he asked.

"No, to that stupid eagle. She's always judging my life choices."

He shaded his eyes against the winter sun and chuck-led. "She's the worst."

She peered into the boat. "Are your weekend guests not joining us for the dive? Unless it was a ruse. You don't need to invent an excuse if you want to hang out as friends, Archer."

"I don't want to hang out as friends," he bit out.

She recoiled. "Oh."

"You know what I mean." He took off his hat and scrubbed a hand through his hair. "Trying to get to being...to being together. While making sure you don't get hurt."

"Except I don't know what you mean," she said softly. "Supporting you while you try to heal *doesn't* hurt me."

"Which you're able to see more clearly than I am. I'm hoping today's going to help me find that clarity." He cleared his throat. "Ah, there they are."

A gorgeous woman in a puffer coat descended the ramp, followed by a tall, lanky teenage guy. She was white with pale blond hair mostly tucked into a slouchy hat. She pulled a cooler by its extendable handle. The teen had the hood of his sweatshirt pulled up. He carried a dry suit. Excitement radiated from his light brown face.

She whirled on Archer. He'd spent New Year's Eve with a beautiful woman? Sure, he'd invited Franci to join them. *Still.* Unwelcome jealousy dug its nails in deep.

"Your friend is awfully pretty."

"My friend is awfully widowed," he said quietly.

Which made her single. What was this?

The closer the woman got to them, the more familiar she looked. *Oh, my God.* She'd seen these people in a picture Archer had on the shelf in his living room. Franci's hands flew to her mouth. "Your godson," she said, words muffled by her gloved fingers. "And his *mom.* Your Coastie friend's family."

"The very one."

"And you want me to dive with him?"

"No. Just to be here. For me." He put a hand on her shoulder. His eyes pleaded with her. "If you're okay with that."

Archer's strange behavior, his emphasis on this being important… Everything fell into place. And she felt so, so guilty for her initial jealousy. "You're doing his test for him."

"Yeah," he croaked, gaze fixed on the newcomers.

The second the teen got to the dock, Archer's vulnerability vanished behind a mask of joviality. The trio was all hugs from the woman and shoulder slaps for the teen. Archer slung an elbow around the kid's neck and pushed off his hood, mussing the dark curls with his palm.

The teen soaked it in, squeezing Archer in a bear hug.

Franci straightened, ready to be there for Archer like he'd asked. If he was willing to face diving with his godson, what might he be willing to face with her?

Maybe love.

Maybe even forever.

Chapter Eighteen

Four dives. A checklist of tasks. Archer had done this hundreds of times since his accident.

He wasn't going to fool himself into believing it would be the same. From the choppy boat ride out past Kettle Beach to anchoring to the buoy to getting into their dry suits, Archer could feel the weight of Eduardo on his shoulders.

Franci read him to the letter, being all the places where he needed her. He could chalk it up to years of working together, but he had a feeling the familiarity came more from the time they'd spent together since Iris's birth. She knew him. Found a million seamless, wordless ways to prove she understood him.

Having her in the captain's chair, chatting with Clara while he checked equipment and ran Daniel through the predive procedures, gave him the extra courage he needed to zip into his dry suit.

Daniel looked as much like his mom as his dad, but his stance was identical to Eduardo's, especially with the teen dressed in dive gear and strapped into his tank and buoyancy compensator.

Daniel's gaze locked on Archer's prosthesis, exposed below the seal and shortened leg of his bespoke dry suit. "I looked it up online and I saw a dive leg with a fin instead of a foot."

"Yeah, that works for some people. My prosthetist offered me one, with a built-in sheath for a dive knife, which was pretty sweet. But I like to be able to stand the second I get in the boat." He lifted the waterproof foot sporting a standard fin. "Once I fix the knee at the right angle, I get decent propulsion. Franci can vouch for me."

"'Decent'?" she said dryly. "He's a bullet. You couldn't be in better hands."

Tell that to Eduardo.

"No," he muttered to himself, stopping the thought before it could take hold.

The other three stared at him.

His cheeks heated despite the chill of the January wind. "I mean, no, stop it. No need to boost my ego."

Lifting his chin, he fell back on his training, taking Daniel through an overview of the skills they would focus on for the first dive.

Clara put a fist to her mouth, her watery gaze locked on her son.

The only thing Archer could do, besides do his damnedest to keep the kid safe, was comfort her. He held his arms out.

She let him hug her for a minute and then stepped

back. "I'm being silly. There are just some days I realize how much he's grown."

"Given he and I are eye to eye now? A lot."

Daniel rolled his eyes. "Chill with the nostalgia,
Mom."

"As if moms have *any* chill," she said. "One day,
you'll have kids of your own and you'll understand."

Archer's throat tightened. Daniel with kids?

Yet another thing Eddy would miss.

His limbs buzzed with the urge to rip off his tank
and pitch it into the water, or maybe do some serious
damage to the bimini.

He clenched his jaw for a second, then relaxed it.
One last glance at Franci, who mouthed, *You've got this.*

He did. "Let's get in the water."

"Yes, please," Daniel said. His smile was bright
enough to light the entirety of the bay where they'd
anchored.

The kid's happiness didn't diminish while they were
underwater, either. Through all the tasks, his gaze shone
behind his mask. He was a natural below the surface.
Smooth movements, confident breathing. Not to mention a heck of a sense of curiosity. Patient, too. He was
willing to wait calmly for the resident pair of wolf eels
to emerge from their den. When the craggy-looking
heads popped out, looking like a cross between a rock
and a troll face, Daniel jolted.

Archer didn't blame him. One of the animals, a
youth, was a vibrant orange, which was startling even
at the depth where the color came out more muted.
Archer grabbed the small flashlight he'd opened from
his Jan-vent calendar this morning. One more perfect

little present to add to the proof his heart belonged to Franci, no matter how hard he'd tried to resist letting that happen.

After flicking the switch, he aimed the beam above the den and slowly lowered it, hoping not to disturb the fish. The light brought out the vivid reds, oranges and yellows that would otherwise be lost to the depth of the water.

Awe brightened Daniel's expression, even through his mask. His gaze drifted down the rock face covered with wispy anemones and then locked on the grumpy-faced animals.

Archer grinned and shot him an okay sign, relaxing a little when his godson returned the message.

Too soon they had to surface. Archer could have stayed under all day. Not unusual, but this was special.

Their heads broke the surface, and Daniel let out a shout of happiness, followed by a joyful curse.

"Oh, sorry, Mom!" he said.

The adults laughed, Clara included.

Both the profanity and the contrition were 100 percent Ed.

Archer ripped his mask off and dunked his face in the frigid water. Maybe the cold would shock away his tears.

He wiped away the water with his gloved hand. They kept rolling, scalding his ocean-chilled skin.

Hell no. He did not want to fall apart like this.

Once Daniel was out of the water and recounting everything he'd seen to his mom at a mile a minute, Archer stood at the stern, back to his friends.

His *family.*

Unbidden tears streamed down his face. He wanted to take off his tank and buoyancy compensator, but his hands were shaking too hard.

"Hey," Franci whispered, scooting between him and the stern rail. "Need an assist with those buckles?"

"I'm fine," he croaked.

She took off one of her gloves and brushed away some of his tears. "You don't have to be fine."

"What right do I have to put my sadness on Clara and Danny?" The words shuddered from him. "Diving with the kid was a privilege, and I—"

She unfastened the straps, freeing him from the burden of his tank.

But the weight of grief and guilt threatened to drive him to the stainless steel decking.

"Why do I get to experience that privilege instead of Ed?" His chest heaved as the words forced themselves out.

"Hey," she said. She pulled him toward one of the side benches and made him sit, and then coaxed him into a hug.

He buried his face into the crook of her neck.

A keening sound split the air.

A bird?

No. Me.

He had to control himself.

A large hand landed on his shoulder and squeezed.

Daniel. Goddamn it. The comfort was supposed to go the other way. But the only thing Archer could do was cling to Franci and try to breathe.

"One, two, three…" she murmured, then took the count all the way to ten before reversing. He focused on her voice. The familiar, gentle tone was more soothing than the easy waves rocking the boat from side to side.

"Sometimes you gotta cry, man," Daniel said.

He didn't want to. His body had other opinions.

Years of strain pulled him from side to side, painful punches. He held on to Franci, knowing if he let go, he might slide off the bench.

Daniel's hand stayed firm on his shoulder.

Clara added hers.

His head sloshed like prop wash.

Who knew how long he sat there, but they kept him upright.

When he finally got a hold of himself, he straightened, wiping his eyes with the back of his hand. He was trying to gather his thoughts, trying to apologize, when Daniel cleared his throat.

"Thanks," Daniel said, voice serious.

Archer fixed his godson with a look. "For having a damn breakdown?"

Daniel sat next to him. "Well, yeah. It's easier to deal with my own feelings when I know the guys in my life have them, too."

He put an arm around the kid's shoulders. Franci stood and motioned for Clara to sit. She busied herself with the equipment, letting the three of them be together. Cry some more. Hug. Laugh at how much they were crying.

"The boat's never been this soggy," Archer joked, holding Clara and Daniel tighter.

"We asked too much of you," Clara said.

"I get it if you can't go on more dives," Daniel said.

"No. You need to finish."

"I can step in if you need," Franci said quietly. Her gaze was serious. "Complete the assessment."

He would have accepted the offer if it was necessary. "I can do it."

What have I done to deserve them all?

Clara glanced at him.

Ah, that had been his outside voice.

"Everyone deserves love, Archer," Clara said.

"Dad would have been so pissed at us if we deserted you," Daniel added. "He loved you. Called you his brother."

And I lost him.

A thought he managed to keep inside, thankfully.

Daniel narrowed his eyes. "You think it's your fault, don't you?"

Coming out of his godson's mouth, the belief was hard for Archer to defend.

He lifted a shoulder.

"Must feel awful." Daniel hugged him. "And Mom's told you a hundred times it wasn't. I heard her. But damn."

"I don't know how to let go."

"By doing this more often. Diving. Talking," the kid said.

Archer's throat muscles still gripped too tight, but the tears were gone, at least. "How'd you get so wise?"

"Mom. Dad. You." Daniel cleared his throat. "It hurts to talk about Dad sometimes. Or even to do something he loved so much, like diving. But it's worth it. To feel close to who he was, and to discover new things about all the stuff he loved. To remember the past."

"Facing the pain is worth it to find the pleasure," Archer murmured. "You're brave."

"So are you."

"I haven't been."

"You can only deal with so much at once," Franci said.

He looked at her sharply.

"Seriously. It's okay to manage one thing at a time."

"Maybe it's time to take on a new thing, though," Archer said. *Time to face my feelings every day.*

"That's why I wanted to learn how to dive," Daniel said. "I didn't want to be afraid of it. You've been a badass your whole life. I figured if you were able to get in the water again after what happened to you and Dad, then it was something I needed to try. And damn, I'm glad I did. It's *incredible* down there. When do I get to do my second dive?"

Archer cracked a smile. "You do the math, kid. It's part of your test."

Daniel yanked his dive chart from his backpack and busied himself with calculations.

Archer itched to get under the water again and complete another dive with his godson. He also wanted to be alone with Franci. She was being supportive, but the protective layer she was keeping between them rasped at him.

A few hours later, they were on the docks, cleaning up.

She checked her phone and gasped. "I need to go. Can you finish this?"

He paused. "Yeah, but is something the matter?"

She rushed off without answering.

Staring at her retreating to the parking lot; he shook his head. He wanted her to rely on him.

He had the boat clean and was about to go figure out where on earth she'd run off to when Clara caught his arm.

"Can we talk for a second?" She crossed her arms over her chest, looking uncomfortable.

Instinct tugged at him to follow a certain head of red hair, but couldn't exactly say no. "What's up?"

"So you think Dan could do the instructor course like he wants to?"

"Yeah, the kid's a natural." Daniel had come out of the water after his second dive crowing about wanting to learn how to be an instructor.

It would mean a hell of a lot of hours logged, but Archer had no doubt his godson could do it. He glanced to the boardwalk where Daniel was steering the power wagon with their tanks.

"What if…"

He waited for her to get her words straight.

"Today was hard on you," she finished.

"What if today was hard on me?"

"No." She chuckled. "Today *was* hard on you. And I don't want to make it worse. But Dan and I need a fresh start."

"Yeah? Where?" *Oh. Oh, wow.* He ran his fingers through his damp hair. "Uh, here?"

Her mouth twisted into a grimace. "Is it a terrible idea?"

"No. *No.* I mean, no, it's not a terrible idea, and yes, come here. Because it wouldn't make things worse. Maybe it would help, even. And I'd be a fool to pass up seeing Danny fall in love with diving for the sake of protecting myself."

She grinned and threw her arms around him. "Really?"

"Yup. I'll help you find a place to stay."

"We're thinking temporary. For the summer. Dan will be off at college in the fall, anyway."

He cocked a brow but didn't challenge her claim of a short stay. She'd find out. Once a person settled their feet on Oyster Island for any length of time, they decided they wanted to stay. Clara wasn't going to find who she was again. But she could discover a new path, and he loved the thought of her doing it on his island.

So extend yourself the same grace.

"Archer…" Clara said softly. "You and Francine seem like a good team."

He pinched his lips between his teeth for a second. "She's…she's becoming my everything. And Iris. It's like…if I don't love them, something's wrong. And for her to love me, too…" He cringed. Why was he telling this to someone who'd lost so much? "I'm sorry."

"Sorry you fell in love with someone?" She scoffed. "That's ridiculous."

He shrugged.

"You think I'm not willing to fall in love again?" Her face darkened. "Would you be mad at me if I did?"

"Not if you want to look for love. Why would I condemn you to being lonely? Of all people, I know how awful it feels."

"Stop putting limits on yourself, then."

He stacked his hands on top of his head. "Yeah, I

know. I will. I was going to talk to her, but then she took off."

"So go find her, Archer. This island is tiny."

First, he checked the shop. Sam was in his office at his desk, spinning a pen between his fingers and staring at a spreadsheet on his laptop.

"Where did Franci run off to?" Archer asked.

Sam met his gaze and stilled his pen. "Iris was running a fever."

His heart skipped a beat. "What?"

"Woke up cranky and warm from her midday nap, I guess," Sam said.

The guy wasn't nearly as concerned as he should be. Damn, no wonder Franci had run off like she'd had a mountain lion on her heels. She must be panicking.

"Where are they?" he barked.

"Charlotte and Dad were babysitting at Franci's place," Sam said.

Nodding, Archer took off. He was on his phone with his sister before he even left the store, making sure he knew what to buy from the pharmacy.

Even so, he knew the thing Franci needed most was support.

And after what he'd gone through today, he finally believed he was capable.

Franci's first instinct was to send her dad and sister on their way when she arrived home to her wailing baby, but she didn't want to be alone.

She knew this would have happened even if she hadn't been out on the water, but she still felt guilty for leaving. Was this why Iris had been so upset when she'd left her this morning? Had her baby been feeling sick?

Greg and Charlotte were more than willing to stay. Franci called the doctor at the clinic, who gave her the guidelines for when to seek emergency treatment. Not yet, thank God. So now the priority was to get her stuffy baby to nurse, and then into a lukewarm bath to lower her temperature.

The first didn't go well—Iris couldn't breathe well while trying to suckle and was beyond frustrated, as best as Franci could tell. And the second? Dream on. The bath was the last thing Iris wanted. Her baby sobbed the minute Franci put her in the plastic tub.

Helplessness washed over her. She glanced at her dad, who was sitting at the dining room table, trying to help where he could.

"I don't know what to do, Dad."

"Keep trying, honey," he said. "Maybe keep her out of the water for now. Wrap her mostly in a towel and sponge her one part at a time."

Franci sniffled.

He rose and put a hand on her shoulder. "You're doing what you can. It's never easy when they're sick."

"I thought I'd be calm the first time this happened."

"No parent is," Greg said. "I bet even Dr. Whillans panicked the first time his kid got a stuffy nose."

Normally, she'd be trying to put on a happy face for her father and sister. Not having to was a relief.

A knock sounded. Charlotte went to answer it.

"Who is it, Char?" Franci called.

Her sister didn't answer.

Franci didn't want to let herself hope Archer was the

arrival. He had guests to entertain—surely Clara and Daniel were staying at his place. But still, she would have given anything to have him standing next to her. She *could* do this by herself. But since she'd fallen for him, she'd found she didn't want to. Life was better when she got to share it with Archer. For both enjoying the good moments and supporting each other when things got challenging. He'd let her be that for him today. Was he ready to recognize he'd started to let her in?

Focusing on her baby's face, she kept running the soft cloth over Iris's tummy and chest, whispering hush noises over her cries.

Heavy footsteps approached. She knew that rhythm like she knew her own gait. Warmth flooded her.

A hand landed on her other shoulder, and her dad sat in his chair.

Franci leaned sideways into Archer. "You came."

"You should have told me what the problem was." He slid one arm around her waist and plunked a paper grocery bag on the table with his free hand. "I wasn't sure what you had, and you weren't answering, so I got everything you could need. A thermometer. Saline and a dropper. A nasal aspirator."

A lump formed in her throat. No. She could cry later. "I have a thermometer, but not the other things. Th-thank you."

"Violet said you can never have too many thermometers."

"You called Violet?"

"I needed to know what to bring." He held her tight to his side. "What's her fever?"

"Just under a hundred."

"Good." He wet his free hand and stroked the top of Iris's head. She squawked louder. "Hopefully the bath will get it down."

Greg squeezed Franci's shoulder and retreated to join Charlotte on the couch.

"I'm so sorry," Archer whispered. He kissed her temple. "You're doing great."

Maybe, but Iris wasn't, red-faced and squalling. "She's not calming."

"I'd be upset, too, if I was stuffy and didn't understand it. Let's get her dried off, try the saline and aspirator. Does she want to eat?"

"Probably. She didn't get enough when I tried to feed her."

One task at a time, they worked through it together. It was a haze of tears—hers and Iris's—and Iris's wails. Franci was tempted to follow suit. It would feel beyond good to have a sob. Her dad and Charlotte left once she had Iris dried and dressed, with Greg thanking Archer for taking care of "his girls."

Franci wasn't paying full attention—she couldn't with her baby crying—but the glimpse she caught of the look on Archer's face indicated he thought of her and Iris as *his*.

And if he was ready to leap, she was all for it.

She took Iris over to the couch and got her to latch, and finally, *finally*, the cries faded to whimpers. Franci let out a breath.

The relief of feeding Iris properly was incomparable. Her heart had broken when she'd gotten home and Iris refused to latch.

Archer eased next to them, slower than usual.

"Is your leg bothering you?" she asked.

"A bit." He stared at Iris's little body. "She'll never be less than a miracle to me."

"Why does it feel like the world is ending?" she said, stroking her baby's too-warm cheek. "I know her fever isn't an emergency. I still feel helpless. If I can't fix this small thing, what am I going to do when it's something big?"

"She's your heart, Franci," he said. "You'll always protect your heart."

"I haven't with you."

"Hey." He stroked a hand over her hair. "You don't need to protect yourself with me."

She shuddered out a breath. "That's not what you've been telling me."

"Francine..." His voice was gruff. "Sorry. Thought I was all done with emotions for the day."

"I'm happy to be your sounding board."

"Careful," he said. "I might accept that offer for longer than you mean."

"I don't mean for there to be a limit."

"That's...that's good." He cleared his throat. "It's different now. Iris is my heart, too. So are you."

She wanted to tuck those words around herself like a blanket and snuggle with them. But words and reality weren't the same thing. She tore her gaze from Iris's damp face and stared into his eyes, the limitless depths of blue. "I believe you. But...you can't hold back. Can you reach for me? Wholeheartedly?"

He laughed nervously. "I took a while to realize I

could let you in and you'd be okay. And that I'd be okay. I want to get it right, you know?"

She nodded, sucking in a deep breath.

He picked up the hand she wasn't using to cradle Iris and drew a circle on her palm. "After Iris was born, I realized I was lost. She felt like mine, Franci. *Ours.*"

All her breath escaped her. She had to heave another in before she could reply. "The second I saw you holding her, I was gone. Just gone."

"I was, too," he said. "For both of you."

"Oh," she breathed. She would never get tired of hearing that.

He leaned in for a kiss. Gentle, but consuming. A lifetime of promise in a flash of a touch.

"I'm scared I'll complicate your life," he said. "But I'm willing to work on it. To trust we can figure it out together."

"We can. I want a future. With the man you are now. Grieving, protective, honest, caring—I love you, Archer. I know you have a lot you need to face. But I've seen what some of the work looks like in supporting my dad after the car accident. Like today, when the memories and the grief are too much, I'll cushion you. Wrap enough layers of love around you so the raw parts of your soul don't take up as much space."

"Today was good. Healing."

"It was, wasn't it?" she said softly. She'd loved being with him and his friends on the water, despite his rough stretch after the first dive.

"Makes me want to do it more." He brushed a kiss to her temple. "I know I'll keep hurting. But I was already hurting—silently. Alone. Holding back. Feeling lonely. I think I'd rather face it with the people I love. I don't have to take it all on at once. I can have a cry on a boat, share some of the weight, feel a bit of relief and still go on to live my life."

"Yeah. We're here for you."

"I see that now—it's not the burden I thought it was."

"It's small moments. Tears one day. Laughs another. Therapy. Hugs. *Love*, Archer. People loving you. You loving and being gracious with yourself."

Iris's mouth opened in sleep, and she released Franci's breast.

Archer took the sleeping baby in the gentlest hands, cuddling her to his strong chest while Franci put her bra and shirt back together.

A rush of happiness nearly knocked her over. "There's no separating being in a relationship with someone from being a mom. Would you...would you want to be Iris's dad? If not in name, then in role?"

"Franci, you being a mom only makes you more amazing than you already were."

Her heart skipped. "That's not an answer."

"If you want me in this little girl's life, calling me Dad, even, I want to be there."

Relief whooshed from her lungs.

He chuckled. "These past months with you—they've been the best of my life, let alone the last four years. The one thing I want to take on is a future with you and Iris. I love you."

"I must be lucky to get to hear you say that for the first time on New Year's Day," she said.

He held her closer. "And if I haven't given you a ring by this time next year, I'll be doing life wrong."

"As long as we're together, I don't think *wrong* exists."

Epilogue

Five years later

The fire crackled in the hearth. The lights on the tree glinted on the tinsel—more haphazardly thrown than normal since Iris had joined in on the fun this year. The sun wouldn't rise for another hour.

Even though Franci could have used the extra hour of sleep, she was awake anyway. She didn't want to miss a minute of Iris running down the stairs and bursting into the living room, propelled by the anticipation of Christmas morning and all her five-year-old wishes. Archer puttered in the kitchen, making tea and looking his usual hot self in loose pajama pants and a cardigan hand knit by Winnie.

Mugs in hand, he strolled toward her, all wide shoulders and wider smile. He put the drinks on the coffee table and joined her on the couch.

"Mmm, you're so cozy," she said, curling into his side and sliding her hands around his biceps. The yarn of his sweater was downy soft against her cheek.

"Best way to be on Christmas morning." He laid a loving hand over the Jingle Belly script on the silly maternity T-shirt Violet had ordered for her. Her nine-months-plus stomach was stretching the seams of the green material. "Especially since this one's being stubborn about coming out to meet us."

Unlike Iris with her early delivery, her brother was in no rush to join the festivities. Franci was a week overdue. All her jokes about never having another winter baby had gone out the window with how long it had taken for her and Archer to conceive. After over three long years of trying, she didn't care what part of the year she was pregnant. Their original thought to have a two-ish year gap between their children didn't matter, either. She was just happy to get to add to their little family.

The lack of a forecasted superstorm was a boon, too.

Even with no remarkable weather on the horizon, Violet had considered camping out in the spare room to make sure she didn't miss a minute of Franci's labor this time.

Franci covered Archer's hand with hers and traced his wrist along the outline of his watch. "Ready to count contractions?"

He snapped straight as a spear. His skin went pale under his boat-captain tan. "Are you— Do you think you're having one?"

"No," she said softly. Her back ached, but from gestating a big baby, not contractions. "Trying to will it to happen, though. I'm ready to meet him."

"Sure. And willing things can work." He relaxed again and pulled her closer. "That first Christmas when we woke up on the couch, I was lying there imagining future holidays. Of waiting in the living room for Iris, like my parents did for Violet and me. Watching the sky lighten through the windows. Sharing a moment together and knowing we have so many more to come."

"You imagined this?" She rubbed her swollen abdomen, earning a kick from what had to be her very crowded son. "Even then?"

"Especially then. Seeing all the possibilities was what made me take the leap. Gave me the nudge I needed." Amazement tinged his smile. "And now I can't imagine life any other way."

"Mama? Daddy?" Iris padded into the room, rubbing sleep out of her eyes. Honu followed faithfully, joined at the hip as always with his smallest friend.

The dog made a beeline for Franci and laid his graying muzzle in what was left of her lap. She stroked his ears but kept her gaze on her daughter, who was surveying the room with a critical eye.

"There's my presents," Iris said, scooting past the dog to climb between Archer and Franci. Her little body was still toasty from her flannel nightie and from being under the covers. "But not my brother." She laid an ear on Franci's bump. "Where is he?"

"Still inside, love." Franci kissed her daughter's riot of red curls.

Iris frowned. "But I asked Santa for my little brother."

"You asked Santa for a stuffed Labrador who looks like Honu," Archer said, tweaking her cheek.

Said monstrous stuffy was inside a cheerfully wrapped

box, ready to be lain on and dragged around for many years to come.

"*And* my baby," Iris insisted. "He said. At my picture, he said he'd try."

"Santa's not in charge of babies, honey," Archer said, making a face at Franci, clearly annoyed the Santa at the boat parade had made such promises.

"But he's *magic*." Iris's voice pitched toward tantrum-alert. She glared at Franci's belly. "And he didn't try. I want my baby."

"He meant your brother would come join us *around* Christmas," Franci said soothingly, rubbing their daughter's back. "But look! Your stocking is overflowing. And there's a present under the tree bigger than you."

The red background of the wrapping paper was covered with pictures of dogs wearing reindeer antlers. Iris sent it a mutinous look.

Archer eased off the couch and stood, then scooped up their grumpy elf. "Okay, jellybean. Let's eat something real quick before we open presents." He kissed her forehead as he spirited her toward the kitchen. "Do you think your brother is hungry, too? Will he want Mommy to eat chocolate chip waffles or the blueberry ones?"

Iris cupped her hands around Archer's ear and whispered her answer, quiet enough Franci didn't catch it.

"You bet," he replied, setting her on the edge of the counter. "All the extra whipped cream on Christmas."

Franci gave the dog one last scratch and then used his shoulders to hoist herself off the couch. Groaning, she straightened.

Her stomach tightened, and she splayed a hand on the underside of the swell.

"Oof. Archer, I—"

Pop.

"Oh, my goodness!"

Her water hadn't splashed on the floor, but it was close. So much for her pajama pants.

Honu looked at her with doggy alarm and whined.

Archer's gaze zeroed in on her face. "You okay, wildflower?"

"Can you, uh…" She sucked a breath between her teeth. "Call Violet and wish her a happy holiday?"

"On it." He pulled his cell out of the pocket of his flannel pants. "She'll be thrilled to join us for Christmas."

"Yeah. Though she'll be working," Franci said.

Archer let out a chuckle. "She won't mind."

"Will Auntie Violet sleep in my room?" Iris chimed in.

"Auntie Violet won't be sleeping at all," Franci said under her breath.

And maybe, if things went quickly, Iris would get her little brother for Christmas after all.

* * * * *

Look for Violet's story,
The next installment in
USA TODAY *bestselling author*
Laurel Greer's new miniseries
Love at Hideaway Wharf
Coming soon to Harlequin Special Edition!

And don't miss Sam and Kellan's story,
Diving into Forever
Available now, wherever Harlequin books and
ebooks are sold.

#3013 THE MAVERICK'S HOLIDAY DELIVERY
Montana Mavericks: Lassoing Love • by Christy Jeffries
Dante Sanchez is an expert on no-strings romances. But his feelings for single mom-to-be Eloise Taylor are anything but casual. She knows there's a scandal surrounding her pregnancy. But catching the attention of the town's most notorious bachelor may be her biggest scandal yet!

#3014 TRIPLETS UNDER THE TREE
Dawson Family Ranch • by Melissa Senate
Divorced rancher Hutch Dawson has one heck of a Christmas wish: find a nanny for his baby triplets. And Savannah Walsh is his only applicant! Who knew that his high school nemesis would be the *perfect* solution to his very busy—and lonely—holiday season...

#3015 THE RANCHER'S CHRISTMAS STAR
Men of the West • by Stella Bagwell
Would Quint Hollister hire a woman to be Stone Creek Ranch's new sheepherder? Only if the woman is capable Clementine Starr. She wants no part of romance—at least until Quint's first knee-weakening kiss. But getting two stubborn singletons to admit love might take a Christmas miracle!

#3016 THEIR CONVENIENT CHRISTMAS ENGAGEMENT
Top Dog Dude Ranch • by Catherine Mann
Ian Greer is used to finding his mother, who has Alzheimer's, anywhere but at home! More often than not, he finds her at Gwen Bishop's vintage toy store. He admires the kind, plucky single mom, so a fake engagement to placate his mother—and her family—seems like the perfect plan. Until a romantic sleigh ride changes their holiday ruse into something much more real...

#3017 THE VET'S SHELTER SURPRISE
by Michelle M. Douglas
Sparks fly when beautiful PR expert Georgia O'Neill brings an armful of stray kittens to veterinarian Mel Carter's small-town animal shelter. Mel has loved and lost before, and Georgia is only in town short-term, so it makes sense to ignore their mutual attraction. But as they open up about their pasts, will they also open up to the possibility of new love?

#3018 HOLIDAY AT MISTLETOE COTTAGE
The McFaddens of Tinsley Cove • by Nancy Robards Thompson
Free-spirited photojournalist Avery Anderson just inherited her aunt's beach house. And, it seems, her aunt's sexy, outgoing neighbor. Hometown hero Forest McFadden may be Avery's polar opposite. But fortunately, he's also the adventure she's been searching for.

HSECNM0923

Get 3 FREE REWARDS!

We'll send you 2 FREE Books plus a FREE Mystery Gift.

FREE Value Over **$20**

Both the **Harlequin® Special Edition** and **Harlequin® Heartwarming™** series feature compelling novels filled with stories of love and strength where the bonds of friendship, family and community unite.

YES! Please send me 2 FREE novels from the Harlequin Special Edition or Harlequin Heartwarming series and my FREE Gift (gift is worth about $10 retail). After receiving them, if I don't wish to receive any more books, I can return the shipping statement marked "cancel." If I don't cancel, I will receive 6 brand-new Harlequin Special Edition books every month and be billed just $5.49 each in the U.S. or $6.24 each in Canada, a savings of at least 12% off the cover price, or 4 brand-new Harlequin Heartwarming Larger-Print books every month and be billed just $6.24 each in the U.S. or $6.74 each in Canada, a savings of at least 19% off the cover price. It's quite a bargain! Shipping and handling is just 50¢ per book in the U.S. and $1.25 per book in Canada.* I understand that accepting the 2 free books and gift places me under no obligation to buy anything. I can always return a shipment and cancel at any time by calling the number below. The free books and gift are mine to keep no matter what I decide.

Choose one: ☐ **Harlequin Special Edition** (235/335 BPA GRMK)   ☐ **Harlequin Heartwarming Larger-Print** (161/361 BPA GRMK)   ☐ **Or Try Both!** (235/335 & 161/361 BPA GRPZ)

Name (please print)

Address   Apt. #

City   State/Province   Zip/Postal Code

Email: Please check this box ☐ if you would like to receive newsletters and promotional emails from Harlequin Enterprises ULC and its affiliates. You can unsubscribe anytime.

Mail to the Harlequin Reader Service:
IN U.S.A.: P.O. Box 1341, Buffalo, NY 14240-8531
IN CANADA: P.O. Box 603, Fort Erie, Ontario L2A 5X3

Want to try 2 free books from another series! Call 1-800-873-8635 or visit www.ReaderService.com.

*Terms and prices subject to change without notice. Prices do not include sales taxes, which will be charged (if applicable) based on your state or country of residence. Canadian residents will be charged applicable taxes. Offer not valid in Quebec. This offer is limited to one order per household. Books received may not be as shown. Not valid for current subscribers to the Harlequin Special Edition or Harlequin Heartwarming series. All orders subject to approval. Credit or debit balances in a customer's account(s) may be offset by any other outstanding balance owed by or to the customer. Please allow 4 to 6 weeks for delivery. Offer available while quantities last.

Your Privacy—Your information is being collected by Harlequin Enterprises ULC, operating as Harlequin Reader Service. For a complete summary of the information we collect, how we use this information and to whom it is disclosed, please visit our privacy notice located at corporate.harlequin.com/privacy-notice. From time to time we may also exchange your personal information with reputable third parties. If you wish to opt out of this sharing of your personal information, please visit readerservice.com/consumerchoice or call 1-800-873-8635. **Notice to California Residents**—Under California law, you have specific rights to control and access your data. For more information on these rights and how to exercise them, visit corporate.harlequin.com/california-privacy.

HSEHW23

HARLEQUIN
PLUS

Try the best multimedia
subscription service for romance
readers like you!

Read, Watch and Play.

Experience the easiest way to get
the romance content you crave.

Start your **FREE TRIAL** at
<u>www.harlequinplus.com/freetrial</u>.